To Love and Protect

It was dark when she awoke. Someone had tucked her in a bed.

"I fear your maid suffered an injury. Her arm was sprained. The apothecary gave her a sedative after binding up her arm, she is sleeping at present. Perhaps I may be of assistance?"

Nympha turned her head at the sound of a beautifully rich male voice coming from the other side of the room. Once she saw the identity of her speaker she closed her eyes again. It couldn't be. Fate couldn't be that cruel.

"Lord Nicholas!"

"The very same," he replied in a dry manner. "And the innkeeper's wife sits close to you at the moment. Never fear, I observe all proprieties."

"Oh, lud!" she whispered. This was not a good beginning to her journey. Not good at all.

Lord Nick's Folly

Emily Hendrickson

A SIGNET BOOK

SIGNET
Published by New American Library, a division of
Penguin Putnam Inc., 375 Hudson Street,
New York, New York 10014, U.S.A.
Penguin Books Ltd, 80 Strand,
London WC2R 0RL, England
Penguin Books Australia Ltd, Ringwood,
Victoria, Australia
Penguin Books Canada Ltd, 10 Alcorn Avenue,
Toronto, Ontario, Canada M4V 3B2
Penguin Books (N.Z.) Ltd, 182–190 Wairau Road,
Auckland 10, New Zealand

Penguin Books Ltd, Registered Offices:
Harmondsworth, Middlesex, England

First published by Signet, an imprint of New American Library,
a division of Penguin Putnam Inc.

First Printing, September 2002
10 9 8 7 6 5 4 3 2 1

Printed in the United States of America

PUBLISHER'S NOTE
This is a work of fiction. Names, characters, places, and incidents either are the product of the author's imagination or are used fictitiously, and any resemblance to actual persons, living or dead, business establishments, events, or locales is entirely coincidental.

I dedicate this book to Sandra Heath in appreciation of her generous help with information on the Nottingham area, not forgetting her assistance on "standing for the Commons." Sandra, I couldn't have done it without you!

Prologue

"You must go, whether you wish it or not, my dear." Mrs. Herbert looked up from the sewing draped across her lap to fix a stern gaze on her next-to-eldest daughter. "My aunt Letitia is not only a very dear lady, she is one of immense wealth. You cannot afford to ignore her summons!" She concluded her pronouncement with a firm nod of her head, dislodging a gray curl from beneath her white day cap, a confection of cambric trimmed in pretty lace.

"Yes, Mama." Nympha Herbert grimaced while smoothing out the petticoat she had been sewing. It truly needed a bit of lace trim, and that was a rather dear item for a rector's daughter to come by. Even if her papa had a separate income to supplement his church living, with six children and a wife, he was always short of funds. "Although I believe Dru would best serve to help Great-Aunt over her injury. Dru is always so good with the sick. I do not feel much like going anywhere."

Priscilla gave her older sister a sympathetic smile. "It is time and more that you cease thinking about the handsome lord who married Lady Harriet. You might have known that Lord Stanhope would marry a titled lady. Perhaps you may meet a good-looking gentleman when you are visiting our great-aunt? Surely Nottinghamshire must have its share of refined men? Would you not agree, Mama?"

"Perhaps," their mother admitted, studying the dress

in her lap. "I can only hope that the gentlemen in that area are not too demanding as to styles. I have tried, but this gown is not quite what I would have you wear, my love."

"I would be the veriest peagoose to complain, Mama. If a gentleman does not like what I wear—well, he must be a sad rattle!" Nympha smoothed a blond curl back away from her face, her eyes taking note of how tired her mother appeared. It would be good for her mother to be rid of another daughter for a time. Five daughters to rear, plus one son to educate, had taxed the rector's resources greatly. Even with Claudia wed, there were still five children remaining. If, by visiting her great-aunt for a time, she might reduce expenses, it behooved her to travel, even if Nottinghamshire, and the town of Mansfield in particular, seemed like the other end of the earth.

"Watch your language, Nympha. Aunt Letitia does not approve of using slang." Mrs. Herbert gave her daughter a frowning glance. "This could be an important visit for you—in more ways than one. Your father mentioned that the chap who is spending some time in our area intends to head north to visit a friend. Lord Byron, if I make no mistake. Newstead Abbey is not so far from where Aunt Letitia lives." Mrs. Herbert shook out the gown she had been sewing, gave a sigh of resignation, then set it aside.

Knowing full well that her mother had not read the poet's work and would disapprove of any of her daughters mooning over him, Nympha merely nodded. "He seems a most elegant gentleman."

"That remains to be seen." Whether she meant Lord Byron or the man who had visited Lord Nicholas she didn't say. As a matter of fact, her mother had not had a word to say about the stranger in their midst. Yet Mr. Jared Milburn seemed agreeable, according to comments made by Papa. But then, one never knew. Appearances might be deceiving.

"Yes, Mama." Deciding it was best to turn her mother's attention from a stranger in the village to something more practical, Nympha queried, "How many days will it take me to reach her home? I vow that her little town seems a great distance away. You believe the roads will be in good repair in early March? Mansfield seems so remote."

"I truly have no idea. You will travel in style in a fine carriage. No matter how long it takes, you shouldn't mind, for she sends money to pay for your stay at the necessary inns. However, your father intends to give a sum for you to spend while there. Great-Aunt Letitia's home is close to Nottingham, I believe, so there will be shopping there, if not in Mansfield."

Tabitha, the youngest of the rector's progeny, piped up. "It is close to Sherwood Forest, as well. Perhaps you will meet a romantic gentleman who will sweep you off your feet—like Robin Hood."

"Highly unlikely," Mrs. Herbert said, giving her youngest a dry look. "It has been my experience that those thieving men are low creatures, and nothing at all to look at."

"But you might have some exciting adventure on your way," Tabitha persisted, seeming reluctant to give up the notion of a dramatic event for her sister, one with momentous significance.

"Great-Aunt wrote she will be sending a traveling coach for me. I suspect it will be a proper one, as staid and as dignified as she likely is. It isn't the sort to encourage a romantic villain." Nympha smiled at her youngest sister. Tabitha was the romantic one of the family.

"I still say it is a good thing for you to go away for a time." Priscilla gave Nympha a meaningful look, but she said nothing more on the matter of Nympha's hopeless fancy for the man who was the son of her father's patron.

Once Lord Stanhope married Lady Harriet all Nympha's dreams had crashed. And now with the soon-to-be birth of his expected heir, Nympha admitted it would be distressing to be at home. No woman liked to be reminded of a failure! He had never had eyes for anyone but Lady Harriet once he saw her, try as Nympha had to interest him.

"I shall welcome a change," Nympha said, giving Priscilla a rueful look. She turned her attention to the garment in her lap. "They make lace in Nottingham, do they not? Perhaps I can buy a length to sew on this dreary petticoat. What a blessing no smart gentleman is likely to see it!" She chuckled at the mere thought, joined by Priscilla and Tabitha.

"What gentleman is likely not to see your dreary petticoat?" Drusilla inquired as she entered the drawing room where the women of the family customarily gathered, the rectory not having a morning room large enough to accommodate them all.

"Dearest Dru, no gentleman at all! I shall have a most unexceptional trip to Mansfield. Uneventful. Dull, I am persuaded," Nympha concluded, with a gentle smile for the sister closest to her in age.

"Well, I brought something to cheer you. Mrs. Wyndham loaned me her latest copy of *La Belle Assembleé* to peruse. I think we might make you the pink crepe dress in it with a bit of alteration. You would not want something quite so elaborate, I am persuaded." She handed the small magazine to Nympha, who promptly opened it to the illustration in question.

"Heaven forbid! I could never hope to copy such an elegant creation as this." She studied the picture of the pink crepe gown and gave a huge sigh. "I am not sufficiently skilled with my needle!" Turning a page, she studied the other illustration for the month. "Now this white crepe gown is simple. I might manage the short full sleeves, and perhaps some trim around the hem. I would not wish to embarrass our great-aunt by looking shabby or too provincial. But I do like pink. 'Drake's neck' is said to be a favored color. What do you suppose that is?"

"A sort of iridescent green, perhaps?"

Her mother peered over Nympha's shoulder. "The neckline is a trifle low, to my thinking."

Nympha and Drusilla exchanged wordless looks.

"Did you have a good walk this morning?" Dru asked. "I saw you heading for the Folly and the new house. What has Lord Nicholas done now?" Drusilla plumped herself on a chair close to Nympha, looking quite prepared for a long recital. They called the greens the Folly as it seemed a silly thing for a man to create.

"The men appear to be finished with the outside of the house he is building. It overlooks his golf links, as he calls that odd stretch of land that has sand traps and water holes and gorse where you would least expect it. I watched for a time. From a safe distance, you may be sure," she added as Dru gave her a skeptical look. "Although I must say I wonder what the interior will look like."

That she had studiously avoided an encounter with Lord Nicholas was not mentioned. Her sisters were well aware that Nympha harbored no interest in *that* gentleman. Indeed, Nympha might have assisted him from time to time, but it had been more in aid of seeing something of his brother, Lord Stanhope, rather than spending time with the most aggravating man on earth—Lord Nicholas. And he, in turn, appeared to view Nympha as a plague placed on earth simply to annoy him. No, she might have some curiosity about the house, but not that far-too-rugged specimen of manhood. When he entered a room it was as though he brought all the out-of-doors with him. He would scarcely fit into a fancy drawing room! Imagine him bowing and paying pretty compliments! Or dancing! She shuddered at the mere thought of it.

"Does Mr. Milburn play golf?" Tabitha wanted to know.

"I saw him near there this morning. I cannot say I paid much attention to him. He was with another gentleman, slightly older, and they were arguing about the game. At least I suppose they were. It seems that men argue quite often over scores or something." Nympha grimaced at that.

"Well, I think it very nice that the marquess gave Lord Nicholas land for his own home and his golf." Mrs. Herbert rose, gathering the gown she had worked on in her arms. "Come Nympha—I wish you to try this. I do hope it will fit. What a pity you lost weight this past year."

Nympha escaped in her mother's wake, happy to be leaving her sisters and their teasing tongues. As to the gown, if it fit, she hoped her mother would assist her in making a pattern of the simple white dress featured in the magazine. Her mother could do anything.

Nick stood at his front door surveying the scene before him. The late-February sun warmed his face, and he leaned against the door frame to study his land. A mild breeze ruffled his hair, bringing the promise of an early spring with it. The smell of sun-warmed earth, robins singing, the new green leaves on the trees, made him itch to get out with his clubs. Sheep grazed on his green at present, a clever means of keeping the lawns short, and providing a bit of mutton at the same time. Perhaps he could take time to play a round? With a good wool jacket against a chill wind, he couldn't see why it wouldn't be possible.

The view of his nine-hole golf links satisfied him. On his one visit to the famous St. Andrews links he had sketched out the lay of the land as best he could, with a helpful bit of advice from a local man. While it was nigh impossible to duplicate that course, he had made the attempt. Perhaps his nine holes would never be more than his own folly, to be played by his personal friends. Still, he was pleased with it.

As a single man, he had no wife to nag him about his hobbyhorse. His smile widened. With his older brother about to produce an heir, the burden of being the heir presumptive was off Nick's shoulders. Of course there was the possibility of a female, but with Philip's conviction that this would be Baby Mark, Nick was sure it would be so.

"It goes well, Lord Nicholas," Mr. Heron declared, the roll of house plans in his hand as he paused by the entry door where Nick stood. "Supplies have been delivered with better speed than I dared hope. We shall finish on time, I vow. Perhaps you might stop by the library in a little while to decide on what wood you want for the paneling. I suggest oak, but you choose anything you like, of course."

Nick promised to come shortly.

The workmen had agreed to get the house done over the summer. Pericles Heron, the architect hired to design and oversee the construction, managed to see supplies were available when needed and that the artisans required presented themselves on time. The house had been started the previous year, and the interior finishing was well underway.

At the rate the men worked, it was quite possible Heron's pledge would be realized. Nick was quite tired of living at the main family residence, Lanstone Hall. Although his parents were still in Italy, Nick was impatient to have a house of his own, designed to his own taste and furnished to please him.

A movement to the far side of his course caught his attention. One of his men—it appeared to be Otway, the head gardener—was coming up from the greens in a great hurry. From the way he was rushing along there was something amiss.

Nick ran down the front steps to meet him. "Is there a problem?" He stopped on the sweep of the eventual drive to await the man, who was quite out of breath. Nick waited patiently while his trusted employee gained a measure of calm. The chap took great gulps of air to regain his composure. With a deep breath, he began to explain.

"Well, I figure as how there is, milord. Saw these fellows out on one of the greens some time ago. Didna pay much attention to them. Considered they might be your friends, you know, playing a round of golf."

Nick fell into step beside Otway as they turned to head back onto the greens. They walked at a decent pace. Until he knew precisely what the problem was, there was little point in rushing pell-mell down the grass. "And so?" he prompted.

"Looked around later, and there was no one in sight, so I forgot all about it. You know how it is—a chap gets busy, and not apt to think on something so ordinary."

"And what is the problem now, if I may know?" The

chap might be as trustworthy as they come; he also took his time in getting to the point.

"Well, now, I chanced to see one of the sheep nosing about the far side of the seventh hole. Thought to see why. Normally they have nothin' to do with the sand bunkers." The wiry man half-turned to look at Nick, expectant to see his reaction, most likely.

"What did you discover?" Nick asked quietly as they increased their speed. Call it a premonition, he knew he was in for trouble. That it had something to do with his golf links made him even more uneasy.

"A body." With this dramatic statement, Otway clearly expected some manner of amazed reaction.

"Good grief, man. Injured? Should we get help for him? Or . . . is he dead?" Nick assumed that whoever it was the sheep discovered, it had to be a man.

"I believe he's dead. No sign of life that I could see. Don't recognize the feller. Maybe you will?"

There was a question in his last remark. Nick wondered who those two arguing men might have been. And who was the mysterious body in the sand bunker? And why in the sand?

It took a little time to reach the spot where the body sprawled, facedown, in the depression of sand. Nick quickly ascertained that the man was indeed dead. No help for him now. "Murdered." Nick rose to his feet after discovering the injury to the head, feeling a little ill at the sight before him. Blood had seeped into the sand, forming a stain of dark claret red.

"Know him?" Otway inquired.

"Face seems faintly familiar, but I couldn't put a name to him." Nick studied the area where they found the man. Other than the head injury there appeared to be no mark on the man. At least, his clothing was not awry, nor was there a sign of a struggle. A single blow to the head had accomplished the deed. It had required a heavy object, and someone who possessed a modicum of strength.

"Milord, isn't this your club?" Otway held up one of Nick's golfing clubs, one with a solid wood head to it.

"Looks as though it might be mine," Nick allowed. He recognized it well, having ordered it while in Scotland. How it got into the hands of a man intent upon committing murder he didn't know. As evidence it was circumstantial. While it might be his own club, there were any number of people who could have taken it when he wasn't around. However, were he a member of a jury, he would think it more than possible that the owner of the club had done the deed.

"Also looks as though that's how this chap be done in," Otway murmured.

"From the impression on his head, I agree. I expect we send for a doctor or an apothecary. I think we need some sort of certificate. Not having been in this situation before, I'm not sure." Nick rose from where he had knelt by the body. "Perhaps the magistrate?"

Hoping to discover the identity of the stranger, Nick searched the dead man's pockets. In one of them he found a slip of paper such as given by a shopkeeper. The name of the shop was Binch's, a haberdasher in Mansfield, a town north of Nottingham.

"Mansfield? What on earth is a person from that part of the country doing here?" he said. "I had better get counsel."

"Well, if you want, I kin ride to Sir William's. If he bain't the one to do the duty, he will know," Otway offered.

"No, I had best go myself. But thank you, just the same. Please find something with which to cover the body." He added a few requests, then returned to the house, where he entered the completed stables around back to find his horse. Within a brief time, he was trotting down the graveled drive in the direction of the local magistrate, Sir William Tabard.

Sir William listened to his tale and made a few notes. Then he joined Nick in his return to the "Folly," discussing the murder as they rode.

It was a relief to have the body taken away. There would be an inquest, of course. But after that Nick decided he would head north to the town of Mansfield to see what he might learn about the mystery man.

His trip to the village had yielded nothing. No one appeared to claim the body, and no one had seen him hereabouts. The innkeeper knew nothing. So . . . where had he been staying? With whom? And why didn't he or they question the disappearance of a guest?

The days slipped past; the inquest was held. It was determined that the stranger had died of a head injury given him by persons unknown. That he had no friend come forth to claim him, that nothing was known about him, did not help Nick's quest.

Nick discussed the matter with Sir William. "As soon as I am able to get away, I intend to go north to discover what I might. I made a sketch of the man—as best I was able, given my poor talent in that line." Nick grimaced at Sir William, who nodded in understanding. "I will be curious to see what can be learned about the chap—if anything."

"You know that no one around here suspects you of the deed. We have known you all your life. This man was a stranger. I think it is most kind of you to investigate his identity. Not many would bother." He gave Nick a quizzical look.

"I thought that perhaps if I learn who he was, I might also learn who killed him."

Sir William gave a sage nod. "You might also find yourself in a bit of trouble, my lord. Someone who has murdered once might not think twice about murdering a second time, if you see what I mean."

Nick agreed. "Yet this is something I must do. The roads are like to be bad yet. As soon as it clears enough so I don't have to go through axle-deep mud to get there, I'll head north." And, he decided, as long as he was that far north, he might as well go to Scotland. It would be agreeable to enjoy the St. Andrews links again. He might well pick up a few more pointers.

Chapter One

"Well, I think it a great shame that we have a mystery right here in the village, and no one seems the slightest concerned about the poor man who was killed." Tabitha flounced on the sofa, drawing all eyes to her frustrated little self.

"Dear, I am certain the authorities will do all that is necessary." Mrs. Herbert frowned at her youngest. "It is not something a young lady should consider. Murder!"

Nympha shivered from the Gothic image summoned at the very word. It might not be romantic in the true sense of the word, but it brought forth images of dark forms in the night, skulking shadows, daggers, all the things Tabitha found in the Gothic novels from the lending library.

"Soon it will be March. Will Great-Aunt Letitia's traveling coach come before long?" Nympha smoothed the hem of the white crepe dress that had turned out far better than she had dared to hope. Priscilla had created a puffed trim for the lower part of the skirt that was immensely clever. Nympha might not be deemed a dreadful dowd after all. Even if Great-Aunt Letitia was recovering from a fall, surely she would want to see her friends, perhaps attend a local assembly when she felt better. There were a fair number of peers located in that area, not that she expected to encounter the Dukes of Portland or Newcastle, much less the elderly Earl Manvers. She had checked the peerage found in her father's crowded library shelves to see who might reside there. Of course, Lord Byron was younger, but he was also much sought after. Why, even that man visiting the area, Mr. Jared Milburn, declared he intended to spend some time at Newstead Abbey.

It sounded romantic. An abbey. Visions evoked from Tabitha's favorite books, read aloud in the evening, popped into Nympha's mind. Haunted, ivy-covered ruins.

But there must be other, younger, more available gentlemen around. Surely there must be someone who would be presentable and perhaps on the lookout for a wife? That she needed to be wed was undeniable. That no eligible male existed around here was equally true.

"Nympha! Do you hear that? A carriage has drawn up before the rectory. Do you suppose? . . ." Priscilla dashed to the window. "Oh, it is, and it is a splendid coach! You will travel in great style!"

And so she did. Nervous, uncertain as to what was ahead of her, but anxious to depart, Nympha set forth the next day. Instructions to write immediately when she arrived, fond wishes for a fine trip, and hopes that something "good" would come of her journey rang in her ears as the coach moved forth from the rectory drive. A wide-eyed maid—Annie, who had been shared with Priscilla—went along.

The same morning, up at the Folly, Nick entered his traveling coach, his valet seated across from him as usual. On a trip of this duration, proper garb and a superior valet guaranteed him the attention he enjoyed—good meals, decent accommodation, and passable horses. It as the only way to travel, in his estimation.

Another small yellow chaise, fondly called a yellow bounder by many, also set forth from the village, headed due north. The horses were not of the highest quality, nor was the postilion inclined to do his best, given the acrimonious nature of his employer. That moody, yet exultant gentleman reclined against the squabs of this vehicle, counting his success before he had achieved it.

Nympha perched on the edge of her seat, smoothing

the luxurious velvet while admiring the many fine appointments in Great-Aunt Letitia's traveling coach. Mama said her aunt had a lot of money. That was most likely true, if this coach was anything to go by.

Annie sat opposite her, round-eyed and given to breathless comments. She gestured to the little vase mounted on the interior side. "Real flowers, those be, miss. This be a real treat, traveling in style!"

"Delightful, are they not? My, this is the first style of elegance. I wonder what her house is like?"

This thought sent both of them into deep contemplation, although it didn't last long, there being so many things to catch their attention along the road. Farms, flowers, trees, animals, plus a village here and there that they thundered through.

They paused briefly for a bite of nuncheon, the elegant coach commanding the innkeeper's attentiveness and civility. Nympha nibbled her way through a variety of offerings, deciding that if one must travel, this was the way to do so.

It was late in the afternoon when it happened: they hit a portion of deeply rutted road. Although the coachman did the best he could, the coach lurched, seemed to right itself, then lurched again. And slowly, slowly turned on its side.

"Lawks, miss!" Annie cried before a bandbox tumbled on her. She said no more.

"Annie, are you hurt? Oh, dear me," Nympha cried while attempting to open the door that would be closest to the ground. She could make out sky through the other one, and thought that way unsafe to venture.

When the door gave way, she tumbled forth, hitting her head on a rock, her petticoat in a froth about her face. Annie landed right on top of her.

Her head ached. Annie was heavy. Nympha yielded to the overwhelming desire to shut her eyes. Oh, she hurt.

Dimly she heard voices above her. Too full of aches and pains, she ignored them. Then comforting arms picked her up, holding her close to a warm, firm body that smelled somewhat of costmary. She vaguely perceived being placed inside a coach, and knew no more.

It was dark when she awoke. Someone had tucked her in a bed. She didn't ache *quite* so much anymore. "Annie? Are you here?" She hoped her maid was recovered and feeling quite the thing. Nympha's head might be a bit fuzzy, but she thought she might get out of bed with help.

"I fear your maid suffered an injury. Her arm was sprained. The apothecary gave her a sedative after binding up her arm. She is sleeping at present. Perhaps I may be of assistance?"

Nympha turned her head at the sound of a beautifully rich male voice coming from the other side of the room. Once she saw the identity of the speaker she closed her eyes again. It couldn't be. Fate couldn't be that cruel.

"Lord Nicholas!"

"The very same," he replied in a dry manner. "And the innkeeper's wife sits close to you at the moment. Never fear, I observe all proprieties."

"Oh, lud!" she whispered. This was not a good beginning to her journey. Not good at all.

Chapter Two

Her petticoat! The last recollection of that dreary garment she so disliked was that it had covered her face when she tumbled from the coach. Whoever had rescued her, whoever had held her close to a comforting chest, must have seen it. How mortifying! She strongly suspected she knew who had observed that intimate bit of apparel, not to mention her white silk stockings and laced blue leather slippers.

"I believe I must thank you for the rescue, my lord," she said with frigid politeness.

"I would have done the same for anyone in that predicament." He continued to lean against the fireplace mantel, one leg casually crossed before the other while he watched her like the neighbor's peregrine falcon watched its prey. Only Lord Nicholas had dark, unfathomable eyes that seemed to see far too much. His hair had that carefully tousled look gentlemen attempted nowadays and few achieved to perfection. He did. That he also possessed a certain air that true gentlemen aimed to achieve also set him apart from ordinary men.

Why did the dratted man have to possess the most marvelously rich voice, the sort that sent little shivers down one's back? It was strange she hadn't noticed it before, but then, it might be that the knock on her head had affected her mind—just a trifle. She grimaced, and immediately the innkeeper's wife, her starched apron crackling as she moved, offered a glass of barley water.

Compelled to sip merely by the look his lordship sent her, Nympha did as was expected of her, then sank back onto her pillows. "How soon may we depart?" Barley water was not her favorite beverage.

"What with all this rain, the road's become a quagmire. Until it is reasonably dry, I fear we must remain here. Besides, your maid is hardly in any condition to travel just yet, nor is your coach repaired." He rubbed his jaw, studying her as if he didn't quite know what to do with her.

"Do not feel compelled to remain here merely because your rector's daughter is slightly inconvenienced." She wanted to order him gone, but she doubted anything she said would have the slightest effect on what he did or didn't do. He truly possessed a lordly air. Now that she thought about it, he was quite as aristocratic in his mien as his older brother, who was heir to the marquess.

"I should say more than slightly." His lopsided grin did the oddest things to her heart. Really, she must have had quite a thump to her noggin. She had known Lord Nicholas for ages, and he had never affected her like this in the past. True, she had never been alone with him like this before, either. The innkeeper's wife didn't count. The woman sat as still as a mouse and said not a word, peering at them from beneath a crisp mobcap as though observing a game of tennis.

"I shall be up and about before you know it," Nympha declared with stout resolution. "My great-aunt will be expecting me in Mansfield soon. I'd not have her worry."

"You will remain in that bed until I say you may get up." He snapped out that order with the lordly manner of one accustomed to being obeyed. "I feel certain your aunt will understand that weather oftentimes interferes with travel."

Nympha merely glowered at him, her mouth set in an obstinate line. "We shall see."

He looked at the innkeeper's wife, then firmly added,

"I trust you to keep an eye on her. Miss Herbert's father is a highly respected rector. I believe he rather dotes on this daughter."

Well! Nympha thought, he didn't have to sound as though he couldn't imagine why Papa was fond of his children, and her in particular.

The deferential reply from the lady who perched at Nympha's side soothed her frayed nerves a trifle, although Nympha suspected her regard was because of his elegant lordship, not the rector, much less his daughter.

"I shall see how your coach progresses. The repairs may not take too long if the proper wood can be located—that axle was badly cracked. I know the road was not in best condition, but scarcely bad enough to cause such an accident. Tell me, do you have any enemies?"

His study of her was intent. "Not an enemy in the world that I know about," she said with a pertness she did not feel. Surely there was no one who would wish her ill? Utter nonsense.

He said nothing in reply to her declaration. Rather, he promised to check on her later, and left the room.

Odd, how empty the chamber seemed with his aggravating person gone. She relaxed on her pillow, wondering how many feathers it took to fill it. That was better than wondering what it might be like to make Lord Nicholas smile—a genuine smile of delight.

Her sight of the offending cambric petticoat where it was draped across a chair turned her thoughts to the ignominy and total unfairness of being the owner of such a garment. Oh, she would look for lace the first chance she had! To hope that Lord Nicholas hadn't taken note of that unadorned petticoat on his foray into her bedchamber was too much to expect. He likely thought it was most suitable for a rector's daughter to own. And if that wasn't a dreary notion she didn't know what was.

She wished her mother were here. She had never traveled alone, much less had an accident. And now—to be in such dire circumstances, alone with Lord Nicholas Stanhope—well!

And yet, in a way she was having an adventure. Oh, how Tabitha's eyes would open wide when given an account of this journey! Nympha almost smiled at the very thought of it.

"Ye look like ye be feeling a mite better, Miss Herbert. If ye have no objection, I'll fetch ye a bowl of porridge topped with our own cream and a dab of butter and sugar. I'll warrant ye will feel yerself in no time." The innkeeper's wife rose from the chair, bustling to the door as though she couldn't wait to be out and about her business.

With mixed emotions, Nympha watched her leave the room. The door had barely shut when it opened again. Annie entered. With her arm bound up and an eye that appeared to be turning every color of the rainbow, she looked a sorry sight.

"I'm that sorry you had a knock on the head, Miss Nympha." The maid came to the side of the bed and smoothed down the coverlet with her good hand. Her blue eyes held an anxious look, and her hand trembled just a little.

"I am quite all right. You look to have suffered far more than I did, poor girl. I trust they attended to you properly?"

"Indeed, miss. I've been treated ever so nice."

"If these people would simply allow me to get up, I should manage very well. I hope that the coach has been repaired, and that we may leave as soon as possible. All of a sudden I long to be at my great-aunt's home." Nympha wiped a tear away with a resolute hand. She would not mope. She never moped. But she did feel a trifle lost and out of her depth in a strange area, with only the aggravating Lord Nicholas to assist her.

Annie patted Nympha's hand, nodding. "I agree, that I do. Oh, that gentleman what was staying in the village, the one your papa introduced to you, is here as well. Small world this be."

Nympha, much subdued, agreed. "How curious." She hadn't been much taken with the gentleman, but she did wonder where he was going.

Rain spattering on the window was the only sound to be heard for a brief time, during which Nympha reflected on the caprices of travel while Annie attempted to see to Nympha's belongings.

Nicholas paused outside Miss Herbert's bedroom to consider what he ought to do next. The wheelwright had promised his best, but it could take a few days to make the repairs if he encountered complications. How to cope with a determined young miss who didn't particularly like him was a matter upon which he preferred not to dwell. What was odd was that she made her dislike so obvious. He was not accustomed to that attitude from unmarried women, or women in general for that matter. Even though he was not in direct line for the peerage, there were any number of ambitious mothers who felt that his proximity to the title was quite good enough. He could always count on some female throwing herself in his way. Nympha Herbert looked as though she'd gladly run a mile in the opposite direction just to be rid of him. And he couldn't allow that. He took a step toward the stairs.

"Lord Nicholas, how fortunate to encounter someone I know! Little did I think that when I left Lanstone Hall I would meet you again so soon."

Nick turned to see a familiar face, most unexpected on this road heading north. "Milburn, good to see you, although I am surprised to find you going north. Thought you would head for London. Difficult time of the year to be traveling, considering the state of the roads and all. Never know when rain will cause a problem." He gestured to the window at the top of the stairs where rain pelted the panes.

"How true. What brings you away from your home and links? Scotland, perhaps? A thought to study the lay of their land again?" Milburn gave him a knowing smirk.

"Perhaps I may. Who knows?" Nick had said nothing to his casual guest of his plans. It was none of his business. For that matter, nothing had been said about the mysterious death on the seventh green, either. Milburn had not attended the inquest. There had been no reason for him to do so. "First, I must escort a neighbor's daughter and her maid to their destination. I believe she is to spend time with a great-aunt somewhere to the north," Nick replied with a wave of one hand.

"Ah, the nursery brigade?"

"Not precisely. Reverend Herbert's second daughter is to visit her mother's aunt, as I understand it."

"Duty calls, and all that. I suppose this great-aunt is wealthy? Esteemed aunts often are, especially if widows." Milburn sauntered down the steps at Nick's side, his query sounding mildly curious.

The query seemed polite, even innocuous. Nick did not care for it, however, and replied with deliberate obscurity. "Well, you know how elderly relatives are, wanting a bit of attention now and again." With that, he continued down the stairs, Milburn following in his trail.

The wheelwright was sorry, but the axle would take another day to replace. The carriage was of high quality and deserved a fine bit of wood. The coachman had insisted it have only the best, and the wheelwright was the only man in the area capable of making any manner of repair.

"These wretched roads," Milburn said as they left the wheelwright's workshop under the protection of the innkeeper's best umbrella. "I hear tell that some chap has devised a scheme to improve the roads so they won't disintegrate into a mire of muck and stone with every rainstorm."

"Hmm," Nick murmured. "Name of McAdam, I believe. Part of *this* road is macadamized, I think, but farther to the north. Quite an improvement for carriages." He glanced at his companion, wondering what was troubling him. Nick didn't know him all that well, but it seemed to him that Milburn, for all his well-tailored garb and polished looks, was uneasy about something. Nick had been an easygoing host. He offered Milburn accommodation at the family hall, but had not gone out of his way to entertain a casual acquaintance. He'd been preoccupied with house construction details, leaving his uninvited guest to entertain himself.

"Pity that Miss Herbert's coach should meet with a disaster. It is a fine vehicle, the highest quality, in fact—which tells a good deal about the great-aunt, wouldn't you say? Kind of you to oversee its repair." Milburn chuckled, then added, "I must say, I was surprised to find *you* tarrying at this inn. I cannot recall when I have had an instance where I happened on two people I knew while traveling."

"You know Miss Herbert?" Nick frowned, then wondered why it annoyed him that Milburn was acquainted with his nemesis, Miss Herbert. It was nothing to him if she was known to any number of gentlemen.

"Only from the village near your home. The rector was so kind as to introduce me to her one day. I met her mother as well—in church, you know. I can scarce say I *know* Miss Herbert. Enchanting creature, though. Those blond curls and blue eyes are all the thing in Town."

Nick nodded, deciding he was being very fanciful and suspicious without reason. The fellow merely sounded interested, polite, perhaps a trifle forward. "So, where are you bound, once the roads are decent again? I do not recall you mentioning your destination."

"I thought I'd spend some time with Byron. He ought to be at Newstead Abbey for a bit around now. He usually goes there when he is a trifle dipped. I have an uncle in that area. I ought to visit him as well." Milburn's step was buoyant, as though he relished the coming days.

Nick took a considering look at his companion. He was well enough—likely Miss Herbert would appreciate those dark curls, thinking them romantic. Dark eyes concealed more than blue, Nick thought, and Milburn's were very dark, almost black. And even though the chap had a scar on his chin, a chit like Nympha Herbert would probably think it something to sigh over. Bah!

Of course, Milburn wasn't as tall as Nick, so he had

the advantage of noting that the fellow's hair was a trifle thin on the top. Nick ran a careless hand through his own thick nut-brown hair with satisfaction. His tousled look was simplicity itself to manage. Not for him the hour at the looking glass to arrange each hair on his head just so.

They retraced their steps to the Dog and Drake where Nick spoke to the innkeeper, requesting a nuncheon to be served before long. He left Milburn in the common room, then went up to check on his unwanted responsibility.

It never occurred to him to depart without seeing to her welfare, even if the rain abated and his own coach was undamaged. He—as well as his brother—had been raised to look after their own, and he considered Miss Herbert in that vague category, being the daughter of his rector.

He rapped on the door. Hearing a murmur that could have meant anything, he cracked open the door. "Miss Herbert? I thought to see how you fare."

The door opened to reveal Miss Herbert garbed once again in her blue traveling dress. He stared at the sight of the fetching ruff at her neck, so typical of her attire. She seemed to enjoy muted colors and soft fabrics, from what he could recall—which he had to confess wasn't much. Behind her he noted a blue velvet mantle draped across a chair, as though she intended to depart.

"Going somewhere? I believe I left orders for you to remain in bed."

"As you may see, I do very well. Only the slightest ache remains in my head. Other than the damage to poor Annie, we are fine—quite ready to depart if it is possible." She gazed up at him with naive innocence in her remarkably blue eyes.

She might have known him most of her life, but she still shouldn't trust a man not related to her. Come to think on it, there were a few relatives one shouldn't trust, either.

"I just came from the wheelwright. He says the repair will take until tomorrow at best." At her sudden frown and downcast eyes, he added, "I was just about to partake of a bit of nuncheon. Perhaps you will join us? We appear not to be the only travelers who have sought refuge here."

She nodded agreement, taking a step forward. "Mr. Milburn seems an agreeable gentleman. How odd we should all know one another—even if slightly."

Nick wondered how best to answer the question not asked. Was Milburn not only agreeable but also trustworthy? A gentleman in truth as well as name? He didn't know him all that well. In fact, when he had appeared at Lanstone Hall, Nick had been required to think a few moments to recall his identity.

"As to that, I couldn't say. He is but a casual acquaintance. I could not vouch for him one way or another." The touch of her dainty hand on his proffered arm gave him an odd sensation, like he should be a knight-errant, protecting a fragile yet brave woman who was under siege.

"How strange. I mean, that he would deign to come for a visit when you scarce know him." She gave him a quizzical look, then walked down the steps at his side. Again, Nick was touched at the sign of trust she evidently placed in him. She might not like him, but apparently she trusted him. It was a novel feeling for a gentleman who had been dashing about Town since he left Oxford, cutting a swath in Society before settling down on his land to create his golf links. It made him feel about seven feet tall.

"That sort of thing is far more common than you would believe. In fact," he confided, "I'll have you know there are chaps who barely have a roof to call their own. They simply travel about, sponging where they can."

"How sad," Miss Herbert whispered as they neared the bottom of the stairs. "No roof to call their own."

Nick guessed she spoke softly in consideration of Milburn's feelings. The thought occurred to him that he didn't know if the fellow had any of the more tender emotions or not. Nick did.

The innkeeper had been busy. Or his wife had, for there was a nice collation on the table. Bowls of hot vegetable soup were placed before them as they joined Milburn at the table. Crusty rolls were warm from the oven.

Miss Herbert seated herself with more poise than might be expected, given that she was stranded at an inn in the company of two men, one she didn't like and one she didn't know.

Nick eased Miss Herbert's chair closer to the table with misgivings. While they weren't all that close to one another, it was possible for Milburn's knees to accidentally touch hers. Why, he had done it himself from time to time, but only with those fair damsels who were quite up to snuff. Miss Herbert was anything but up to snuff.

He needn't have worried.

"Mr. Milburn, I fear we are a trifle crowded at this table. Perhaps if I move to another chair you will have enough room? You tall gentlemen have such long, er, limbs. My brother, Adam, is the same. He never seems to have enough room at the table." She gave both men a pleasant look, holding her soupspoon aloft while turning to each.

Nick cleared his throat of a sudden obstruction. What a guileless smile she had offered Milburn. He had turned a beetroot red, moving away in such haste he nearly overset his soup bowl.

"No, I am fine. You must forgive me for chancing to bump you."

Nick caught Milburn's gaze at that point, sending the fellow a message that should have been plain to a dimwit. "The rain appears to be lessening. Do you intend to move on this afternoon, Milburn?"

"Actually, I thought it might be a good idea were we to travel as a party for a time." Milburn avoided Nick's gaze. "One cannot be too careful nowadays. The roads are often dangerous." His dark eyes that met Miss Herbert's were full of meaning, although what he intended to convey escaped Nick.

"Do you mean highwaymen, or merely nasty holes in the road?" she inquired with obvious dismay.

Nick leaned back in his chair, waiting to see what Milburn would say.

This time Milburn did glance at Nick. He gave Miss Herbert a jaunty smile as though to imply he could take care of either one, and replied, "Why, as to that, you need have no worry. Not if we are there to defend you."

Nick wondered if Milburn hoped to leave his hired yellow bounder at the Dog and Drake, presuming to sponge a ride with him. Rather than bring that matter up, he turned his attention to his meal. If anyone were going to change coaches, it would be that he would invite Miss Herbert to share his—in the guise of safety. If that ruse failed, he would offer to join her so that he might be handy if the coach had more trouble.

There was no way of knowing, but he had decided there was something a trifle smoky about Milburn showing up as he had. Nick refused to consider that he might be jealous of Milburn's dashing good looks. After all, Miss Herbert couldn't see the thinning hair atop his head.

It might have been possible for Milburn to learn that Miss Herbert set forth on her journey early this morning. Nick hadn't known, but Milburn apparently had spent time nosing about the village—he'd met the rector and his wife, not to mention wangling an introduction to Miss Herbert, hadn't he?

The meal continued in silence for a time until Miss Herbert commented on the weather, then offered an opinion of village life, followed by a remark about the benefits of fresh air. Nick decided he'd suggest exploring the village. She might like that.

"Miss Herbert, I would deem it a great pleasure if you would consent to stroll along the walk in this village," Milburn quickly said. "I believe there is a clever little shop not far from here. You must have a little memento of your pause here."

Nick waited to see what Nympha would do. He supposed he ought to intervene, but after all, if she was old enough to travel to Nottingham, she should know a lure when she heard one.

Miss Herbert blotted her nicely curved lips with her napkin, glanced at Nick, and then smiled. "I should like that very much, indeed."

She ignored the pudding offered by the serving maid, merely easing away from the table slightly, as though anxious to be gone.

"I will return to the wheelwright's shop to see what progress he has made, my dear," Nick said with a hint of the proprietary in his manner and voice.

"Why, Lord Nicholas, how very kind you are, especially when I am sure you are anxious to be off. You never did say where you are gong." She tilted her head, and the clever little flat hat she wore looked in danger of falling off.

"I believe our destination is the same. Mansfield."

Milburn gave a start. "*You* go to Mansfield as well?"

Nick leaned back in his chair again, surveying Milburn through half-closed eyes. "Is there any reason I shouldn't be going to Mansfield? I was not aware the town was off-limits to me."

"Oh, of course not. Silly of me, to be sure. I was merely surprised that all three of us go to the same town. Seems all the more reason to join company."

"I shall give it some thought, you may be sure," Nick replied evasively. He would need to speak with Miss Herbert alone. All he could do for the present was to let her walk with Milburn . . . unless—"Perhaps you would like to see how your coach proceeds, Miss Herbert? Then after that, we could all take a stroll to the village shop. I daresay there will be something of interest there." He gave Miss Herbert a smile as shrewd as the one she had given him before. He was rewarded with a dashed pretty blush.

"That would be lovely. My great-aunt's coachman will likely report, but it would be nice to see for myself."

Nick gave no hint of his satisfaction at this change in plans. Milburn's angry expression was quickly masked with a composed face.

The three left the Dog and Drake shortly after.

Miss Herbert was suitably impressed with the work that needed to be done on the traveling coach. The wheelwright was fashioning the axle even as they entered his shop. A pause by the door proved to be all that was necessary for her.

"My, that was interesting. What skill he has," she declared as Nick lifted her across a puddle. Nick smiled at Milburn.

"Thank you, sir. I vow I had not known you were such a gallant." She peeped up at him from under that ridiculous hat, examining his face. She wore a curious expression that baffled Nick.

"Oh, Lord Nicholas is quite the man with the ladies," Milburn said, his manner and voice insinuating.

"Well, I believe every gentleman aims to be agreeable to ladies. I should hope I'd not be objectionable," Nick replied with easy grace, tucking Miss Herbert's arm close to his side.

"I doubt you could be that," Miss Herbert said with a judicious gleam in her fine blue eyes.

"Do not be too trusting," Nick murmured as Milburn went ahead to open the door to the village shop.

"Of you, Mr. Milburn, or gentlemen in general?" she inquired in dulcet tones.

"All of the above."

She gave no indication as to whether she had heard him or not, entering the shop with obvious anticipation.

Nympha looked about her with more than a little curiosity. Having the attention of two gentlemen of the *ton* was enough to go to a girl's head—if she wasn't careful. She had heard the words of warning offered by Lord Nicholas, including himself in his advice. Why she should *not* trust him, she didn't know. Within her memory he had never by word or deed indicated he was untrustworthy. Of course, they were far from home now. And Mr. Milburn was an unknown quantity.

She examined the bits and pieces offered for sale in the shop. There was a card of lace, but not the sort to trim a petticoat. It still rankled her finer senses that his lordship should have observed her odiously plain garment.

Mr. Milburn insisted upon buying her a twist of peppermints. Lord Nicholas smiled at that, then found a box of bonbons recently brought from London by the hopeful owner of the shop upon his return from an annual restocking trip.

Nympha grinned inwardly at the thought that such elegant gentlemen were vying for her attention. She knew full well that it was because she was the only presentable female around, and suspected gentlemen found the appeal of competition irresistible.

The wind had risen while they were in the shop. Nympha pulled her velvet mantle closer about her, wishing it had a fur lining like one she had seen in *La Belle Assembleé.* She didn't dawdle, but stepped forth with haste, anxious to return to the comfort of a brisk fire at the inn.

The gentlemen kept pace with her, saying little in the face of the wind. Once they achieved the inn, Lord Nicholas slipped her mantle from her shoulders, then guided her to the fireplace. She had been right to suppose a good fire would await them.

Milburn left them to return to the room he had engaged for the night, promising to rejoin them shortly.

Nick watched as Miss Herbert stretched out her hands to the fire's warmth. He dropped her mantle on a nearby chair, then walked to her side.

"I believe you and I ought to join forces for the trip to Mansfield. Your traveling coach may well be repaired, but given the state of the roads, I would be much happier were I able to be close by in the event of trouble. After all, what would your esteemed father say if he knew?"

"My father knows you well, Lord Nicholas. However,

I cannot imagine what he might say to our traveling together."

Nick thought he knew, but refrained from comment. "Please think about it. I'll not press you, but I will ask again come morning. With any luck at all, the wheelwright should have the coach ready following our breakfast."

Nick decided then and there that he would ride with Miss Herbert. Precisely how he would manage to evade Milburn he didn't know, but he would. Oh, yes, indeed—Milburn would find his scheme to fix the attentions of the lovely Miss Herbert, doted on by a possibly wealthy great-aunt, to no avail!

Chapter Three

Following a quiet evening spent discussing poetry and various writers, Nympha went to her room in the inn. She was quite bemused by what she had learned about the man she had disliked for so long. He was not at all shallow, nor was he even strongly opinionated. He had treated her thoughts and offerings as though they mattered, a novel thing when most men appeared to believe women had no brains worth mentioning. He did not seem at all disdainful that she had been raised to engage in meaningful conversation as a result of her father's unusual belief that God had created woman to be a man's helpmeet.

Nympha enjoyed a sound sleep, undisturbed by worries of traveling on the next day. After all, Lord Nicholas had promised he would look after her—more or less. Nympha had discovered she was not one of those stalwart girls who thought they could manage everything. She was well aware of the dangers that might befall her. To her way of thinking, having both gentlemen to hand was sensible. Interesting, too. Although, she mused as sleep crept up on her, she wasn't too sure about Mr. Milburn. She recalled her mother's voice, saying, "Handsome is as handsome does," and Mr. Milburn was handsome in his way.

And she sensed there was something between the two gentlemen. Quite what it was she couldn't say. Perhaps it might be nothing more than a feeling of antagonism on the part of Lord Nicholas. But as to Mr. Milburn, she rather thought his attitude was more a veiled hostility. She caught a hint of it every now and again in the looks he gave Lord Nicholas when he was otherwise occupied. Just why Mr. Milburn should dislike Lord Nicholas she couldn't begin to imagine. His lordship was all that was amiable, certainly helpful. Maybe Mr. Milburn envied his lordship's position, or his handsome face.

While Nympha had been raised not to judge a person by his appearance, she had to admit that that romantically tousled brown hair falling over a noble brow and gleaming dark eyes filled with mysterious depths had it all over Mr. Milburn's pleasant countenance and black eyes that seemed to lack any warmth. At times Lord Nicholas was inclined to thin his mouth into a firm line, but her father praised him for his astute management of his new estate.

Nympha snuggled into the coverings of her bed while pondering the nuances of the two gentlemen with whom she now traveled. It was a pity that once she reached her great-aunt she'd not see more of them, for that was a highly unlikely prospect. She had truly disliked Lord Nicholas in the past. Now she was revising her opinion slightly. He had looked after her splendidly, even if he tended to be a bit high-handed! On that thought, she slept, forgetting the thoughts she usually directed to his older brother.

Annie managed to bring in the tray set with chocolate and rolls while another maid opened the door for her. "Morning, miss."

Nympha inhaled deeply when the aroma of hot chocolate drifted to her nose and opened her eyes. "How is the weather? I do hope the rain has gone."

"Yes, miss. The sun might not be warm like summer, but it shines. I expect as how the primroses will be peeping out before long." She waited while Nympha settled against her pillows, then placed the tray before her.

"Spring," Nympha said with a sigh of satisfaction at the mere thought. "Do you know, I have not the least notion how long Great-Aunt Letitia intends me to visit with her. I imagine I'll stay for a while." Nympha polished off her chocolate and two of the rolls. Having not the slightest ache in her head this morning, she rose, dressed with what little help Annie could offer, then set off for the common room, intent upon finding Lord Nicholas if possible. She wore her blue traveling gown again, having little by way of wardrobe from which to choose.

Pausing at the entrance to the common room, she took note of the occupants. As yet, neither seemed to be aware of her presence. Both gentlemen were garbed rather finely for travel, she thought. However, she suspected that Lord Nicholas, even though he looked casual, was the more dashing of the two. His bottle-green coat worn over biscuit breeches with a waistcoat of muted rust-and-gold weave would send her brother, Adam, into transports. They fit his lordship superbly. Mr. Milburn wore a brown coat of undistinguished cut with tan pantaloons and a peacock-blue waistcoat. She couldn't see the buttons, but she would wager they were large. He seemed inclined toward the dandy, whereas Lord Nicholas wore more refined garments. Compared to Lord Nicholas, Mr. Milburn, in spite of being very nice looking, seemed lacking.

She couldn't see their boots, but would also wager they were highly polished. Her own half boots of Moroccan leather, so sensible for traveling, could have used a touch of polish. Perhaps she would seek out the valet Lord Nicholas brought along to see if he might assist Annie with the polishing since she was incapacitated, more or less.

Lord Nicholas glanced at the door, and she was discovered. He promptly rose from the table. Gesturing to the vacant chair, he urged, "Please join us. I doubt your chocolate will sustain you for long. I hope to put in a few hours on the road before we must pause for a lunch."

"Then we are to go this morning?" Nympha was delighted, hurrying forward to join them. The thought of keeping her great-aunt waiting was not pleasing. She slid onto the chair between the two men, sparing a glance at Mr. Milburn before turning her attention to Lord Nicholas again. "The coach repair is completed? I am set to go?"

"Well, yes and no. I thought that perhaps you and I might forge on ahead. The wheelwright ran into a problem with the coach. Your great-aunt's coachman agreed that it is better to get a really good repair rather than to have a shabbily done job that requires redoing, or worse yet, have another accident. So, instead of waiting here, I hoped you might agree to proceed in my carriage. Your maid will join us, and Simpson can either ride on top or inside, depending on the weather. What do you say?"

Nympha nibbled at her lower lip, confused and a bit annoyed. She had relished traveling in the elegant coach sent for her, and was reluctant to forego that luxury. Yet, she truly hated to linger here, alone, when she could be on her way to the north. As to having the company of Lord Nicholas all that distance, she preferred not to consider her feelings.

"Very well, if you think it best," she replied with all the reluctance she felt. "After all, I have known you for ages, and you seem more like my brother than a stranger." She offered a bland smile before spooning some buttered eggs and a bit of gammon onto her plate. Mr. Milburn proffered toast, and they ate their meal in a silence broken only by requests for salt and jam.

Nick wordlessly fumed while consuming a hearty meal. He was not accustomed to being treated like a brother by a perfectly presentable female not related to him. In fact, she was more than presentable if you studied her a little. Why, dressed in the height of fashion she would shine at any ball or social event. He hoped her great-aunt actually *was* warm in the pocket, able to buy her young relative a few pretty creations—if such things were available so far north.

He intended to see something of her once in Mansfield. Her great-aunt might be of help in his quest to discover the identity of the murdered man. At least, he hoped so, if she was the sort of woman who knew everyone for miles around. Having Miss Herbert in his carriage meant he would have to deliver her directly to her great-aunt, thus offering him an opportunity to meet the elderly lady, perhaps gain a chance to call on them.

"I was hoping that we three might travel on together," Milburn inserted, giving Nick a sullen look. "It is more congenial when there are several in a party. The larger the number, the less likelihood there is to cause gossip, don't you think? Not that I expect to see more people I know along the way, but one never knows . . . ," he concluded in a rather suggestive manner with a raise of a shrewd brow.

Dash it all, Milburn did have a point. And the last thing Nick wanted was gossip. One look at the dainty miss with her blond curls peeping from under a small chip bonnet, and his goose would be cooked. Or Milburn's. Either way, it was not to be considered.

"I take your meaning. Very well. I see no reason why our carriages cannot make a sort of cavalcade out of the trip. If you feel your post-chaise can keep up with mine, by all means join us." Nick knew a certain satisfaction frustrating Milburn in his attempt to rid himself of the expense of his hired post-chaise by traveling in Nick's vehicle. Were it another man, it would likely have been different. But Nick felt he didn't know Milburn well enough. Besides, why should he and Miss Herbert be cramped merely to accommodate a near stranger? Dash it all, he simply wanted distance between Milburn and Miss Herbert! He did not examine his reasons closely—not at all—but there it was.

Milburn compressed his mouth in what seemed to be silent annoyance. Obviously, he had hoped the matter would be resolved to his liking. "I look forward to our meeting at meals and the evenings, in that event," he said with reluctant grace.

The maids and Nick's valet had been busy while they were at their morning meal. All their baggage was in the process of being stowed in the boot of his carriage when they left the inn. Nick had settled the account for himself and for Miss Herbert, after murmuring to her that the coachman had a purse with him sufficient to cover his expenses as well as the coach repair.

He was pleased that she didn't argue with him as some forward misses might have. She behaved with unexpected propriety, not that she had been all that disgraceful in the past. However, she had admired his brother and had gone to great lengths to attract his attention. Perhaps that was the reason she had no interest in him? Well, Nick couldn't compete with the heir to the marquissate. He wouldn't even try!

Milburn crossed to where his Yellow Bounder awaited him. He exchanged a few words with the postboy. Garbed in white corduroy breeches and a bright yellow jacket, the postboy was booted and spurred, ready to leave.

Because the morning was so fine, Annie decided to sit up with Simpson on that seat designed for servants. The valet was a very superior sort, and Nick suspected Annie wished to learn as much as she could from him. Either that, or flirt!

"I will keep a record, sir, and you shall be reimbursed once we reach Mansfield and my great-aunt," Miss Herbert declared as Nick assisted her into his family coach.

"As you wish, Miss Herbert."

The mud from yesterday's trip had been washed away, and the family crest gleamed in all its bright paint. While Nick didn't usually hold with display, he'd found when traveling that a crest made a world of difference in his treatment. He did enjoy good meals and fresh, lavender-scented sheets.

Nick flashed a smile at her as he joined her in the coach once she had settled. A touch of independence did not harm the pretty girl he had chosen to rescue. "I shall report to your relative all that has been done, my dear."

Nympha eased back on the seat, wondering why she hadn't insisted upon Annie joining them. The girl had looked so eager to join the impressive valet that it seemed cruel to deny her the pleasure. Besides, what could happen inside a traveling coach in broad daylight?

Looking about her, it was clear she wouldn't miss the elegance of her great-aunt's carriage in the least. The Stanhope coach was equal to or surpassed it in refinement, with all manner of little touches to ensure one's comfort. Her great-aunt's coach did not have a sword case built in—Nympha supposed she didn't feel the need for it. The squabs, or cushions, were silk covered, and there were venetian blinds on the windows. Nympha suspected the carpet that covered the floor of the coach was a Wilton, for it was thick and richly colored.

"You travel well, I believe," Nympha said at last to break the silence.

He had chosen to sit opposite her, so she didn't have to turn her head to speak with him.

"I find it agreeable not to arrive aching and miserable at my destination." He reclined against his seat, crossing one knee over the other once the coach had set forth and the pace was determined.

Nympha nodded, wondering again what was taking him to Mansfield. "Do you know anyone in Mansfield, sir?"

"Well, I daresay I know Byron as well as anyone does. Portland and Manvers as well. Lord William Bentinck comes from around there, and I've run into him at the various clubs and social events when in Town. Nice chap."

She knew that Portland was a duke and that Lord Manvers was an earl. Hadn't Papa mentioned that Lord William was aiming for a seat in the House of Commons? Nympha settled against the cushioned seat as though she could sink into it. This was high-flying for the daughter of a rector, no matter how well connected he might be. "I see."

"I imagine that your great-aunt is well acquainted with those in the area. Perhaps she may be able to recommend a good inn in Mansfield?" He rubbed his well-shaped chin with a hand that looked strong and capable. It was surprising how she had never observed much about him before. It was merely because she was in such proximity that she looked more closely at him now—that was surely it. But she began to find him appealing, surprisingly so. He might be decidedly masculine, but his consideration for her comforts and well-being charmed her. He proved to be far more complex, more tantalizing than she had suspected.

"I feel certain she will." The thought occurred to her that her relative might well be pleased to house the son of the Marquess of Lanstone for a time. After all, he possessed his own status. Lord Nicholas Stanhope was a gentleman many hostesses would eagerly welcome.

"What do you plan to do on your visit?" he quizzed. "I suppose you intend to survey Sherwood Forest? You hope for your own Robin Hood to find you?" His lordship cast her a look that bordered on teasing.

Nympha knew she blushed at the gleam in his eyes. "I'd like to see that, and perhaps Newstead Abbey as well. I suppose if Byron is in residence that wouldn't be possible. Young ladies do not visit the residence of a bachelor. Papa said that some gentleman discovered two Roman villas nearby a few years ago. Come to think on it, that might be more interesting than seeing the abbey."

"I've been told that when he is bored Byron shoots at the walls for amusement. It tends to pass the time when it is raining outside."

"Mercy! I do not think I will have anything to do with the place in that event." She was shocked to think a gentleman could behave in such a manner.

She studied the scene out of the window, wondering what else to discuss with his lordship. She had always ignored him in the past. Now, she was finding it quite difficult to do so. She was aware of him every second. He stirred something deep within her she didn't understand.

Eventually, he pierced the quiet with a comment on a book he had read that she had also enjoyed. This led to a discussion of other books they both liked, thus passing the time until the coach drew into the courtyard of a superior coaching inn. His consideration in helping her from the coach flattered, and his touch aroused a warm feeling inside her. She liked laughing with him.

The Bell possessed a charming exterior and an equally agreeable interior. As Nympha followed a mobcapped maid down the hall to a room where she might refresh herself, she could hear Mr. Milburn's voice complaining to Lord Nicholas about the road he was compelled to endure.

Well, it was his notion to follow them. He might be a handsome gentleman, but she wasn't drawn to him at all. The thought that Lord Nicholas was more to her liking was set aside as impossible. She reminded herself that she did not like the man, and that was that!

One day followed the next in fascinating order. She couldn't get enough of the scenery. They were blessed with fine weather and roads that had at last dried out. Mr. Milburn complained of the dust at every stop. Yet, when Lord Nicholas suggested he leave them, Mr. Milburn stuck like a burr.

She was very glad to have company on her journey north. She confessed as much to the gentlemen who were so kind as to join her for meals each day, although it was Lord Nicholas to whom she was most grateful.

"We are the ones who are in your debt, Miss Herbert," Lord Nicholas replied with more gallantry than she expected. "We would be a pair of dull dogs without you."

Mr. Milburn echoed this sentiment with equal courtesy.

But it was Lord Nicholas who captured a corner of her heart with his pleasant conversation, his little attentions, and his consideration of her wishes. She hadn't met many gentlemen, hadn't experienced hours of challenging discussion as she did with Lord Nicholas. He had a keen mind, yet teased her with silly games to pass the time.

He saw to it that she had her favored tea when they paused for lunch, and requested biscuits to take with them. His kindness, his charm, quite won her over.

By the time they reached Nottingham, all three had become a bit more informal. Still, Lord Nicholas did not invite Mr. Milburn to share his traveling coach—in spite of its spacious interior. He explained to Nympha that if it chanced to rain, he would want Annie and Simpson to be inside, dry and not likely to come down with the ague.

As the coach traveled north from the larger city, Nympha drew forth the detailed instructions for reaching her great-aunt's home that the coachman had dictated to her before they parted ways.

"Here, my lord, the instructions your coachman needs to find the house." She offered them to his lordship, aware that his touch affected her oddly—even through her gloves. She dismissed the effect as of no consequence, purely an accident. But it was unsettling, nevertheless.

Nick accepted the proffered papers, studying them with care. Miss Herbert had a fine hand, very easy to read. "It seems we shall be there in no time at all. I'll wager you will be glad to see the last of us." A smile lit his eyes, even if his face was sober.

They had to change horses one more time, during which Nick explained to his man where they were to turn off to reach Coxmoor Hall.

Returning to his traveling coach, Nick glanced at his passenger. He would be sorry to part with her, he realized with a start. The girl he had considered a peagoose had turned out to be far more substantial—witness the books she enjoyed reading and her insightful comments on poetry. Not that Nick was that well acquainted with poetry, but he had perused some of Byron's. It was the sort of stuff that sent impressionable young women off to the woods to declaim favorite passages to the ferny glades.

"I want to thank you for your kindness on this journey," Miss Herbert ventured. "You have made what would have been a dreary trip most pleasant. I confess that I thought you to be immersed in golf to the exclusion of all else, and you proved me wrong. I apologize, if that thought offends you." She smiled, a delicious little smile he found rather tantalizing. But then, he had learned there was a lot about Miss Herbert that attracted him.

Before he could reply the coach turned off the main road that had brought them north to a side avenue.

"I believe we are near the end of your journey, Miss Herbert." Nick peered out of the coach window, hoping to see a glimpse of Coxmoor Hall. The avenue was well tended, the gravel neatly raked. To either side of the avenue was a lush parkland with deer roaming beneath spreading oak trees of stately size. Banks of rhododendrons were massed here and there, their lavender-tinged buds beginning to open.

This was not a modest estate.

A glance behind showed that Milburn had elected to follow them. Evidently he hoped to make the acquaintance of the widow much as Nick did, but probably for vastly different reasons. Milburn was not a poor man, and he had hinted he was to come into a comfortable inheritance before too long. Yet Nick doubted if a man of his tastes ever had enough money. Nick wanted information, and he hoped Mrs. Coxmoor would be a fountain of facts and possibly figures.

He returned his attention to Miss Herbert when she cleared her throat.

"I suppose it is silly, but of a sudden I am a bit nervous." Nympha gestured with her hand to the exquisite parkland to either side of the coach. "I truly had not expected this. I thought perhaps a modest villa or a neat manor. But this . . ."

"Cheer up, I won't leave you until you are comfortable here. Sometimes it helps to have a familiar face about when you are thrust into a strange situation."

"As I said before, you are amazingly kind. You make me ashamed of some of the thoughts I harbored about you. And I will *not* share them now, but know I find you admirable. Most of the time," she amended when she recalled a few of his more autocratic decrees given along the way. That attitude had been bred into him. He could no more *not* be that way than not breathe!

At last the coachman drew them up before a very large residence built of warm-tinted stone. It rose three stories, with an impressive portico in the center front. This was not an unassuming dwelling, not in the least.

There was a flurry of activity as the groom opened the door, then let down the steps. He offered his hand, and Nympha hesitantly stepped from the coach to gaze about her. Her first thought was that she wished her mother could see this magnificence. Her second was—what in the world was she doing here?

Lord Nicholas followed her from the coach. As they slowly walked up the stairs to the entry level, Mr. Milburn left his post-chaise, paying the postboy before he hurried to join them while his baggage was unloaded. It would seem he intended to beg transport from Lord Nicholas. Nympha stole a glance at his lordship to see if he indicated a reaction to this bit of effrontery.

She encountered a dark-eyed stare that told her nothing. Before she might venture a word, the large and very impressive oak door opened. A dignified butler bowed with exquisite courtesy, then ushered them into the hall.

"Miss Herbert, we have been expecting you." He looked at the two gentlemen with her, his brow raised a fraction.

"I am Lord Nicholas Stanhope and this is Mr. Milburn. We escorted Miss Herbert when the coach in which she traveled met with an accident. If we might speak with Mrs. Coxmoor?"

"Follow me."

And they did. They trod across the marble-paved hall, its black-and-white preciseness a foil for the lush red of the silk wall hangings and the rich paintings hung on them. Nympha's gaze darted about her, taking note of probable ancestors, interesting people.

Annie was taken in hand along with the luggage, heading up the stairs, leaving Simpson standing quietly near the door. The maid's eyes looked as though they were about to start from her head at the sight of such splendor.

The footman stationed outside the drawing room threw open the double doors.

"Miss Nympha Herbert, Lord Nicholas Stanhope, and Mr. Milburn, madam." The butler bowed, then backed from the room as though Mrs. Coxmoor were royalty.

Nympha advanced into the room, awed by all around her. She could easily spend days absorbing the details of this particular room. The walls here were also hung with red silk, and there was a magnificent looking glass topped by a gilded eagle above the fireplace. A tall, slender lady rose from a sofa of red figured silk. Slender, garbed in a beautiful gray silk sarcenet gown of utter simplicity, she did not appear her age, which Nympha knew approached seventy.

"So you are Nympha!" Great-Aunt Letitia quickly crossed to wrap her grandniece in a swift lavender-scented hug. "How like your mother you are—when she was a girl. I recall her well."

"Thank you, ma'am. I bring greetings from her and my father." Nympha smiled at her great-aunt, who, in spite of the magnificence of her surroundings, looked cozily as she ought. She shared the family nose, and there was a hint of Grandmother about her eyes.

Mrs. Coxmoor turned to Lord Nicholas and Mr. Milburn, her brows raised in question.

"Your traveling coach met with an accident," Lord Nicholas said, bowing. He went on to explain the decision for the three to travel on together.

"You live near here? Or do you visit? I do not recognize either name." Mrs. Coxmoor's gaze was penetrating.

"I am here to explore the area, perhaps locate someone I know. Milburn is rusticating, I believe." Lord Nicholas turned to look at him.

"I confess, I merely travel about for the pleasure of it. That and to meet a relative of mine."

"We were hoping you might suggest a suitable inn to be found in Mansfield." Lord Nicholas bowed again, displaying the elegant manners Nympha had noted were a part of him.

Nympha was proud to have been a part of such company. "I must say, ma'am, that Lord Nicholas saw to it that we stayed in none but the finest of inns while coming north. I am indebted to him for his concern and care."

Mrs. Coxmoor's gaze raked the two men with a lightning glance. "Please, you must stay with us. I fear the inn in Mansfield would not satisfy you, not if your standards are above the ordinary. After all you have done for my grandniece it is the least I can do. Goodness knows there are sufficient rooms in this great pile of stone."

Neither gentleman was slow to accept. Of course, they made little noises of protest, but brief ones, before agreeing that it would be of all things wonderful to remain in Miss Herbert's company—as well as with Mrs. Coxmoor.

"Good, then it is settled." She crossed to tug a silken rope near the fireplace that brought the butler into the room within moments.

"Foley, see that rooms are prepared for the gentlemen. They will be staying with us for a time."

Foley bowed. "Indeed, madam."

"And Foley, have James bring refreshments."

"Yes, madam."

Nympha wondered if she would ever become accustomed to such austere formality after the simplicity of the rectory.

Mrs. Coxmoor returned her attention to her guests. "Do tell me all about your journey. Precisely what happened to the traveling coach? It was in good repair when it left here, but I know what the roads can be like." She gestured to the sofa opposite the one on which she had been seated, then drew Nympha to sit at her side, facing the gentlemen.

Nick set forth the bare bones of the accident, omitting any mention of his suspicions. After all, nothing else had occurred to mar the trip. Miss Herbert interposed comments where she thought necessary.

"Well, it seems you have had quite an adventure, my dear," Mrs. Coxmoor said with a somewhat arch look at her grandniece. "Let us hope that the rest of your visit will be equally enlivening."

Chapter Four

"Everything is of the finest, my lord. Mr. Milburn has even been assigned a man to do for him." Simpson sniffed his disapproval of any gentleman who would travel without his valet. "This is the best of households from what I can see to this point." He paused in unpacking Nick's apparel to give him a respectful look. The valet was surprisingly fussy about accommodations, expecting the cream for his master. That he would also appreciate nice rooms for the staff was left unsaid. He'd reported that his small room adjacent to Nick's was all he could want in comfort.

"Nice to have your approval," Nick murmured as he casually strolled across to inspect the view from the large bedroom he had been given. The rug beneath his feet was thick and soft, appearing to be of excellent quality. There was a hint of lavender in the room, most pleasant. His room in his new home would likely not suit him better. As a matter of fact, he could pick up a few ideas from this house for his own.

"Madam will tolerate nothing but the latest, I was informed when I inquired about facilities." Simpson unbent enough to offer the faintest of smiles. "Indeed, sir, you have truly landed on your feet."

"Hmm." The view from his window showed a well-tended garden looking its early spring best. Green shoots indicated where perennials would later bloom. Early tulips were in bud. The grass was perfectly scythed—he'd wager a weed wouldn't dare to pop up anywhere it wasn't wanted. He could see a sizable pond in the distance with the willows at its edge showing a tinge of green on their dancing branches.

He turned from this bucolic scene to study his room. A mammoth four-poster bed was centered on one wall. He would hazard it offered utmost comfort. Behind it hung light blue silk with a vaguely Greek motif he liked. A handsome desk equipped with everything he could need for writing was opposite the bed between two windows. Comfortable-looking chairs covered in a dark blue-and-white print were scattered about the room, small tables at the side of each, upon which one might place a lamp or candle, or glass of brandy—a fine bottle of which he noted stood on the dresser where Simpson still fussed.

"Mrs. Coxmoor believes in treating her guests, even unexpected ones, quite well. Wonder how her husband made his wealth?" Unlike many of the *ton*, Nick was not above chatting with his valet. The fellow was a wizard at learning anything of interest, and Nick had often found his knack invaluable.

"As to that, milord, I learned that the late Mr. Coxmoor had interests in a coal mine and a lace factory, among other things. No matter what he turned his hand to, he made money at it. Could have bought himself a barony had he wished. Decided he would rather be a plain mister."

Nick smiled at the disbelief in Simpson's voice. It was hard for his valet to imagine a gentleman not wanting a title to give him a bit of prestige. Most men coveted that distinction.

"Madam did not seem to mind either way, so there you have it," Simpson continued. "The house is not so very old, but she is fond of it, for she and Mr. Coxmoor devised much of the plan. I fancy that is why she remains here, although the house is far too large for one person."

"Yet all I saw coming up here was in perfect order, so her income has not diminished." Nick went to the neat stand that now held his shaving gear, a bowl of warmish water, and anything else he might wish. His beard grew far too fast to be pleasing, so he took care of that before dressing for dinner. Simpson deplored his habit of shaving himself; Nick always replied he needed the practice in the event that Simpson might not be around at some point in the future. Surprisingly enough, the meal was to be held the same time as one might expect in London. He wished to be down early so to possibly chat with his hostess.

He wondered briefly how Milburn fared with the borrowed valet, then dismissed the man from his mind. Far better to speculate on how he was to approach Mrs. Coxmoor regarding the identity of the murdered man.

In a very large bedroom on the far side of the house Nympha plumped herself down on a chaise lounge to study her room. My, it would be difficult to return home after this magnificence. If she had thought the exterior impressive, the interior of the house was awesome.

Delicate gold-and-white striped paper adorned the wall, with pretty Dutch landscapes hung here and there. The four-poster bed was exquisitely carved in walnut, and the pale rose-figured bed covering looked sumptuous. More pale rose and a fragile green had been used in covering the chairs, and the colors were echoed in the fanciful thick rug she suspected came from China. Best of all was a wonderful walnut desk outfitted with rich cream hot-pressed paper. The bottle of ink seemed to be green. She couldn't imagine what Tabitha would say to receive a letter written with green ink!

"Best change for dinner, miss. You do not want to be rushed," Annie cautioned.

"Little difference it would make. None of my dresses will do justice to this house—or my great-aunt's elegance. Wait until you get a glimpse of her. She is remarkable. No one would ever believe her to be my *great*-aunt."

But Nympha submitted to a change of garb, and thought that the simple white crepe she and her mother had made looked just what it was, simple and homemade. Having been preached to all her life of the dangers of pride, she sighed and picked up her gloves and reticule before leaving her room.

The stairway was in the center of the house, and here Nympha encountered Lord Nicholas.

Nympha smiled, pleased that her relative could offer such fine accommodations to her friends, for she now considered them as such after days of traveling in their company. She supposed some high sticklers would have insisted Lord Nicholas had compromised her by traveling with her in the carriage. But with Annie and Simpson often inside for one reason or another, she doubted that argument would hold water. Besides, she was the rector's daughter, wearing drab clothes. Who would believe the handsome, dashing Lord Nicholas would give her an amorous look?

Quite as though he had seen into her mind, a smiling Lord Nicholas immediately offered his arm to her. "Settling in nicely?"

"Have you looked from your windows? Mine reveals a lovely prospect. I had no idea that Nottinghamshire was so pleasant."

"Hmm, indeed. Looks quite civilized, in fact." Lord Nicholas exchanged an amused glance with her, and Nympha felt the most peculiar little jolt to her heart as her eyes met his. It must be the aftereffect of such prolonged travel. It could be nothing else!

Mr. Milburn trotted down the stairs to join them. He refused to be excluded from any conversation, and immediately commenced what amounted to a lecture on the beauties of the area, particularly Sherwood Forest, until they reached the open door leading to the drawing room.

"Ah, I see you all are recovered from any ill effects of travel." Mrs. Coxmoor swiftly took in her grandniece's simple white crepe. "White is supposedly the only color for a young miss who is making her come-out. Somehow, I believe otherwise. I cannot see where the palest green or blue would not do. What do you think, Lord Nicholas? I would wager that you have spent time in London."

"True, white is widely worn, but I agree with you regarding pale colors. White is not always kind."

"And," Nympha inserted with a look at his lordship, "it becomes dirty if one so much as looks at it."

"Tell me of your plans, gentlemen. Mr. Milburn, you intend to find a relative? What is his name—perhaps I may know of him?" Her great-aunt studied the somewhat overdressed gentleman with what Nympha considered a very assessing look.

"Sir Cosmo Milburn, ma'am. I am not certain where he lives. I know his son better. We went to school together, but we didn't spend any time visiting back and forth, if you know what I mean." Mr. Milburn appeared a trifle uncomfortable with the question, which Nympha thought harmless, indeed, nothing more than any polite hostess might ask.

"I have heard of the baronet, but he is somewhat of a recluse, and seldom goes into company. His son is rarely seen." Her great-aunt turned to Lord Nicholas, but did not quiz him on his plans; rather, she merely gave him a look that seemed full of speculation.

"I intend to do a bit of seeing the sights around here." Lord Nicholas gave the elderly lady a disarming smile. "I imagine your grandniece is anxiously looking forward to viewing a bit of Sherwood Forest."

"He thinks I should like to discover a Robin Hood there. I fancy that would be the last thing desired!" Nympha's voice was full of her disdain.

At that fortuitous moment Foley appeared in the doorway to announce in a grand manner that dinner was served.

As they walked into the imposing dining room, the walls of which were covered in the same red silk, Great-Aunt Letitia drew Nympha to her side. "And what would you like to do, dear? I am persuaded you would enjoy hunting for lace. You must have some for yourself, and perhaps your mother and sisters would welcome some as well? We can go to the factory and select whatever you wish, you know."

Visions of lace danced before Nympha for several moments. Sensible of the cost this would represent, Nympha hedged. "Perhaps a bit of lace, ma'am. There are several garments I should like to trim." She glanced down at her white crepe, with puffed trim but sadly lacking any lace, and thought of her petticoat. "It would be very nice."

"We shall see." Great-Aunt Letitia smiled, a pleased sort of expression that told Nympha nothing more than she would have her wish to acquire a bit of lace.

"I must apologize for my subterfuge. I was not injured. I merely wanted the pleasure of a visit from you. I feared your father might thwart my wish."

"I did wonder. I'm happy to see you in good health, ma'am." Nympha speculated as to why her elderly relative wanted to see her.

The dinner was all that any of them might expect in so fine a house, and more than Nympha had imagined. Great-Aunt Letitia casually mentioned that she had begun to employ the latest style in serving—*à la russe.* "I observed it while in Russia last summer. I think it an eminently sensible way to serve guests."

Nympha looked to the sideboard where, rather than arranged on the table, the serving dishes were set out in splendor. The footmen handed them around to the guests in strict rotation. The plate of soup set before her had a heavenly aroma, one she couldn't identify, but delicious to her taste. The footman whisked away her soup plate the moment she had finished, to replace it with a pretty china dinner plate.

It amused her to have first the fine beef roast served, then the potatoes, followed by beans smothered in a cream sauce, and lastly a marvelous sauce for the meat. The various aromas teased her nose. She would have to let Drusilla know about that sauce, for it not only had a heavenly scent of sage about it, but also other subtle flavors.

The same routine was repeated with the desserts, a lemony pudding in a meringue basket and a chocolate soufflé. Nympha elected to have a bit of each—how could she choose only one!

The soufflé floated down her throat in an essence of chocolate delight. The lemon and meringue was unlike anything she had tasted before combining those two—sharp yet sweet, light yet rich.

A glance at Lord Nicholas revealed that he appeared to be enjoying the food as much as she did.

The service *à la russe* seemed very practical from Nympha's limited experience. When she had dined at Lanstone Hall, it had been a mad confusion of serving dishes here and there on the table, and she often did not have access to the foods she particularly enjoyed.

Mama would be amazed to learn that you could have far fewer dishes to be served, limiting the work in the kitchen. It might be easier on the budget as well.

By the time they left the dining room the hour was late, and Nympha longed for her bed. Some of her fatigue must have shown in her face, for it was suggested by her thoughtful great-aunt that she retire at once. "It must have been a long day for you, dear girl."

"Thank you, most observant of great-aunts. I am very tired and will welcome that lovely bed in my room." Nympha managed a graceful curtsy.

Mr. Milburn offered to see Nympha to the top of the stairs, holding her candle for her most gallantly as they walked up the stairs together. He spoke softly to her as they went up the steps. Whatever he had to say made her laugh.

Nick stood by Mrs. Coxmoor. He hoped he might have his opportunity now to speak about the identity of the murdered man.

"I gather you want to talk with me. Come, we can have a few minutes of peace before your friend returns." She led the way into the drawing room and she immediately crossed to the sofa where apparently she liked to sit.

Thanking his stars that he had tucked his sketch of the murdered man inside his waistcoat in case of just such an opportunity, he hastily pulled it forth. "Do you by chance recognize this man?"

She considered the drawing for several moments before answering. "I have seen such a face—but it is not one I can put a name to right away. I gather your friend is not included in your search?" She again studied the sketch in her hands, then looked up at Nick.

"I prefer to keep this to myself for the moment. Your grandniece is not aware of the sketch either."

Footsteps alerted them to Mr. Milburn's imminent return. Rather than hand the sketch to Nick, Mrs. Coxmoor tucked it into her reticule, then began a conversation on the local attractions.

"Sherwood Forest, by all means," Nick said as though it had been offered him.

"I intend to give a ball—perhaps a masquerade where Nympha can be Maid Marian. You can portray Robin Hood if you should like."

Nick grinned. "How clever of you to think of that. I believe Miss Herbert would enjoy that very much. I know she looks forward to buying the lace."

"Everyone does," Mrs. Coxmoor replied with some complacency. "Every petticoat requires a few rows of lace; every white gown would benefit from it as well. There is a great deal of lace made hereabouts, as you may know."

"I understand your husband had a lace factory?"

"He also employed a considerable number of women who did cottage work, making the lace at home. There are some patterns that are as yet difficult to produce by machine. And there are people who prefer to buy lace that is handmade." She turned her head toward the door. "Ah. Mr. Milburn, we were just discussing the sights to be found in this area."

"Your grandniece mentioned some Roman ruins nearby," Nick said as Milburn sat down on the other end of the sofa Nick occupied.

"What about Newstead Abbey?" Milburn looked from Mrs. Coxmoor to Nick, his brows raised in query.

"I do not know if Lord Byron is in residence. I hope that Nympha is not one of those girls who sigh over his poetry." Mrs. Coxmoor frowned at the very thought.

Rather than answer, Nick rose and bowed to the elderly lady he estimated must be tiring, in spite of appearing twenty years younger than she was. "It has been a long day, ma'am. We rose early to make certain we would be here before dark."

"And you do not stay up late in London?"

"Perhaps, but I expect you do not."

She gave him a rueful smile. "Very thoughtful of you, young man. I took a fine nap this afternoon so as to be fresh in the event you arrived this day." She gave Milburn a speculative look.

He rose at once, bowing politely to his hostess. "Yes, it is time we all headed for our bed, I'd say. I must thank you again for offering your hospitality to a stranger. Much appreciated." He glanced to Nick, then walked at his side as they left the room.

Behind them, Foley marched in to see to his mistress.

"So, you entertained Miss Herbert on the way up the stairs." Nick glanced at Milburn, surprised to see a red flush creep up his face.

"Well, she is a shy young thing. I'd not do anything out of the way, you know."

"No need to be defensive, Milburn. I know you to be a gentleman." But Nick didn't think Nympha Herbert the least shy, young though she might be. After listening to her opine on everything from poetry and novels to scenery, he knew she was far too opinionated to be called shy.

Alone in his room, Nick mulled over Milburn's behavior and decided there was nothing improper there. Yet Nick experienced a strange compulsion to protect Miss Herbert from any attentions Milburn cared to send her way. What had he said to her to make her chuckle in such an engaging manner? He'd give a monkey to know.

* * *

Morning brought Nympha bright eyes and curiosity about her surroundings. With the sun shining, albeit through clouds here and there, she wanted to explore outdoors.

Once she had finished her chocolate and rolls, she bade Annie help her dress—which was becoming easier as Annie's wrist returned to normal.

"I don't hear anyone downstairs, miss. House be as quiet as a tomb."

Nympha donned her cloak with haste, tying the tapes with eager fingers, then pulled on gloves. "I wish to explore a little, see something of the gardens. I shall return in time to partake of a light breakfast."

She skimmed down the central staircase. No matter it was early, Foley materialized to open the front door for her. "The early tulips are to the left, miss. Quite nice, they are, too."

With a word of thanks, she marched down to the gravel path, then turned to the left. It didn't take her long to find the enormous beds of barely opened tulips. The first bed was of red tulips for the most part, with two stripes of white dividing it. Oh, how her mother would have enjoyed seeing this display. She wandered on to admire a bed of early pink, still in bud, with the greenery of later-blooming tulips around them, and a border of hardy blue pansies. Another bed of short yellow tulips interspersed with white were quite showy, even if short of stem. Purple pansies bordered this bed. She bent over to pick a few of the fragrant blooms.

"Good morning, Miss Herbert. Out and about early, I see."

"Mr. Milburn! Fancy seeing you here." Nympha shot up, staring at him with surprise. On their journey north she had the impression that Mr. Milburn had a difficult time waking and took his time dressing. He did not believe in the simplicity of garb that Lord Nicholas did. However, his cravat appeared hastily tied, and he had the look of one who had been in a rush. In a hurry to see her? She found that difficult to believe. Clutching her pansies in uneasy fingers, she took a step toward the house.

"It is a lovely morning. Why not see a little of the grounds as long as we are out and about?"

She felt flustered. If Annie were here, she would not hesitate. Then, spotting a gardener up ahead, Nympha nodded agreement. Naturally, Mr. Milburn would not do anything out of line, but she felt better knowing someone else was around.

"I suppose that accustomed to living in a village where nothing exciting ever happens, you are finding this trip to be delightful," he said.

Nympha imagined that most people who lived in London or a larger town would think the same. "The trip has been lovely, but you must not think that village life is always dull. Why, not too long ago we had a murder in the village. Or, I should say, on the golf links that Lord Nicholas created. It caused quite a sensation."

"I heard a rumor of the violent end to a life. Tell me, did anyone see who did the deed?" He took hold of her arm to guide her around a wheelbarrow that had weeds and dead leaves heaped in it.

If Nympha thought this was an exceedingly peculiar conversation to have early in the morning while walking in the gardens, she didn't say so. "No, and that was frightening. But Papa said whoever killed the person was likely long gone by the time the body was discovered."

"So, they have no clue as to who might have murdered him?"

"Not really. Oh—did you happen to see any strangers about when you were talking to that man? I saw you out near the links that same day, only earlier. 'Tis such a lovely area, with the trees, ponds, and neatly scythed grass, that I go there often simply to enjoy it—much like a park."

"Ah, no, not in the least. The chap I spoke to was an old acquaintance, and we chatted briefly before I returned to my lodging. And," he continued with a smile, "I remained in the village for some days following."

"What a pity. That is," she hastily added, "that you couldn't have helped to find a clue."

Clouds obscured the sun, and Nympha found the air becoming a trifle chilly. She changed her direction, slipping away from Mr. Milburn's hold, to return to the warmth of the house.

He followed closely at her side, chatting about the scenery and the gardens.

Nympha would not have thought him a chatty man. They reached the house without her having to utter a word.

Once inside, she handed her cloak to Foley, and when he informed them that a meal was to be had in the small dining room, she went that way. It would be lovely to have a cup of hot tea.

Lord Nicholas was seated at the table reading a newspaper from Nottingham. He displayed astonishment at the sight of them. "Egad, Milburn, out and about at this hour of the day? Good morning, Miss Herbert. It does not surprise me in the least to see you with pink cheeks and sparkling eyes. I've seen them often enough. But Milburn?"

She shot him an annoyed look, then busied herself with the offering of foods at the sideboard.

"Actually, I found it quite invigorating. Rare display of tulips, wouldn't you say, Miss Herbert?"

"That is certainly true." She glanced at the two men, then applied her attention to the assortment of food on her plate. What really captured her thoughts was the unusual amount of interest Mr. Milburn showed in the village murder. But then, since murder was not committed every day, perhaps it was not all that strange.

"What do you have planned for the day, Miss Herbert?"

"She will go with me to Mansfield to select some lace," Mrs. Coxmoor said from the doorway. "I fancy that is at the top of her list of things to do. Am I not right?"

Nympha gave her great-aunt an amazed look. She had not expected to see her relative so early in the day.

"I should like that very much. Lord Nicholas, do you intend to go into Mansfield as well? Perhaps you might find the person you seek?"

"By all means, Lord Nicholas, do join us." Her great-aunt turned her attention to Mr. Milburn. "Should you wish to ride while we are gone, there are mounts in the stables that might please you."

So . . . Mr. Milburn was not invited to go with them. Nympha found this odd, but she wasn't about to say anything. Although she had believed she didn't care for Lord Nicholas, she found she far preferred him to Mr. Milburn.

"I should enjoy that very much, ma'am. The country hereabouts looks interesting, and I would learn something of my uncle. Perhaps he is at home and will receive me."

"There, then. I suspected that is what you would prefer." Mrs. Coxmoor accepted the cup of tea Foley poured for her, then sat next to Nympha. "We shall have a fine time hunting for lace. I am determined to send packets to the other ladies in your family."

For perhaps the hundredth time Nympha wondered why she had been selected to visit instead of one of the others, and this time she set the question forth to her great-aunt.

"You have my middle name. I am Letitia Elspeth and you are Nympha Elspeth. You did not know that?"

"No, indeed, I did not. How lovely," Nympha said truthfully. She was coming to like the sprightly lady more and more.

"Well, once you are all satisfied here, we will be off to the delights of the lace to be found. I trust you will occupy yourself, Mr. Milburn? If we are late to lunch, I have instructed Foley to see that something is served in the event you become hungry."

Mr. Milburn expressed his appreciation even as Lord Nicholas and Nympha left the table to prepare for the excursion to the town where such gorgeous lace might be seen and bought.

Thus it was that when Nympha entered the shiny landau to head for Mansfield, she caught sight of Mr. Milburn headed down the avenue ahead of them.

"He looks to be going the same direction as we shall," Great-Aunt Letitia murmured to Lord Nicholas. "I wonder why he did not say he intended to go to Mansfield? Not that it would have made any difference, mind you."

If Nympha was curious to know what her great-aunt meant by this observation, she wasn't to know. Nothing more was said on the matter as the carriage rolled down the avenue.

Chapter Five

After a bit of silence Mrs. Coxmoor asked, "Do you play tennis, my lord?"

"Tennis, ma'am?" Lord Nicholas looked as confused as Nympha felt.

"I have had a neat little court some distance from the house. I thought perhaps one or both of you might enjoy the game. Perhaps Mr. Milburn as well?" Mrs. Coxmoor folded her hands on her lap, looking for all the world as though she sat in her drawing room rather than bouncing along a country road in a closed landau.

The carriage rolled onto the main road leading to Mansfield.

"As to that, ma'am," Nick replied, "I have played some while in London. There is a tennis court just off Piccadilly. Several of us enjoy a hard game now and again. Scropes Davies is a splendid player and a good opponent—almost a professional. Have you learned the game, Miss Herbert?"

Nympha calmly returned his look. Did he assume she was so provincial she wouldn't have even heard of it? "My father does not consider it seemly for us to play tennis, although I have observed the game. My sisters and I have played battledore and shuttlecock, sir,"

"Similar games," Great-Aunt Letitia declared. If she observed Nympha's annoyance when Lord Nicholas addressed her, she gave no indication of it. "I would appreciate it if you would teach Nympha, my lord. Do you know if Mr. Milburn also plays?"

"I believe I have seen him at the London court, although he's not been my partner."

Nympha frowned while staring out of the window. She couldn't imagine why her great-aunt was the least interested in their playing tennis!

"And archery? I trust you both indulge in that sport?" her great-aunt persisted.

Nympha shook her head, definitely puzzled.

Lord Nicholas smiled. "You are trying to make me out the sportsman, I gather? I also enjoy archery, although I do not belong to the Toxophilic Society. Our Prince Regent used to be active there, I believe."

"But now he is too fat, I imagine." Great-Aunt Letitia sniffed. "I think were he to exercise more, and eat less, he would find himself in better health. I enjoy a number of outdoor activities. I was used to play tennis, but my health no longer permits it. However, archery is one of my enjoyments. We shall indulge in a few matches while you are here."

Nympha exchanged a guarded look with Lord Nicholas. She had observed his mother walking across the fields to paint a watercolor. It was quite something else to partake of a round of archery with a lady who was rising seventy!

The matter was set aside when they approached the town. A neat wooden sign proclaimed they were entering Mansfield Woodhouse.

"You merely call it Mansfield. It seems to have another name attached." Nympha gazed about with curious eyes as the carriage jounced on the cobbled street.

"Simpler to keep to the one. Now, we shall meet in the Mansfield Arms for a nuncheon. We shall be mostly in the marketplace, but I think we will also stop at a few of the shops on Stockwell Gate. I requested we be set down in front of Binch's. I want some silk thread, and I am persuaded that Nympha had best select a few ells of silk and muslin. Will you join us, Lord Nicholas?"

Nick immediately agreed, recalling the slip of paper he had found in the dead man's pocket that had the name of Binch on it and that his hostess had slipped into her reticule. He was not certain what Mrs. Coxmoor had in mind, but he would take advantage of so innocuous a visit.

Miss Herbert gave him an apprehensive stare that quite decided him. Did she think he might poke his nose into her selection of fabrics and color? Upon reflection, he might.

"I should be pleased to join you, ma'am." He exited the carriage first and assisted the women. Mrs. Coxmoor wore lemon kid gloves of the finest quality, and stepped from the carriage with smart confidence.

Miss Herbert placed her hand in his with obvious reluctance. He noted she wore exquisitely mended white cotton gloves. Her hand trembled slightly, and he wondered why. Surely she did not believe he would think ill of her for having mended gloves! He was too well aware of the circumstances of her family to censure her for that. He could only admire her poise in the face of something that must cause her chagrin.

Mrs. Coxmoor swanned into the shop with the assurance worthy of a duchess. Mr. Binch—Nick assumed that must be the chap—bowed to her with considerable deference. Well, that wasn't surprising. She could probably buy the entire town of Mansfield and not notice a loss.

"Good morning, Mr. Binch. I require some silk threads, blue, mostly. And my grandniece wants some of your finest silks and muslins. I intend to have Mrs. Rankin make up some dresses for her." She proceeded to a case where the packets of silk thread were to be found, but not before she had a chance to hand Nick the sketch of the dead man.

Nick waited until the array of silk and muslin fabrics had captivated Miss Herbert before he motioned to the shopkeeper. Offering the drawing to him, he asked if the face seemed familiar.

"Aye, it does somewhat, although I cannot recall why.

I know I have seen someone who had those looks. Searching for a gentleman, are you?"

Nick ignored the curiosity in his voice and eyes. "That I am, or someone who recalls seeing him." He would give no particulars. How could he come out and say he hunted for relatives of a dead man killed with his own golf club? That might bring an interesting reaction, but hardly the one he desired.

"I will be staying in the area for a time with Mrs. Coxmoor. Should you think of anyone who looks similar to this drawing, I would appreciate it if you could get word to me."

"Now if you were to leave that drawing with me, I might be able to reflect a bit, have it come to me."

Nick wasn't about to let his original drawing out of his hands again. "Tell you what, I'll make a copy and leave it with you as soon as I can."

The fellow looked disappointed, but not for long.

The widow found the silk thread she wanted, then moved to where bolts of fabric were arranged.

Nick sauntered over to join the ladies.

Miss Herbert appeared on the verge of objecting to the purchase Mrs. Coxmoor had in mind. "I do not require so many gowns, ma'am. Half a dozen!"

"Lord Nicholas, indulge me with your opinion. I say this blue silk, that lilac India muslin, the cherry-striped percale, and I believe the blue-spotted muslin. Perhaps some of the fine white satin as well. What do you say, my lord?"

Nick glanced at the embarrassed Miss Herbert and barely suppressed a grin. "My sister-in-law favors white muslin for morning wear. Why not add a length of this . . . What do you call this?" he asked the proprietor, gesturing to a bolt of pale pinkish fabric.

"That is our finest blush-colored sarcenet, my lord," Mr. Binch replied in an obsequious manner.

"The very thing, sir." Mrs. Coxmoor gestured to the stack. "We shall have lengths of them all, Mr. Binch."

While she oversaw the cutting of each length, checking

for any flaws in the fabrics, Miss Herbert motioned Nick to the other side of the large shop. Suspecting he was in for a scold, Nick suppressed a grin and followed her.

"Lord Nicholas, I do not approve of such extravagance. You did not have to abet her!" She sounded like his nanny.

"But, my fair one, she wanted me to do just that."

"I am not your fair one!" she insisted with a flash of her very fine blue eyes. Her cheeks were flushed with indignation.

He was tempted to tweak the curl that peeked out from under her chip bonnet. He enjoyed teasing her. She was such a responsive woman. He couldn't help but wonder what she would be like in his arms. He suspected the blushing that so often cursed fair-skinned blondes concealed a passionate nature.

"I am glad I suggested that sarcenet. It will flatter you no end. The blue silk as well. Come now, you cannot deny you would like a few pretty gowns? If it gives your great-aunt pleasure, give in gracefully. Besides, it is my understanding she has no children. Pray, who else will she spend her money on?"

"I did not come here to spend her money," Miss Herbert said with the characteristic stubbornness Nick was coming to know. How could she in the past have listened to him without comment when he talked about his golf links? Or had she pretended her attentiveness? Had he been so absorbed in his own passion for golf that he totally missed her reaction?

"What are you thinking about?" she quietly demanded so as not to draw attention to them.

"I am wondering about you, Miss Herbert. The real you." He tilted his head to study her, realizing he did wish to know more about her, what pleased her.

"I fear there is nothing to know about me that you do not already know. After all, we have seen each other most of our lives." Her eyes held a wary note in them.

"Ah, there you are wrong, my dear. I am coming to believe there is a great deal to you that I wish to know."

He particularly wanted to know why Milburn had made such a dead set at her since their arrival at Coxmoor Hall. Nick watched her closely. She looked flustered, fidgeting with her reticule.

Nick smiled inwardly. He was about to rejoin Mrs. Coxmoor when Miss Herbert spoke. "It must be difficult for you to leave your home while it is so close to being completed," she blurted, surprising him with the change of topic. She did *not* want to talk about herself.

But it was her words that returned his gaze to her. "And how do you know the house is close to completion? I was unaware that the village knew what was going on in the interior."

"Rubbish, my lord. I have viewed the exterior from a distance, and know it is almost finished—save for a bit of trim. Word has it that the only lack inside is finishing—like the paneling in your library, and the color for the silk to be hung on your drawing-room walls."

Nick grinned. "How fortunate that Napoleon didn't have spies as good as our villagers. You forgot the wainscoting for the dining room, as well as the paper for the walls above it. How is it that you are able to see the exterior so well? You cannot see it from the road."

She looked uncomfortable, remarkably so. She shifted from one foot to the other. He'd be willing to bet that she would have escaped from him if she could see a way around him. As it was, slipping past him would require a touching of bodies, something he suspected would cause the pretty Miss Herbert to blush more than pink.

"Well, tell me. I must rectify the lack of privacy." He decided to tease her a bit, for she was so rewarding to torment.

"That I won't, for the view is beautiful." The blue of her eyes darkened as she defied him, tilting that determined chin just so.

Nick thought a moment, then pierced her with his dark gaze. "It would have to be from one of the greens. I would hazard a guess that it would be just beyond the seventh. Do I have the right of it?"

She clamped her lips shut, glaring at him.

Not for the first time Nick took notice of those delicate lips, beautifully shaped and looking as tender as a newly opened rosebud. He wondered what it would be like to kiss her, feel the softness, taste those charming lips. She smelled of lavender. He liked that. Most of the time her voice had an oddly seductive quality to it. It was strange he hadn't noticed that before—when they were at Lanstone Hall. Goodness knows they had sat beside each other at enough of his mother's tedious dinners.

"I shall be certain to study the view when we return home, you may be assured." He hoped to goad her into protest.

"Nicholas Stanhope, if you destroy the very fine view of your home, I shall . . . shall . . . do you violence." She compressed her lips again.

Looking about him, Nick could see that not a soul in the shop was paying the slightest attention to them. The other customer was avidly watching Mrs. Coxmoor, to see what she bought. He turned back to Nympha. Lightly lifting her chin, he raised it just so, then laced an all-too-brief kiss on the most delectable lips he had touched in a long, long time.

"You . . . you . . . villain," she whispered, her ire losing something with the lack of volume he knew she longed to use.

"Oh, I do not think I am a villain. Perhaps an opportunist?" He smiled.

Nympha glared at him, hating the color she knew must stain her cheeks. "I was under the impression you were a gentleman, sirrah!"

"I am as human as the next chap. You know," he said in a conversational tone, "I had not realized what a charmer you are. There must be something in the air here. You do not seem the same."

"Nor do you." She tried to sound very indignant. The

trouble was that she did not *feel* very indignant. Rather, she wished he would kiss her again! And was that not a fine thing for a rector's daughter to confess—even if only to herself.

How in the world could she have been interested in his lofty brother when the dashing Lord Nicholas was around? It was beyond comprehension.

"Nympha, dear, come," her great-aunt called. "The parcel will be delivered to the carriage by the time we are ready to depart." Assuming the two would follow in her wake, Mrs. Coxmoor set forth from Binch's shop like a ship in full sail.

"Hurry. I have no idea where she plans to go next." Nympha grabbed his hand, and Lord Nicholas trailed close behind her.

They caught up with the older lady as she turned onto Stockwell Gate. "First to Cursham's. I believe we need gloves. Plus scarves and a muff, and perhaps hose. Ah, I see he has a new shipment of bonnets. Perhaps we can find something there."

Feeling as though a whirlwind had swept her up, Nympha obediently followed. "Yes, ma'am."

Lord Nicholas took one look at the shop and said, "I shall meet you at the Mansfield Arms about noon, if that is agreeable? I fear Miss Herbert would never forgive me if I assisted in selecting her gloves, not to mention hose."

Sending him a scandalized glare, Nympha hastily opened the door to Cursham's shop, holding it for her great-aunt.

Mrs. Coxmoor paused. "There is a rather nice bookseller along this way. 'Tis a new shop—Langley. You will find books, not to mention sundries like medicines and lottery tickets."

Lord Nicholas smiled. Nympha could see he charmed her great-aunt—just as he charmed her, unfortunately.

Why had she thought it might please her great-aunt if Lord Nicholas stayed with her? Such complications as had arisen hadn't occurred to Nympha's innocent mind. Now that she thought on it, the journey north was probably scandalous as well, even though nothing had happened other than him having captivated her heart.

Her sister Drusilla would likely say it served her right for not remaining with the traveling coach sent to convey her north.

"Wake up girl. We still have things to buy. With the new shipment of goods, I'll warrant you find as nice a selection here as you might in London."

The shopkeeper assured Mrs. Coxmoor—the wealthy and influential Mrs. Coxmoor—of just that.

In shorter time than Nympha would have believed possible, she was the happy possessor of a dozen pairs of hose in fragile pink silk, a half-dozen of excellent white cotton, and a dozen pairs of gloves in a variety of colors made by Mansfield's own glover, Mr. Hinde. The crowning touch was an ermine muff. She was overwhelmed.

Great-Aunt Letitia consulted the watch pinned to her pelisse before instructing Mr. Cursham to deliver the parcels to the carriage. "Come, Nympha, we are to meet Lord Nicholas for our nuncheon."

Nympha suspected that her great-aunt enjoyed tossing out the title. She knew how impressed all shopkeepers were by that. Never mind that Mansfield occasionally saw the Duke of Portland and Earl Manvers, this was one of their own people having a guest related to the Marquess of Lanstone and Earl of Stanhope. There were few shopkeepers who catered to the upper classes who did not study a copy of some peerage. They knew.

They walked across the street and along to the Mansfield Arms where they found Lord Nicholas waiting for them. He carried a small package under his arm.

"I trust we have not kept you waiting long?" Mrs. Coxmoor asked politely.

"Not at all. I picked up a few things, then came here. Langley's carries some interesting books as well as fine drawing paper."

Nympha wondered at the look he gave her great-aunt. For strangers, they had achieved a rapid rapport.

"Quite so. I should have thought of that. Come, they

will have a meal ready for us." She led the way to a neat parlor where a table was set for them.

Never once was Nympha allowed to wonder what might be in that mysterious cream package now resting on a chair nearby. Excellent food was set before her, tempting her appetite. Lord Nicholas demanded she give an account of her shopping, particularly the ermine muff.

Great-Aunt Letitia said she'd sent word to Mrs. Rankin to come to Coxmoor Hall two days hence. Nympha wondered what the good lady did if she had other, quite as important, customers to serve.

Lost in her musings, she contemplated the package and its contents. Drawing paper? What, pray tell, did his lordship want with drawing paper? If she recalled correctly, Lord Nicholas had always turned to his brother if he wanted a sketch of his links. Since his brother was absent, what use would drawing paper be to Lord Nicholas? Unless he did portraits, not landscapes? If so, of whom?

"Miss Herbert, you are not attending. Where, I wonder, is your mind?" Lord Nicholas sent her a quizzing look. His eyes seemed to dance with mischief. Did he guess that she longed to know what was in that package?

Alas, it was not to be. Following their nuncheon they took the carriage to the lace factory where Great-Aunt Letitia invited them to see the new machines that produced the lace. Two colors were available, white and blonde, which was the color of raw silk.

They entered the weaving room, a noisy place that had Nympha putting her hands over her ears. Along the brick floor stood a great many machines close together, each spinning forth an array of fine silk or cotton lace.

"These are the looms using the new Jacquard method of weaving. Once we leave here I can show you what it is like. Come." As usual, she led the way.

They obediently followed—Nympha most thankfully. Lord Nicholas guided her down the steps. He was merely being helpful, but she found his closeness disturbing to her hard-won composure. Did he guess how he affected her?

When they reached a tiny office, Great-Aunt Letitia pulled out a chain of cards from a drawer, each one with holes punched in it, evidently creating a pattern of sorts. "This is one of the Jacquard patterns we use to create the lace here. The cards make an endless chain so the design keeps repeating over and over. I will not bother you with details, but you, Lord Nicholas, may come to look again if you so please. I fancy that Nympha has her heart set on lace for her own use."

By some mysterious means, a young man had been summoned. He entered the room with many cards of lace and a fine white lace shawl, very long and embroidered with an exquisite design.

It didn't take long to select what she wished. The edging, her great-aunt explained, came from another factory, brought here especially for Nympha.

When they left, Nick had nothing but the greatest admiration for the woman who appeared to direct the factory. That she knew every in and out of the business was evident. This was not a woman who merely sat back to allow her manager to administer it for her. Well, she certainly must keep the fellow on his toes.

The landau awaited them at the edge of the pavement. Within a short time they had left the cobbled streets of Mansfield behind them. The seat next to Nick was piled high with parcels, most of which he could readily identify.

They were nearing Coxmoor Hall when he spotted Milburn dashing through the woods on his borrowed horse. That he was also headed the same direction as they were was obvious. Where had he been for so long? And with whom?

They met in the stable yard.

"Ah, Mr. Milburn." Mrs. Coxmoor stepped down from the landau to greet her guest. "Did you have luck in finding the gentleman you wanted to see? Your uncle, was it not?"

Nick almost laughed at the expression on Milburn's face. It was a cross between astonishment and vexation.

"Actually, I did, ma'am. I hope to see him again before too many days pass."

"Fine." Mrs. Coxmoor revealed no curiosity about the person Milburn had gone to see. Nick resolved to find out more if he could. He hadn't known Milburn all that well, but of a sudden he was curious and wanted to know more about this mysterious uncle.

While Mrs. Coxmoor was directing the servants who had come out to fetch the parcels, Milburn was making up to Miss Herbert. Nick noted Milburn didn't cause Miss Herbert to blush. How curiously interesting. He smiled.

Why did Nick find his compliments so odious and overblown? It wasn't mere jealousy—not that Nick could be jealous of a fellow like Milburn. The man was a bit too ingratiating. He'd like to see the last of him.

Then awareness that Milburn likely believed Miss Herbert might inherit all the Coxmoor fortune occurred to Nick. Would she? She could, given Mrs. Coxmoor's obvious fondness for the girl. The thought put a different complexion on Milburn's fascination with Miss Herbert.

There was no way that Nick would allow that fellow to entice Miss Herbert. Nympha deserved far better than Milburn. Dash it all, she was a good sort. She had tramped all over his links with him in the early days of planning. No matter that she had hoped to interest his brother; she had offered sensible suggestions and carried supplies for him without complaint. And now he was discovering she had other, more fetching qualities.

"Suppose we go into the house, Nympha? Mr. Milburn and Lord Nicholas are doubtless wishing for a drink, and I will perish if I do not have a cup of tea."

Nympha hurried after her great-aunt, darting a look at Lord Nicholas as she went. It was to be tea . . . then what? She soon found out.

Following a generous tea, complete with cakes, biscuits, and wine for the men, she was told.

"I wish to watch Lord Nicholas and Mr. Milburn play a game of tennis. Foley will bring along the rackets and balls. Come! We will go now."

There were no excuses allowed, no requests for digesting the large tea, or a respite from the activity of the day to this point permitted.

The men meekly rose to accompany their hostess. Nympha followed in their wake. Goodness, what would her rather eccentric relative think of next!

The tennis court her great-aunt brought them to was in a neat building with narrow high-set windows. Inside, a net was strung across the center of the court that had been marked off with white paint on what appeared to be slate. A bench sat to one side where the ladies could observe.

Her great-aunt must have left instructions for this to be arranged before they drove to Mansfield!

Lord Nicholas looked around with obvious approval while he stripped off his coat and neckcloth. Mr. Milburn seemed uneasy, but then Nympha noted an almost calculating expression flicker across his face. It disappeared so fast she was not quite sure what she had seen, as he seemed his usual self soon enough. He joined Lord Nicholas in removing his coat and cravat.

Lord Nicholas took off his boots with a look at her great-aunt. "Better to play in stocking feet than boots. In the future I shall find a pair of tennis shoes."

Foley offered the men a choice of rackets; then after they decided Nick would serve first, he handed him a dull gray tennis ball.

Nympha had watched a game once before, but it hadn't captured her attention like this one. She admired the fine muscles Lord Nicholas displayed in his thin linen shirt. Broad shoulders, narrow waist, slim hips—she ought to be blushing at the direction of her thoughts. She scarce noticed Mr. Milburn. Her focus remained with Lord Nicholas, the movement of his body.

Nick won the first serve and sent the ball soaring across the net with his usual verve. Milburn returned it with better skill than Nick had expected. The volley continued until Milburn was in the far end of the hazard side. Milburn then hit the ball with a stroke that appeared to take every bit of strength he possessed.

The report of the racket hitting that ball sounded much like a shot. But instead of the ball coming anywhere within the confines of the court, it zoomed straight to where Nympha sat, hitting her square on her forehead!

Nick dropped his racket and dashed across to where she had toppled. He gathered her up, looking at the swelling lump with more than a little dismay. "Nympha!" He glanced up at her great-aunt, then back to the woman now in his arms. "Ice would help, I believe." Somehow he knew this formidable woman could conjure up something as unusual as ice.

Foley appeared on an instant, then ran off at Mrs. Coxmoor's bidding for the ice.

Milburn had hurried up right behind Nick, exclaiming his horror and apologies for what had happened.

Mrs. Coxmoor brushed him aside, commanding Nick, "Take her to the house. It is growing chilly out here."

That Nick was still in his stocking feet and without his coat or cravat she ignored. Knowing it was important that Nympha be treated at once, Nick did as bade, carrying the unconscious girl with the greatest of care.

Foley held open the door, and Nick charged across the entry hall, demanding the location of her room as he went.

Annie appeared at the top of the stairs, gasping at the sight of her mistress. But she kept her head, leading Nick down the hall until they reached Nympha's room. After hastily tossing the bedcovers aside for him, Annie waited for orders.

Nick gently placed the still form down on the large bed, adjusting her legs and arms just so, then turned to greet Foley as he entered with a basin. Ice.

"A cloth, Annie. We shall wrap the ice in it, keep it on that lump." He had to remain coolheaded, competent.

The requisite cloth was promptly handed him, and

Nick applied the ice at once. He could only pray that serious damage had not been done to her brain. He had seen chaps knocked unconscious like this, only to be witless once they finally regained awareness of their surroundings.

"How does she do, Lord Nicholas?" Mrs. Coxmoor silently walked to stand beside him, staring down at her grandniece with a strained expression.

"Too early to tell. A doctor?"

"Closest one is in Nottingham, some fifteen miles from here."

"I'll fetch him," Milburn offered. "Just tell me his name and direction." He stood just outside the room, his face a dull gray in color.

Mrs. Coxmoor replied without taking her eyes off her grandniece. "Thank you, but I have already ordered the groom to ride there. The doctor should be here within two hours."

Nick hoped that he would not be too late.

Chapter Six

The house remained strangely silent while they waited for the doctor to arrive. The tick of the upstairs hall longcase clock marked the passage of time. When it sounded the hour, Mrs. Coxmoor made a little sound of dismay.

"Surely he will get here soon. It seems like forever since I sent Henry to fetch him." She stood by the window, staring off at the gardens for a time before pacing about the room. "I should like to soothe her brow." The elderly lady looked drawn and anxious to do something for her grandniece.

"I will not leave Nympha." Nick felt as though he should be in command, although he had no right to assume this. "I know her parents, known *her* most of her life. I could not leave her now," Nick insisted in an undertone that would not disturb their patient. Of course his reasoning made little sense. He couldn't explain why he deemed it so important, but he knew it was.

He kept the ice in place, pleased to see the lump subsiding a little. "Foley, is there any more ice where this came from?"

"Indeed, sir. I shall fetch some directly." The butler had stationed himself by the door, intent upon helping if he might. Annie anxiously hovered on the far side of the bed.

It was a measure of the butler's concern that he sought the ice himself. In a brief time he returned with the bowl holding small chunks of ice. "I thought it better to bring just a few, milord. It does melt, and best to leave the rest where it is for the moment."

Nick didn't bother to ask where that might be. He wrung out the cloth, wrapping it around a piece of ice. Her forehead would turn all colors of the rainbow later. Now it simply looked bruised, and the lump a nasty gray and bluish red.

He thought she moved slightly, and wasn't that the faintest of moans? He bent his head so he might catch any sound she made. The scent of lavender clung to her, teasing his nose with her fragrance.

On the far side of the room Mrs. Coxmoor stood, watching. The fire had been built up, and the room soon became pleasantly warm.

"You don't think it too much heat?" He gave Nympha a worried look. She felt cool to the touch, but would it be bad for her to become overly warm?

"It should counteract the ice, I am thinking," Mrs. Coxmoor replied.

Nick made no response to that, merely tugging the light coverlet over Nympha. She stirred slightly. Nick bent over again, hoping she might say something. Oh, he hoped she made sense!

"Oh, how cold that is," she murmured. "What happened?" She batted a hand at him as though to brush away the ice.

Breathing a sigh of relief, Nick kept the ice where it was. "You were hit by Milburn's ball when we were playing tennis. Be still. You have a great lump on your head. I'm trying to help by placing ice on it. Supposed to reduce the swelling—at least I have seen it work before."

"I do not remember a ball," she said in a vague thread of sound.

"Do not worry your head about it now. All we want is to see you better." Nick smoothed her hair away from her face. He looked to where Mrs. Coxmoor now stood at the end of the bed. Her autocratic face was crumpled with worry, and she wrung her hands.

Nympha said no more, but Nick thought she seemed to rest a bit easier. Could she be sleeping, rather than unconscious?

The hall clock chimed the hour. A sound of footsteps echoed in the entry hall below. Foley shortly returned with a tall, lean gentleman who possessed an imposing set of side-whiskers. "Dr. Graham, madam."

The ex-Scotsman assessed the patient with an experienced eye, and then ordered them all from the room save for Annie. Mrs. Coxmoor refused, her voice and manner brooking no argument.

Nick left with reluctance. Somehow he felt as though Nympha ought to be in his care. "Mind the ice."

Dr. Graham gave him a stare, and Nick shut the door behind him as he left. The hall clock ticked loudly as he passed it on his way to the stairs.

When he reached the ground floor he wandered into the library. Here he found Milburn, his hair every which way, his jacket and shirt untidy.

Foley entered with Nick's coat, cravat, and boots. "The under gardener brought these up, milord."

Nick tossed the cravat aside, then shrugged into his coat and tugged on his boots. Once dressed, he wandered over to stare out of the window at the early-spring scene beyond.

Mr. Milburn appeared disconsolate, pacing back and forth in the library until Nick objected.

"You'll wear out the carpet at the rate you go. Try the hall tile." He eyed Milburn with dislike. At the moment there was nothing Nick would like more than to see the fellow at land's end.

Milburn paused, staring at Nick as though first seeing him. "Do you think she will pull through?"

"I could not say. She did rouse for a few moments, but sank back into whatever state she was in before. The doctor seems competent enough," he added thoughtfully. He left the window, hearing footsteps on the stairs.

Mrs. Coxmoor entered the room, crossing to where a tray held a number of bottles. "He insisted I had to leave." She poured out three glasses of brandy, offering each gentleman a glass before she took one with her to stand by the fireplace.

"What has the doctor to say?" Nick glanced to Milburn before returning his attention to Mrs. Coxmoor.

"Not much, as yet. He ordered me from the room, but made no pronouncement regarding Nympha. I merely objected to his bleeding her. Seems to me that it did my late husband no good." She cast Nick a belligerent look as though he might argue with her. He didn't.

Milburn left the room as though he could bear to hear no more. Within moments they heard the front door shut.

Nick slouched down in a great winged chair near the fireplace, where a fire flickered at a neat stack of logs. Like everything else in this house, it was perfectly laid, and burned enough to offer pleasant warmth. He leaned his chin on his left hand, which he propped on the chair arm, mulling over what had occurred. Seemed to him Milburn was a sponger. Nick had suspected that on the trip north. It wouldn't be easy to dislodge him from a pleasant spot.

"I like an apple-wood fire." Mrs. Coxmoor stared into the flames a time before turning to Nick. "Milburn has gone outside. Can you tell me what you think of what occurred out there? We have a bit of time on our hands before the doctor will offer his report."

"I have been considering that last shot of his. There is, of course, no explanation as to why he sent the ball that particular direction—other than to beat me. I must say, he hit that ball with remarkable drive and energy. Haven't seen the like of it before—other than in a champion match, that is. I cannot see why he felt it necessary for a little game between friends. Perhaps he just likes to win. There was no way I could have returned that shot."

"And is he a friend of yours?"

"I can't say I know him well. I have seen him about London, of course. We have not moved in the same circle, but still, London isn't all that large—at least the West End where the *ton* resides."

"Mr. Milburn lives there as well?"

"Don't know his direction precisely. I believe it is the Albany."

Nick rose as they heard steps coming down from the first floor. In moments Dr. Graham appeared in the doorway, looking to Mrs. Coxmoor at once. Nick took a step in his direction, then paused. Mrs. Coxmoor must have precedence. She was a relative; he was merely a man who has known the girl most of her life.

"Well, how is she? Will she mend, do you think?" Mrs. Coxmoor walked to where the doctor stood. She gestured him to enter, then walked at his side to the fireplace. All the while she studied his face.

"The ice was a good idea. She would have had a truly nasty lump had you not applied it so promptly. As to her mending, yes, she will. I suggest she remain quiet for a few days. When she feels more the thing, perhaps a light activity would be acceptable. Keep her quiet."

"Her mind does not seem affected?" Nick asked, his fears pushing to the fore.

Dr. Graham bent to the fire to warm his hands. "No. It is my thinking she had a nasty knock on the head, but no permanent damage has been done. She seemed lucid when I finished with her."

"Thank God," Nick murmured. "I was worried."

"You were right to be concerned. I have seen cases where the senses are totally disordered. I would say that is not the case with the young lady." He gave Nick a curious look, quite as though he wondered what the connection might be.

"I have known Nympha Herbert since she was a little girl. I'd not wish to see anything happen to her."

Dr. Graham nodded. He discussed the patient's treatment with Mrs. Coxmoor while Nick listened.

When the doctor had departed Nick resumed his seat near the fire. "Surprised Milburn hasn't returned to see what the doctor had to say." He finished the brandy Mrs.

Coxmoor had handed him, then set the glass on a small table close by.

She drank the remainder of her brandy, took her glass along with Nick's to set on the tray. "I am sorry I invited the man to stay here. I had no idea he was intent upon doing away with my grandniece."

"Surely you do not think his action was deliberate?" Nick rose again to face her. "I don't much like the chap, but would he resort to murder? Why? What could be his motive?"

What she might have said in reply was not to be known as Milburn reentered the house, coming directly to the library in great haste.

"I saw the doctor's carriage go down the avenue. What did he have to say about Miss Herbert?"

For a moment Milburn's face was illumined by the setting sun. Nick thought he saw genuine concern there. Mrs. Coxmoor had to be wrong. Why would Milburn want to kill Nympha? Rather, he ought to be wooing her for the fortune she most likely would acquire.

"She will do well enough. Rest and quiet was what he prescribed." Nick watched Milburn carefully to assess his mood, his reaction to Nick's words.

"That and willow-bark powder for her aching head," Mrs. Coxmoor added. "I intend to give her some of Dr. Boerhaave's Infallible Red Pills. They always work for me when I have aches or pains. I suppose you favor Dr. James's Powders? I know many do," she said to Nick.

"I am never ill, ma'am. But I believe my mother does favor Dr. James's Powders," Nick said with a half smile.

Milburn smiled as well. Granted it was a strained smile, but he seemed genuinely relieved. "Perhaps I could just look in on her before dinner?"

Nick met Mrs. Coxmoor's intent gaze, wondering if she would permit Milburn this privilege.

"I think you might, providing you do not disturb her. Annie is with her. I will arrange for my own abigail to stay with her during the night. She will not be left alone. Not as long as she remains in this house."

"I'll go as well," Nick vowed, determined to see Nympha again to make certain she was continuing to improve. He wasn't jealous, not in the least. He simply cared.

When they peeked in to check the patient, Nick was pleased to note she had more color in her cheeks when she turned her head to see them.

Dinner was a light meal, and partaken of even more lightly. Only Milburn seemed to have any appetite. Once the meal ended, Nick pushed back his chair, turning to Mrs. Coxmoor with an unspoken question in his eyes.

"Go on up," the elderly lady said with a shooing motion. "I trust you will find her better."

Nick ran up the stairs, striding to Nympha's door while wondering if there was a cautioning in the words from Mrs. Coxmoor. He hoped to see that Nympha had regained more of her color.

Pausing outside her door he rapped lightly and eased it open. He nodded to Annie, then crossed over to the bed. Nympha looked very small and fragile in the vast bed. Her eyes were shut.

"Has she spoken again?" Nick studied the oval face with the blond curls spread over her pillow. How he wished he could see those saucy blue eyes now.

Annie still held a bit of ice to Nympha's forehead. "No, milord. She answered the doctor's questions, but has said not a word since."

"I do not think I wish to take up tennis."

Nick's gaze darted to the still figure in the bed. "Well, I shall teach you anyway. Your great-aunt wishes it."

"Impossible. I cannot run fast enough."

The words were whispered, a mere thread of sound again, but still heard clearly in the silence of the room.

"Bathe her forehead in lavender water. My mother swears it is good for a headache. Perhaps it will help Miss Herbert."

"Yes, milord. Mrs. Coxmoor brought in a bottle of it for our use. If nothing else, she will like the scent."

Nick vowed to buy a large bottle of the stuff for Nympha if only she would recover.

They took turns watching her that evening, Nick stubborn in his insistence that he remain close to her. He told himself that he did so because he knew her parents.

When Nick finally returned downstairs late that night, Milburn expressed no desire to see Miss Herbert again, leaving the nursing and care up to the others. "Although, dear chap, I wonder at your sitting with her so often. Is it the done thing? For a gentleman to enter the bedroom of a young lady?"

"I have known her forever, Milburn. I cannot see that it presents a problem. Besides . . . who would spread the tale abroad?" Nick shot a meaningful look at the man who had almost killed Nympha. It was inadvertent, true, but that did not mean Nick had to like the fellow.

"True, true. I meant nothing by the remark I assure you. *I* will be as mute as a fish. But on occasion servants do talk. I imagine the Duke of Portland's and Manver's servants occasionally meet these servants. Were the Coxmoor people to chat, tell about the near disaster . . . well . . ." Milburn's voice trailed off.

Nick stared at him, and Milburn backed off.

"Just wanted to point out a possible difficulty, old man." Milburn took another few steps backward.

"Perhaps you can remove to your uncle's now?"

"No, no, the old fellow cannot tolerate noise or company. I merely check on him as often as I can."

Nick cynically wondered if Mrs. Coxmoor's food was better. He returned to the wing chair near the fireplace, plumped himself on the cushion, and proceeded to stare into the flames while wondering what could possibly happen next.

The maids took care of Nympha during the night, although Mrs. Coxmoor rose once to look in on her. Nick had been unable to sleep until he also checked to see how she fared.

Odd how she had established such a place in his life. At first he had thought her a dratted nuisance, and he did not like her attraction to his brother. He wondered if she still nurtured a *tendre* for him. From little things she had dropped, he rather believed she had put that infatuation behind her. He hoped so.

First thing in the morning Nick made it a point to check on Nympha. He rapped lightly on the door, which was promptly opened by Annie.

"How is she?" Nick peered around the maid. He was overjoyed when his gaze met Nympha's bright blue eyes.

"Mrs. Coxmoor, she says as how you can come in, but only for a few minutes," the maid said with the air of one who has memorized a message.

Nick ignored Annie. He rapidly crossed the room to the bed.

"Before you can ask, I am better." Nympha gave him a cross look. "My head aches some. I should like to know how that ball hit me when I sat on the sidelines." Nick thought that were she able to be up, she would be tapping her foot in annoyance, her arms folded before her.

"I cannot say," Nick answered candidly. "I cannot believe he intended to do you any harm. I have seen tennis balls go every which direction." They hadn't gone with the deadly speed of this particular ball, but what did he know about stray balls?

"Oh, yes, I remember. You belong to a tennis club in London and you play golf at home. What else do you do to occupy your time?" Although serious, her eyes held enough curiosity to please the vainest of men, although Nick was not a vain creature.

"Archery, as I said before. Oh, I also like angling. I ride, but I am not much at hunting." He smiled at Nympha, glad to see her less pale, even if her forehead was a nasty purple, with hints of yellow and green. The lump had subsided quite a fair bit, to his satisfaction.

"I think you are a man of the out-of-doors." She made

that pronouncement as though it gave her pleasure to have a first opinion justified.

"You might say that. When you are feeling more the thing, what say we go to that Roman ruin site? I should think it would be a gentle excursion. Dr. Graham said you could have a quiet outing. I should think that exploring the past would be peaceful."

He reached out to pick up her nearest hand. "You had us all very worried." All? Dash it, he had been beside himself with fear and dread. And he had wanted to crown Milburn, and not with a tiara.

"I am sorry you were all so worried. Papa says I have a hard head. Perhaps that helped?" Her smile was brave, and although she seemed tired, she clung to his hand with surprising determination.

"I fancy recuperation gets boring. You are too old to whine and too young to be crotchety. Pity you have the headache. Otherwise I could find you a book to read. Unless . . . you would like me to read to you?"

The door opened and Nick half-turned to see Foley entering with a tray, upon which reposed a bowl of gruel along with thin slices of toast and a dab of cherry jam.

"If you feel up to the toast and jam Cook says you may have them after you finish the gruel." Foley placed the tray on her lap with great care, then retreated with his usual dignity.

"Thank you, Foley." When he had gone, she gave the gruel a rueful look, took a few spoons, then set on the toast and cherry jam with far more enthusiasm. "That gruel tastes like yesterday's dishwater. The jam is heavenly. Annie—toss the gruel out of the window." Nympha cast a mischievous glance at Nick. "I'd not wish to hurt Cook's feelings."

And so the day went, with Nick dancing attendance on her, reading to her from a novel entitled *Emma.* Mrs. Coxmoor kept busy planning things to do when Nympha totally recovered. Milburn disappeared for hours at a time. No one asked where he went. It was a relief to have him gone, if truth be known.

Upon his return following an afternoon ride, he presented Nympha with a slim package. Opening it, she found an exquisite lace fan. She thanked him fervently, making Nick wish he had thought of the gesture. Well, it was nice of Milburn, the very least he could do.

Before dinner Nick met with Mrs. Coxmoor. He explained his feelings about Milburn. "He's a sponger, and they are the most difficult of guests to speed on their way."

"I see what you mean," she said, her expression reflective. "Like you say, there really is no reason for him to harm her." She folded her hands before her, looking extremely regal in her pale gray gown with an overskirt of sheer lace. Her cap was also of the most gossamer lace, resting on her silvery white hair as though the lace had been created just for her. It probably had, come to think on it.

"If, as I believe, you intend to make her a major beneficiary, you would expect him to court her. Witness his present of the lace fan. It is something a suitor would give a young lady. Am I right in my assessment of the situation?" Nick fiddled with the papers scattered over the library desk before glancing up at Mrs. Coxmoor.

"Indeed, you are. Since I have no close family remaining, other than my niece, I thought to provide for the girl who carries my name." She gazed at Nick as though expecting his reaction.

"It is often done that way, I believe." He spotted Foley standing at the library door, and moved to escort Mrs. Coxmoor to the dining room.

"Nympha will be recovered before you know it." He offered comfort, but truly didn't know how the girl would be. How could he? He'd rarely been around her much until the past year when she had haunted the links while they were under construction. Naturally, he had chatted with her at those dinners. He once suspected his mother planned to have him marry Miss Nympha Herbert! Impossible. Yet, he'd do all necessary to keep her out of

Milburn's covetous hands. He strongly suspected Milburn wanted the money.

In the days that followed Nympha rebounded with the stamina of one who is naturally of good health. She fretted over her multicolored forehead, arranging her blond locks in such a way as to hide it.

At last the day arrived when Mrs. Coxmoor and Nick declared her well enough to venture forth on a gentle excursion. Mrs. Rankin had been put off for a time.

Nympha was almost sorry to be going out. She had enjoyed having Lord Nicholas read to her. The novel was an excellent story, more like real life than the gothic tales that Tabitha favored.

"I fear you have not made any headway in finding that man you hoped to locate while here," she said. Although she knew full well that he had a goal of his own to perform, she had treasured her time with him—even if she had an aching forehead for part of it. That was a surprising reaction she had never expected—to enjoy time spent with Lord Nicholas Stanhope.

She had felt well enough to get out of bed and sit near the fireplace the last two days. Her great-aunt was overly protective, but it was nice to be so cherished. Growing up in a large family gave one little individual attention. Not that she didn't love her sisters; they were as dear as could be. But a mother could only offer so much attention to each one.

They plodded along in the landau at a moderate pace. It enabled all to admire the scenery around them. It was a splendid day with perhaps a hint of rain in the clouds overhead. Nympha thought it a trifle chilly out, and she was thankful for her cozy muff into which she had tucked her hands. Great-Aunt Letitia insisted she have a warm scarf at her neck and a new velvet bonnet to protect her head.

"I contacted Rooke, the owner of the property. There will be no difficulty in our access to the ruins."

"How did he discover them? I imagine they were buried beneath a foot or more of dirt." Nympha turned her attention to her great-aunt, who had thought up this jaunt to entertain her.

"Some years back, around seventeen eighty-six, I think, Hayman Rooke spotted some small tiles, the sort the Romans used in their pavements. They had been working in the north field, and these turned up. Curious, he got his men to dig around, and they found a wall about a foot below the surface. It turned out to be a fair-sized villa with nine rooms, with a hypocaust that showed evidence of having been used." She smiled with appreciation of the slight gasp from Nympha. "Whoever lived there liked bright colors, I must say. Wait until you see them."

Before Nympha could persuade her to reveal what she meant, they arrived at the site.

Lord Nicholas hopped out to first assist Mrs. Coxmoor. He handed Nympha from the carriage as though she was made of spun glass. It was a novel sensation to be treated like a princess. A girl would only be human to respond to that!

Mrs. Coxmoor marched ahead of the others, leaving Lord Nicholas to walk with Nympha. A neat path had been set out so they didn't have to plod through a rough field. When they reached the exposed ruin, Nympha was fascinated by what she saw. "Oh, my! I see what you mean about colors. Look, there are stripes of purple, red, yellow, and green on that wall!" Nympha cried when they reached the dig. "It must have been cheerful in the chill of winter."

"I am surprised to see stucco," Lord Nicholas said. He let go of Nympha's arm, to crouch down, touching the revealed stucco with a tentative finger.

"You must see the mosaic. Come," Great-Aunt Letitia said in her most imperious manner.

Nympha and Lord Nicholas dutifully followed, admired the superb example of mosaic pavement, then wandered about to study the other painted walls, the hypocaust with its little pile of ashes, and a tessellated pavement along a hallway.

Another building close by looked to have storage and perhaps a necessary convenience. "They had a cold bath here." Lord Nicholas pointed at a neatly lettered sign.

"I cannot think I should like a cold bath," Nympha stated firmly, shivering as the wind picked up. "Brr. Isn't it possible they heated the water?"

"No evidence of it." He turned to Great-Aunt Letitia. "Mrs. Coxmoor, I suggest that it is time we return to the Hall. The wind has risen. Nympha looks chilled. It is possible that rain could come at any time. Look how the clouds have come over us."

The three hurried to the landau, settling in it just as the rain began to fall in a gentle drizzle.

"Do you wonder what happened to those people all those years ago?" Nympha cast one last look behind them before the carriage turned onto the main road.

"Well, at least nothing happened to you on this excursion," Great-Aunt Letitia said. She exchanged a look with Lord Nicholas that had Nympha wondering just what had occurred while she was in bed with a wounded head.

She had said nothing about the absence of the other guest at the Hall. Mr. Milburn might be a handsome enough gentleman, but it seemed he did not get along well with Lord Nicholas. After being hit on the head by his tennis ball, she was just as pleased not to deal with him.

Although, to be fair, she was well pleased with his thoughtful gift of a lace fan. It was the prettiest fan she had ever seen, much less owned. And as an atonement, it served extremely well.

Perhaps she would have to do as her father would no doubt advise—forgive and forget. She studied Lord Nicholas again. Just where did he fit into the scene?

Chapter Seven

Nick took the many copies he had made of the sketch of the murdered man, folded and tucked them carefully in his inner coat pocket before setting off for the stables. He had briefly explained to Mrs. Coxmoor that he wanted to explore the town of Mansfield and at the same time mouse about to see if he could learn more regarding the identity of the mysterious dead man. He had the notion of handing out the sketch to various shopkeepers to see what reaction he might get. He'd stop at Binch's first.

The sketches had occupied his time when Nympha had been recovering and he'd had little to do. Somehow he had been reluctant to avail himself of the horse and saddle his hostess had offered him. He'd no wish to go haring off with Milburn, who had grabbed onto the offer like a drowning man would a piece of flotsam.

Nick still had no clue as to precisely where Milburn went on his jaunts, as the man was as tight-lipped as could be about his uncle's condition. Nick wanted him gone, yet could scarce push him out the door.

"I wish you the best of luck with the sketches—you will likely have need of it," Mrs. Coxmoor had said in parting. He left the house feeling somewhat disheartened.

"Lord Nicholas! You are off to Mansfield?"

Nick turned back to see Nympha hurrying across the cobbled yard to where he waited.

Miss Herbert wore a simple cream dress over which

she had tossed a scarlet cloak. On her blond curls she had perched the same chip-straw hat she'd worn before. She made a rather fetching picture, and smelled even better when she came close, a light scent of lavender clinging to her.

She was a dainty morsel, and one he ought to stay clear of if he had any sense. He tried to tell himself he wanted to remain free to do as he pleased, that he wanted no entanglements, but Miss Herbert seemed to make mice-feet of his intentions. He doubted if she had the slightest idea of the effect she had on him. He was just becoming aware of the magnitude of his feelings himself.

She carried a stack of precisely folded missives. "These need to be sent. If you could manage that while in town, it would save sending someone else with them."

At his raised brow, she continued. "They are invitations for the masquerade ball my great-aunt insists she must give. She said something about celebrating my recovery, but it is a rather grand way to do that!"

"To ease your mind, she did mention a masquerade before," he reminded, while imagining Nympha in an alluring costume that would do justice to her slim, yet very elegant figure.

"Still, it will be a vast amount of work, I will wager." Nympha's smile looked a bit rueful, as though she was well aware on whose shoulders the work would fall.

"Your great-aunt will undoubtedly have others to do most of the work involved. I have observed she is very good at deputizing the jobs to be done."

"I know. But thank you."

He accepted the faultlessly folded notes, admiring the thick cream paper and beautifully inscribed addresses. "I'll be off." Her wistful expression caught at his heart, and he almost asked if she would like to come along, but she might interfere with his investigation.

"You have errands, I suppose?"

"Would you like to come with me?" Where had those words come from?

He supposed she could stroll about the town, perhaps giving him ideas as to where he might leave a copy of the sketch. The notion that he would enjoy her company flitted through his mind to be dismissed at once.

His spontaneous offer was met with an ecstatic smile. "Indeed, I would! Let me fetch my reticule—I'll be but a few moments."

He was an idiot. Certifiably. He reminded himself of his original intentions, wryly surmising that whatever they had been, they had fallen in a heap when he had insisted that Nympha travel north with him.

His traveling coach with his grays in harness was brought forth from the excellent stables. His coachman had befriended the chap who had driven Mrs. Coxmoor's vehicle and remained with it until repaired. There was a bit of mystery there as well. The wheelwright had insisted that there was no reason the accident should have happened. Every other part of the coach had been in tip-top condition, and too new to fall apart.

Nick decided he wasn't all that fond of mysteries.

Miss Herbert was as good as her word. She hurried from the house to join him, popping into the coach with a pleased grin lighting her attractive face. "The maids were all occupied so I decided to go without one. It ought to be acceptable? Surely your company is as good as a footman's?" Her eyes teased.

"I should think so." Odd, how Nick hadn't truly realized what a lovely girl she was. Even when he spent hours reading to her while she recovered, he had never seen her looking anything but nice. Her hair was always brushed, a smile—even if wan—hovered over her lips, and her polite manners all seemed a part of her nature. She had been well raised.

"I do enjoy looking about. Even if I do not buy a thing, it is lovely to see what there is on offer." She folded her hands in her lap and gave him a sparkling look.

What a decidedly novel notion. Nick tried to imagine any of the London beauties he had met offering such a naive remark and couldn't. Perhaps that was one thing that appealed to him about Nympha Herbert—her freshness and lack of Town boredom.

She wore a pair of her new gloves. He saw her secretly admiring them, smoothing them over her graceful hands. He was glad she had acquired something she so obviously wanted; then he grimaced. Good grief, he was becoming a sentimental bore.

"Do you have many errands in town?" Her query was diffident, quite as though it mattered not to her.

"Perhaps you may help me. I made sketches of the man I am trying to locate. I would like to place them about in the hope someone might recognize him." Nick almost kicked himself for blurting out this information, but on second thought it might be wise to do just this. But Miss Herbert had a winsome way about her. He would wager that a person might be more inclined to favor her instead of him.

"That is why you wanted the drawing paper! I confess I had wondered about that. You always had your brother creating drawings for your golf links. I could not imagine what you might sketch. May I see it?"

The coach rumbled into Mansfield as Nick pulled the batch of papers from his pocket. He peeled one paper from the collection and offered it to her.

She gasped.

"What is it?" Nick was confused. No one else he had talked to knew the identity of the stranger. How could Nympha Herbert recognize him?

"I have seen a man who appeared remarkably like this person. He was with Mr. Milburn. They were on your golf links, and I suspect they were arguing—you know, like you do when you perceive a play to be other than your opponent declares? Do you know what happened to him? I did not see him after that. I never gave him a thought, to be truthful. But I did not forget him completely." She studied the drawing again before handing it back to Nick.

"Remarkable. I have sought answers everywhere, and

here you are." Nick wondered if he should reveal what had happened to the mystery man. Clearly, Miss Herbert was not made of spun sugar. On the other hand, he wondered if it was better to remain silent. What she didn't know couldn't hurt her. And Miss Herbert had a penchant for falling into difficulties.

"I told Thursby to set us down at the inn. I imagine the locals fetch their mail from here?"

"I have no idea, but perhaps you have the right of it." She spoke with the assurance that comes from living in a village and knowing the ways of rural society.

Nick had handed the stack of invitations back to Miss Herbert when he dug out his sketches. Now she sat primly holding them on her lap.

The coachman deposited them directly in front of the inn. Nick gave Thursby instructions for the day. Miss Herbert accepted Nick's proffered arm with polite decorum.

She walked into the inn with him to hand the invitations over to the innkeeper, who nodded his concurrence with Nick's supposition.

"These will be sorted and picked up by the various grooms and maids today, to be sure."

Nick and Miss Herbert left the inn to make their way along the main street to the marketplace.

"We shall stop at Binch's first." Nick gestured to the shop across from where they walked. "I showed him the sketch before. He wanted one to keep."

"Mrs. Rankin is to come tomorrow. In addition to my new dresses—and there are far too many of them—I am to have a costume for the masquerade. What shall you wear?"

"If you are to be Maid Marian, as your aunt suggested, I shall be Robin Hood. Perhaps you would like to go to Sherwood Forest to absorb some of the atmosphere? You might have better feeling for the sort of costume you should wear."

"I suspect Mrs. Rankin has made a great many Maid

Marian costumes if she has been a mantua maker here for many years. I would wager it is a popular costume."

Nympha went ahead into Binch's, followed closely by Lord Nicholas. She waited politely while his lordship handed the sketch to the proprietor. There most definitely was recognition in Binch's eyes. It had flared briefly, but it was there.

"You recognize the man?" Nympha queried.

"Can't put a name to him, but he has been in here. Paid cash for his purchases. Never gave his name."

Nympha shared a look of disappointment with Lord Nicholas. "Thank you." She was about to leave with his lordship when she paused. "If you can think of anything else, please let us know." The image haunted her and she pushed it away; determined not to allow her sensibilities to surface.

Once they returned to the pavement, they continued on to the next shop.

"Paying cash is not that unusual, I suppose," Nympha ventured. "Papa said it is always best to pay cash for what you buy. After all, the merchant has bills to pay. I should imagine that if everyone paid bills promptly, businesses would be far better off."

"Spoken like a true rector's daughter," Lord Nicholas said, his tone teasing.

Nympha's heart sank; she felt snubbed. She admired the handsome gentleman at her side, and now he taunted her. They continued in silence, as she had no wish to say anything to him. Should she voice another opinion, he would likely ridicule that as well.

Perhaps he sensed her feelings of umbrage, for a short time later, after calling in at a fair number of shops, he stopped in the center of the market. In his imposing manner, which to be sure was a part of him, he said, "I believe we need a restoring cup of tea and perhaps a biscuit or three." There was no doubt in his mind that she would accept the offer for tea. He probably had women swarming over him when he was in London, ready and eager to do his bidding.

"If you like." She wished she had stayed at her great-aunt's. Misery crept up in her, reminding her of the vast gulf between her and this handsome lord, the son of a marquess. Perhaps inheriting her great-aunt's fortune and estate might make her more acceptable in the eyes of a gentleman. But a man like Lord Nicholas had sufficient in his own right. Could it be that lack of position would not rank all that high in his calculations? And pigs might fly.

She would wager the woman he married would come from a noble family, the higher, the better. Although, what she was thinking of to include Lord Nicholas with a thought of marriage was beyond common sense. It was not so long ago that she had declared she couldn't stand the man. Besides, wasn't he merely being polite to her? Keeping an eye on the daughter of his rector, most likely as a friendly favor?

How often had she heard derogatory comments on cits and their money? If she inherited from her aunt—and it seemed that she might—would she be viewed in the same light? Papa often declared it was the love of money that was the root of evil. Money was nice to have; it made life more agreeable. But she wanted more than money.

Could she settle for a marriage without love? If money made it possible, she would prefer to wait until she could find her ideal, a man she could love and who would love her in return. She knew it would be impossible to live with a man who scorned her very thoughts.

However, money would make her independent. She could pick and choose—and that was a comforting thought.

They settled in a private parlor to the rear of the inn. Tea and biscuits were fetched them immediately. The door prudently was left ajar. Again Nympha watched the deference given his lordship. Yet, she had to admit that she had been treated politely as well. Cynically, she wondered if that was because it was speculated that she might be the one to inherit the vast riches her great-aunt possessed.

"What is it?" Lord Nicholas inquired once she had poured his tea and offered thinly sliced lemon.

"What is what?" Nympha wasn't sure what he meant by those words and she certainly wasn't going to assume a thing. One could fall into a pit of trouble by saying the wrong words.

"Something is on your mind. While I have been chatting up the various shopkeepers, you have been trailing along behind like a disapproving shadow. I said something you did not like?"

She gave him a startled stare. Through the open door to the hall she saw a maid hurry past. The inn was quiet, too quiet. "I do not know what you mean."

"You became silent after your remarks on paying debts promptly. I see nothing wrong with your statement. I did not disagree with you. So what put your back up?"

"But then, I spoke as a true rector's daughter, and I expect I always shall. Once a value has been instilled in a person, I should think it difficult to eradicate."

"Remind me to talk with you after you inherit the vast estate your great-aunt intends to bequeath you." His intent gaze pierced. She almost felt it touch her skin.

Nympha paused, her teacup in hand before her mouth. She stared at him over the brim of the cup. "She said that to you?"

He nodded.

"Oh." Her lone word was a great exhalation of air. "That could present a problem or two." She thought a few moments. "But it would give me the opportunity to help my sisters and Adam. My parents as well."

"What would you do with the lace manufactories? The coal mine? Her other interests?" He held his teacup before him just as she did, like a shield to ward off something unwanted.

"If I marry, my husband might wish to assume the control of them." She continued to hold her teacup in front of her, forgetting she had wanted the beverage.

"I urge you to marry well, in that event. A man who

is astute in business, or gifted with finding good managers." His face seemed carved from stone for a moment.

Her searching eyes could detect no expression of any sort. "Perhaps I should call upon you for guidance in that event." She was goaded into adding, "I fancy you know every gentleman of interest and importance. Better still, you would know who I ought not marry—the wastrels and gamesters. I have heard tales that many of those sort are extremely charming and handsome."

"They live by their wits and charm, most often." At once he softened, yet his gaze seemed probing—for something he sought. "My advice is to take care. Better common sense than charm and wit. There are any number of charming scoundrels around."

He took a long swallow of tea, and Nympha did as well to ease the sudden dryness in her throat.

"Perhaps we should be on our way. I promised to show you a bit of Sherwood Forest. Do you want to pause on the way home, or go tomorrow?"

"Tomorrow Mrs. Rankin is to come. If there is something to see, we had best do it on our way home."

How odd it seemed to call Coxmoor Hall home, yet it would be if she inherited and married a man who would live with her there. She would make a few alterations.

He rose. "You will want to change the wall hangings, I am persuaded. Red is not a good color for you. I think blue would do well there." It was as though he could read her mind. Perhaps it was a logical extension of their conversation. But she found it disconcerting to realize he could sense into her thoughts like that. She left the table with her mind in a whirl.

Since he had handed out all the sketches with scant information returned, Nick decided they might as well return to Coxmoor Hall. He informed Thursby of his intention to pause in the forest. He wished to show Miss Herbert the major oak beneath which it was thought that Robin Hood met with his merry men.

They set off at a good clip. Nick eased back on the rear-facing seat, able to study his passenger without any demur. She remained silent, apparently absorbed in her thoughts.

"Can they be purchased for a penny?" He was surprised to realize that he wanted her to focus on him. He had never considered himself to be a vain creature, but the idea of an appealing young woman so able to ignore him stung.

Startled, she shifted her attention to him. "I scarce think they are worth that much. I was mulling over what I recalled of the Robin Hood legend. Do you suppose he really lived, that he really fought as they say, and that he finally married his Marian?"

"You would like to believe in a happy ending?" He crossed one leg over the other while continuing to observe Nympha closely. She was an entrancing young woman, and why had he not seen it before?

"I think most unmarried young women like to believe such is possible." She folded her hands in her lap, but he got an impression that she wished to do something else. He'd like to know what.

"What happens when you gain your inheritance?"

"We have already discussed that, my lord. Who can say what the future holds for certain? My aunt may live many more years, and I could meet with an accident."

"Be careful as to your choice of husband and you should have no problem." What in the world possessed him to offer her advice that would be better coming from her mother? Even her father had that privilege. Why should she pay the slightest attention to what he, Lord Nicholas Stanhope, had to say?

"As I said before, perhaps I may trot him past you for approval." She dropped her gaze to where her hands folded demurely in her lap, but not before Nick spotted the teasing glimmer in her delightful blue eyes.

Her eyes truly were a remarkable blue. He had seen lapis lazuli that color, a rich tone with flecks of gold in their depths. He wondered if she had ever worn the gem. It was not a highly valued stone such as a diamond, but not common, either. Of a sudden he had a wish to present her with a necklace of lapis, with ear bobs to match. They would become her well, and with perhaps a gown of white and blue to show off her blond tresses.

He must be losing his mind. He did not go about mentally dressing a young woman. More than often it was the opposite!

The coach rolled to a halt. Nick could see a thickly wooded area, with oaks, beeches, and silver birches in abundance. The woods, with patches of ferns here and there, was almost enough to make him a believer in the legend.

A path wound through the woods. Nick decided to let Nympha walk for a ways. It certainly ought to put her in the mood for her masquerade and costume.

He stepped from the coach, turning about to face the door. "Come, I'll help you." He worried that she was not totally recovered from that thump on her head.

When she appeared—her scarlet cloak flaring about her slim form—he reached to pick her out. Only once he had her in his grasp, he knew the most peculiar urge not to let her go. She became oddly tense as well, as though she knew his reaction and perhaps felt the same.

With more reluctance than he could believe, he set her on her feet, then offered his arm. "The path will be uneven. You had best take my arm, lest you fall. We do not want another accident."

"If it was an accident."

"Why would you think it wasn't? Surely Milburn would have nothing against you." Unless he had seen her near the links on the day he argued with the stranger. No, it was far more likely that Milburn would decide to court her when he realized she was to inherit that vast estate with wealth one usually dreams about. Was that not what had prompted the lace fan?

"I cannot believe that a skilled tennis player would hit a ball that went so far astray." She sounded annoyed.

"As to that, I fear I have had balls go every which way. We cannot accuse him of any crime on such slim evidence." He could not accuse the man, not without proof of wrongdoing.

She remained silent as they strolled along the path that led into the woods. Ahead of them stood a magnificent oak with wide-spreading branches. It was a massive size, and likely hundreds of years old.

Her surprise at the sight before her was a delight to see.

"What a magical place." Nympha stared at the huge oak, her eyes widening at the significance. "They truly think this to be the very oak under which Robin Hood met his men?"

"So they say." He thought her enraptured face utterly bewitching.

"I never thought much of it one way or another. It seems as though I have always been too busy with practical matters to daydream—helping Mother and all. Tabitha would like this—she adores Gothic tales. Since Robin Hood fought the sheriff and the king, freeing his friends, capturing the heart of a beautiful maiden—so they say—it is certainly that. It is a very romantic spot."

Nympha considered the gentleman at her side. He had shown every consideration for her, helping her, teasing her out of her serious reflections. Seeking his help seemed a natural thing to do.

Did he guess how his touch affected her? Could he read her mind with such ease as he had shown before, and know that she was a bit in love with him? She hoped not. She lifted her gaze to his face, wondering what he thought.

She had been kissed but once, and that lightly. Never had she been alone with a gentleman like this—and now she was. Would he risk kissing her? Truly kissing her?

Perhaps he also wondered about her, possibly kissing her. There in the deep silence of the wood, amid the silver birch and oak and masses of arching ferns, he bent his head, and his lips captured hers in the most delicate, delicious kiss she had ever imagined.

She ought to protest; certainly she ought to break away. This was highly improper. She had been taught better; a true gentleman did not dally with a young lady of quality. Her family might not be of the *ton,* but they were still eminently respectable gentry.

He lifted his head a moment to gaze down at her.

Thereupon she became lost in the second kiss. His touch melted her, and she could think of nothing better in this world than to be here with him, in the heart of this magical forest. Sensations whirled within her, creating a swift eddy that threatened to do away with all thought.

Reality set in somewhat like that thump on her head. Perhaps Lord Nicholas had decided that if she was going to inherit vast wealth and property she might make an acceptable spouse? Even though respectable, she knew she was not of his status in society. But from all she had read and heard, money did soothe the conscience, ease the pain of wedding into a family of lower circumstances—if indeed he thought of marriage!

She abruptly pulled away from him—quite as she should have the instant he drew her toward him. What a pity she hadn't taken one of the maids along. It would have prevented this from happening. Or was Lord Nicholas the type who would get his way no matter what? In that respect she hardly knew him well enough to know.

"Thank you for letting me see the tree and a bit of the forest. It was most, er, illuminating." She spun around and stumbled on a root that protruded, her eyes blinded by sudden moisture. He rushed to set her on her feet again, and she carefully removed his hand from her arm.

"Nympha, forgive me if I took unwanted liberties. I did not get the impression that my kiss was unwelcome."

She cast him a glance that she hoped told him nothing. "As to that, you must be aware you are handsome and possess a great deal of address. I have no more immunity against your charm than any other young woman, I suppose."

He sighed, most likely with annoyance at her provincial attitude to a kiss. But he escorted her to the coach with a polite reserve she found chilling.

Once seated in the coach, she regarded him with a brave face that she hoped concealed her bashful heart. Silence was her best refuge.

Nick studied the young woman who perched so uneasily on the seat across from him. Blast it all, what had possessed him to kiss her, and like that?

A gentleman did not overwhelm an innocent, and she certainly was all of that. It was her very innocence that had caught at him, tempted him. He would forever associate the scent of lavender with her; he knew that.

But what would happen now? He doubted she would go to her great-aunt to reveal what had occurred in the forest. The thing was, what would she say?

He found himself hating the thought of putting up at the Mansfield Inn. He had enjoyed staying with her surprising great-aunt. And, he reminded himself, he also needed to keep an eye on Nympha, not to mention Milburn.

It was possible to say she was in no danger, but what about Milburn? Would he pursue a young woman of undoubted innocence to capture her future fortune?

The coach rumbled into the stable yard. Within minutes the steps were let down, and Miss Herbert moved forward to accept the hand of the groom in assisting her from the coach.

So it was to be like that, was it? Nick left the coach, following her into the house.

With an inward grin, he touched her arm before she went up the stairs. "Thank you for accompanying me on my errands. You proved very helpful. I don't know what I would have done without you."

Her wide-eyed stare of surprise was his reward.

"Any luck, Lord Nicholas?" Mrs. Coxmoor inquired as she joined them in the entry hall.

"I think so. At least I have hopes."

Chapter Eight

What did he mean he had hopes? The man was a walking enigma.

Nympha proceeded up the stairs in a thoughtful mood. It had been a disturbing excursion—not so much around the little town of Mansfield. It was the highly illuminating stop at Sherwood Forest that disordered her calm. His kiss had shaken her, still sent tremors through her at the very memory of it.

It was a pity there were so many contradictions spinning through her mind. While Lord Nicholas might have sufficient funds at the moment, was there ever a man on earth who had enough money? That green folly of his, the golf links, must be costly to say nothing of building a house.

And what about Mr. Milburn? She had no knowledge of his finances, but she'd wager he would gaze kindly on a young woman of wealth. If she was to inherit, as Lord Nicholas seemed to believe she would, what then?

She changed from her simple cream dress to the equally simple blue silk, over which she draped the stylish lace shawl. Once satisfied with her appearance, she returned to meet her great-aunt in the drawing room. Dinner would be soon, and Nympha wondered if both Lord Nicholas and Mr. Milburn would be present. She fiddled with her reticule and the lace fan.

"My dear, I trust you had a pleasant day." Without waiting for an answer, Great-Aunt Letitia continued with a surprising request. "Mrs. Rankin comes early in the morning. She has two assistants, so she ought to be able to have a dress or two ready for you soon. After she has taken your measurements, I wish you to join me in the library." She paused for a moment. "I have decided you are to inherit all I have—save for a few small bequests." She beamed an approving smile on her grandniece.

"I scarce know what to say. I am overwhelmed." Nympha's right hand sought her throat; then she clasped both hands before her lest they flutter. She detested fluttering females. So Lord Nicholas had been correct in surmising that she was to be an heiress.

"I will send off a letter to your parents to request that you remain with me here. There is much for you to learn about the properties you are to inherit. I believe your first lesson will be in the morning—when you join me in the library." Seeing Nympha's expression, she added, "It will not be so onerous, I promise. In particular I would not have you ignorant of the workings of the various mills. I wish you to know who is trustworthy."

"Indeed, ma'am, that should be necessary to understand," Nympha replied while she tried to absorb all the many implications of her inheritance. It was vast, complex, and she wouldn't be going home for a long time if what her great-aunt said held true. Nympha couldn't imagine her parents denying her the legacy.

"I have found the businesses all quite fascinating," her great-aunt continued with a distant gleam in her eyes. "At first, after my husband died, they expected me to sell, or at the very least turn over the management of all the properties to a supervisor. It was considered unthinkable that I—a mere woman—could begin to comprehend the workings of a business. I outsmarted them all. My husband had taught me much; I learned the rest."

"That is incredible." Nympha was utterly awed by the woman who sat so composedly on the sofa. "It is a wonder that one of those men did not try to have you declared incompetent."

"They might have tried. But I managed the transfer

well, and soon they came to know that I meant business. The coal mine I leave to my manager, coal not being particularly interesting to me. It is the lace making that fascinates me. When you marry, if I am still around, I will teach your husband. I believe Lord Nicholas is curious about the mills and manufactories. Perhaps I will invite him to join us—in the event he desires to invest in such enterprises."

While Nympha groped for the right words, Lord Nicholas entered the drawing room, closely followed by Mr. Milburn.

"Gentlemen, I see we are to have the pleasure of both your company this evening." Great-Aunt Letitia smiled at them with impartiality. She sat on her favorite sofa, her back as erect as could be, wearing a gown of gray silk that was a wonder of simplicity. Nympha thought that while there was a queenly aspect to her, it was best not to forget her shrewdness.

Lord Nicholas bowed over her hand before going to stand by the fireplace. Nottinghamshire might have a salubrious climate—not humid nor subject to cold blasts from the north—but it could still be chilly on a March evening.

Mr. Milburn also bowed low over her great-aunt's hand, before turning to Nympha, bowing to her as well. He took note of the lace fan in her hands. "I am pleased to see you favor my modest present, Miss Herbert. How gratified I must be to see it has found favor in your eyes."

"I should be a foolish girl to think it other than beautiful. It was kind of you to think of me." Nympha retreated just enough so he would not be so close. While she admitted he was handsome and possessed a polished address, she still could not forget that tennis ball hitting her poor forehead.

She began to see why the fathers of heiresses took umbrage at those half-pay officers and second sons who sought a rich daughter to wed. If this was a small sample of what she might expect, she had better find a husband fast!

"It is good to see you back to normal. I was utterly desolated that by watching a simple game of tennis you would have been so badly injured." He smiled at her with a warmth she had not observed before. It was hard not to be cynical about his interest. She was willing to wager he had learned about her inheritance. The footman who served as valet to him would have been agog with the news. She doubted there was a servant who didn't eavesdrop or gossip.

Dinner was a trial. The food was its usual excellent quality, served with customary style. If Nympha found it a difficult meal, it was because both gentlemen complimented her to a degree beyond what she felt proper. There was nothing outstanding about her blue silk gown; nor was her hair out of the common way. Annie had dressed it simply, drawing it up to the top of her crown, allowing the curls to fall. She thought the two men could as well have dumped the butter boat over her head as well as all the fine phrases!

After the ladies left the dining room and the men behind, she was able to relax with her great-aunt. In spite of her imposing personality, Nympha found she was drawn to her. The more time she spent with her elderly relative, the more at ease she was with her and the better she liked her.

"You must learn to cope with flattery, my dear. I have endured it much of my life. When one is a simple girl with few prospects and subsequently obtains vast wealth, things change. You will have to learn to discern between true compliments and false flattery. You must take note of the eyes, my dear. So much of one's character is revealed in the eyes."

When the gentlemen joined them shortly, both men apparently not given to spending time with each other over the port, Nympha made a point to study the eyes of both men. Lord Nicholas had dark eyes, yet when he had held her close this afternoon she had seen golden sparks in them, a warmth that permeated her to the core. Were they honest and faithful? Was he? At this point she couldn't say. She knew what she wished, but how often did a wish come true?

Mr. Milburn's eyes were almost black. She could detect no sign of warmth in them, no flecks of gold or any other color. As to what character might be revealed in his eyes, she couldn't imagine what it might be. She turned from him to meet her great-aunt's gaze and shrugged.

The conversation was general, with Great-Aunt Letitia commenting on the fate of the income tax that ought to be repealed now that the war was over.

"I understand that the Commons is demanding the income tax be repealed. After all, those men have to be reelected, and it is a highly unpopular tax." She studied both men, likely to gauge their reaction. "We have been taxed on just about everything imaginable. The income tax is tyranny in its worst form!"

"How true, ma'am. It is a good thing they intend to burn all the records," Lord Nicholas inserted. "You think the opposition will succeed in ousting it?"

"Rumors reach us faster than you might think. After all, we are but one hundred and thirty-eight miles from London, give or take a few. A fast courier can have news here in a day or two of hard riding." Her eyes, a sharp blue that appeared to miss nothing, held a gleam of enthusiasm.

"The repeal of the income tax would benefit you a fair amount, I suppose," Mr. Milburn declared. "It is a horrid tax, but is there such a thing as a fair and just tax?"

"The colonials demanded such and did not get it. Let us hope that the members of Parliament learned that particular lesson well. I can recall the nonsense put forth by the greedy hand of the government. They were short-sighted, looking only to the moment, not seeing the side of those people across the Atlantic from us. They dared to call an educated people a clutch of felons. What a slap in the face that must have been."

Nympha listened as Lord Nicholas and her great-aunt discussed the politics of the day. Eventually tiring of the topic, she rose to quietly walk to the pianoforte. Locating a bit of music she knew, she sat down to play, thinking to offer a bit of soft music.

Mr. Milburn followed, offering to turn the pages for her. He glanced at the pair talking politics and smiled.

Nympha thought she detected smugness in that expression. Yet she appreciated his attentions. What woman could resist having a refined gentleman to turn pages for her?

Nick watched Milburn fawn over Nympha. Why, the fellow practically drooled. Not that she wasn't a delectable piece, garbed in a simple blue silk that draped over her slim form to reveal an excellent figure. The lace shawl emphasized her beauty. She merited attention; it simply galled Nick that Milburn was there and he was here. But then, he liked the great-aunt, found her fascinating to discuss matters with—particularly politics. It was amazing how well-informed she was. Politics were oddly fascinating.

Nick hadn't been able to prod Milburn into revealing his financial status. The best he'd been able to elicit was a vague comment on the dearth of heiresses. Milburn had come out with an odd remark to the effect of being glad he was not to be dependent on one of them.

Was he to inherit a considerable amount? From whom? His uncle? And when would this take place? Not that one could always determine when a death might occur.

Unless . . . one arranged for it to happen.

"If you will excuse me all, I am for bed. I cannot remain up as late as I once did," Mrs. Coxmoor said as she rose from her sofa. She waved a handkerchief in Nympha's direction. "Stay if you will. I shall see you in the morning."

Nympha, thinking it far safer to head for her room, rose as well. "I will join you." She curtsied to the men, not looking at either one of them directly. "Good night."

She could only hope that sleep would come quickly.

* * *

Mrs. Rankin appeared bright and early the next morning. Her two assistants carried the baskets of thread and all else required. Nympha met them in the entry hall after leaving the breakfast room. She had eaten quickly and very alone.

The mantua maker was efficient in taking her measurements, then determining which of the fabrics should be made up first.

"I need a costume for the masquerade ball my great-aunt is giving. She wishes me to attend as Maid Marian. Do you have such a costume made, or could you make up a simple garment for me to wear? I want nothing elaborate, just something tasteful."

Mrs. Rankin was no fool. She well knew the importance of the clothes she was to sew for this young woman. If it was true that she was to be the heiress, there could be any number of lucrative orders in the future, providing the results were pleasing. Even Nympha realized this.

"I know the very thing—like this." She hastily sketched a gown fitted with a tight lacing in the back so that it clung to the body. The neck had an interesting design at the opening slit, and the sleeves were long, the points reaching to the knees. "There should be a girdle, high around the front and brought forward at the hips. The ends tie, to hang down almost to the hem. All it takes is fabric and a bit of time. Your great-aunt has all the fine linen you might wish."

"Excellent. My maid can locate what is necessary. Perhaps the housekeeper will know where the fabric can be found. I fear the ball is very soon. What about the gentlemen? Is there a place where they might find the correct attire?"

"Nottingham might have something. Then again, perhaps they could find something in the attics here? No one ever tosses out a thing. There must be trunks full of old clothes up there."

Nympha nodded. She sped from the room after deciding to have the lilac spotted muslin and the blush sarcenet made up first. A tinge of rose stained her cheeks when she thought of how Lord Nicholas had suggested she have some of that fabric. There had been a suspicious glint in his eyes, quite as though he had something more intimate in mind. A glance at the hall looking glass confirmed her high color.

"You are in fine looks this morning, Miss Herbert." It was the very man in her thoughts, Nicholas. "Dare I inquire what has given you those rosy cheeks?"

"No." She was abrupt, but far too flustered to think of a way to explain that glow. She rushed into a change of subject. "If you do not have a costume yet, perhaps we may be able to find one in the attics. Mrs. Rankin suggested you might."

He agreed with alacrity. Nympha sought permission from her great-aunt, who replied, "As long as I am not required to go up there, you may use anything you find. Look in the gray trunk first. Once you have something, I shall see you in the library, my dear. You as well, my lord, if you please."

Nympha found her way to the attics at once, with Lord Nicholas close on her heels. The gray trunk yielded surprising riches.

"Dark green hose will do." He emerged from the depths of the large trunk with a pair of long hose in hand.

He held them up for her inspection. Nympha thought they might be serviceable with a bit of repair. With them came an interesting set of leather strips that she puzzled over until Lord Nicholas guessed at their use.

"I fancy these were used to wind around the leg to hold on the hose. And here are the boots to go with them."

"Here's a green tunic to match—almost." Nympha pulled forth a heavy linen item. "And a hood of a greenish blue. It even has a point in the back. You shall be very Robin Hoodish, I think." Nympha draped all the latest items across him with a gesture of triumph. If she found placing the clothing against him to be disturbing, she gave no hint of her reaction. She tried valiantly to pretend it was no more than her brother standing beside her, and not some dashing and very handsome lord.

Simpson had trailed them to the attics and now retrieved the items of clothing. He could be heard muttering about cleaning and airing and repairing all the way back downstairs.

He left Nympha and Nick alone, which was precisely what Nick had hoped. She knelt at the trunk, replacing items that had been tossed about to reasonable order.

Being alone with Nick was not what Nympha had longed for—she rose at once to follow Simpson.

"Nympha, you cannot ignore me forever, you know."

"Who said I am trying to ignore you, my lord?" Nympha backed away from him in the direction of the door. At least, he suspected that was her intent.

He followed her—equally intent upon apologizing if such was necessary. It was dashed hard to get a moment alone with her.

"You have avoided me since yesterday—Sherwood Forest, to be precise. Must I apologize?" He examined her face, wishing she would look up at him. Her creamy skin was faintly tinged with rose. Lavender scent, uniquely a part of her, drifted over to tease his nose. She was quite bewitching.

She studied her hands, now folded before her in a tight, nervous clasp.

"I guarantee I do not bite, my dear." He eased two steps in her direction.

"I am not your dear. I am not anyone's dear. As to an apology, I am not sure I want it." She backed away two steps.

"You seem torn. Could it be that you enjoyed it as much as I did?" He tilted his head at an angle, giving her what he had been told was a beguiling smile.

"I must go! Great-Aunt said I was to come to the library as soon as we found you a costume. I believe you are to join us." With that, she whirled about, and this time flew down the stairs as though the hounds of hell were at her heels.

There was nothing to do but follow her. Milburn met him on the landing, seeming puzzled.

"Did I not see Miss Herbert come tearing down the stairs? What happened, old man?" He smirked, making Nick long to punch him in the jaw. Of course, that was a common sensation, so it was hardly something new.

"We were hunting for a costume for me to wear. Simpson is even now making repairs on what we found. Have you thought of something? Or will you take refuge in a domino?" Nick smiled, a narrow glimmer of amusement.

"I intend to go as King John, a far more imposing character than that fellow Robin Hood. He was definitely lower class, dear chap."

Nick refrained from reminding Milburn that Robin Hood got the girl.

Leaving Milburn to his dreams, Nick sauntered down the remaining steps to the main floor, around to the library.

Mrs. Coxmoor gave him a searching stare before motioning him to join them. Without comment, she returned her attention to her grandniece, offering information on the business she was to inherit.

As a lesson it was riveting. Nick paid close attention to every word. If things turned out as he was beginning to hope, he would need to know all this. In the event they didn't, the knowledge would be useful for his investments. What a pity they didn't offer lectures of this sort at Oxford. It was far more illuminating and practical than Latin and Greek.

When she concluded the morning's session, Mrs. Coxmoor advised the pair to get a breath of fresh air following their lunch.

"You must allow your poor brains a bit of time to assimilate all I have put in them today. Perhaps in a week or so you will have a basic grasp of the business."

Nympha nodded, leaving the room with her head reeling with facts and figures. And she was supposed to take over the running of it all? She paused at the bottom of the stairs and turned to Lord Nicholas. "I hope she lives for many years—and in full possession of all her faculties. Either that or I shall have to find myself an honest and astute husband quickly!"

"Perhaps you may have both."

When he did not say anything more, she nodded, then ran lightly up the stairs to her room. So . . . he thought she should find herself a husband? What she wanted and what she might have were likely two different things.

Unless . . . Lord Nicholas Stanhope did not have as much wealth as she had thought. Perhaps he needed to marry for money. In that event, she might have . . . what? A marriage such as she feared? A loveless union? His kisses were expert if those samples were anything to go by. He could tease amusingly and converse with sensible comments. But surely there were daughters of peers who also had money. He could aim as high as he pleased.

No, she had better not dream. Best to search elsewhere. Perhaps her great-aunt had someone in mind. She knew the area well. Maybe that was why she planned the masquerade ball! Could it be that she intended to introduce Nympha to those she deemed acceptable partners in more than a dance?

Intriguing thought!

Once she found her pelisse that had a close hood attached, she marched down the stairs, intent upon doing as told—get a breath of fresh air as soon as she had a bite to eat. She had little appetite; a sandwich was sufficient. It took but moments to consume that and a piece of fruit.

She headed for the front door.

Lord Nicholas was not in sight in any direction. Mr. Milburn was. She wondered if he had lain in wait for her.

"Going out? I wondered if you would like to join me for a bit of archery. Your great-aunt said you might enjoy it. What say?"

Nympha gave him an assessing stare. He was neatly

garbed, flatteringly interested in her company, and did not seem as though he wanted to kiss her. There was no heat in his eyes, no warmth in his expression. "That would be just lovely."

They walked in companionable silence until they found where the archery butt had been set up. Apparently Mr. Milburn had planned this in advance, for two bows of different lengths plus a supply of arrows were close by.

"Have you done this before?" Mr. Milburn handed her the sorter of the two bows, before picking up an arrow.

"Not exactly."

He grinned, and Nympha felt more in charity, seeing a more likeable side of the man.

"Allow me to help you, Miss Herbert. You will want to stand at a right angle to the target, like so." He gently positioned her, not permitting his hands to linger at her waist as she might have expected.

She had placed her hand where one obviously was supposed to grasp the bow. She glanced up at him for more help.

He handed her a slim wand of wood. "The arrow."

"I know that," she said, fearing she was a bit curt with him, but heavens above, everyone knew what an arrow looked like. Shooting it was another matter.

He stood behind her, placing one hand over hers. "Now you take the other hand and draw back the bowstring."

When Nympha faltered at this, finding the bowstring taut, he wrapped his other arm about her, to enclose her hand with his. She discovered she was enveloped in his clasp, disconcertingly close to his body. Yet she felt none of the disturbing sensations that had assailed her when she had been so close to Lord Nicholas. "The next step is nocking the arrow, like so." He proceeded to put the arrow on the bowstring with the feather up along the left side of the string.

"Now draw the bowstring back. That arrow ought to be between the second and third fingers. Swing the bow up, aim at the target, and release."

Of course it wasn't as simple as that, but Nympha had tried this once before so she had a vague notion of what she was supposed to do.

The arrow sailed past the butt, landing in the grassy plot behind it.

"Ah, getting a bit of practice in are we?" Lord Nicholas said as he joined them, looking as though he had just returned from a fast jaunt through the gardens.

"Mr. Milburn is helping me with my archery. I seem to have forgotten much of what I learned." Nympha slanted an amused glance at his lordship. He appeared a little annoyed.

"Show me your progress, in that event."

After giving Lord Nicholas a reproving look, Nympha again took an arrow, nocked it, raised the bow as reminded, then released the arrow, hoping it might end up somewhere near the target. It didn't. She sighed in utter frustration and exasperation. Why did she have such a time with any sport?

"May I offer a suggestion, Miss Herbert? You might find your aim better if you try to sight along the arrow, then let the bowstring roll off your fingers. Like this."

Lord Nicholas picked up the other bow, grabbed an arrow to nock it just so.

Nympha watched as he appeared to aim a bit high over the butt—at least it seemed that way to her. It was amazing to watch that bowstring just roll off his fingers. The arrow shot in the air and hit dead center.

She clapped in appreciation, allowing her bow to fall to the ground. Lord Nicholas reached for it before Mr. Milburn could react. He offered the bow to Nympha, stepping behind her just as Mr. Milburn had.

"Now, you do it. You can, you know. You can do anything if you just try. Never give up on a thing if it means something to you." He gave her a steady regard that went straight to her heart.

Again she nocked the arrow to the bowstring, then raised it. Only this time Lord Nicholas wrapped his arms about her, guiding her arm, raising the bow so that the arrow was aimed higher, just as she observed his had been.

"I hit it!" True, the arrow was in the red band, but it wasn't in the grass.

At once she became aware of his proximity, the scent of costmary in his linens, the solid body so close to her. Why, she could feel his waistcoat pressing into her, the lean power of his legs against hers. She ought to be shocked, she supposed. Instead, she found it a rather heady sensation.

He had used a light tangy lotion when he shaved that morning. It still clung to his skin, and it teased her nose with its sharpness.

Had she ever been so aware of another?

He let go of her bow, stepping slowly away. Had he also been affected by their closeness? It was odd that Mr. Milburn's proximity had not had the slightest impact on her, none at all. All of which proved nothing, other than she was susceptible in some manner to his lordship.

She observed the two men eyeing each other like a pair of dogs about to fight. Not if she could help it!

"Please, could you help me once more, Mr. Milburn? I have trouble with the arrow."

Before Mr. Milburn could move, however, Lord Nicholas had picked up an arrow, stepped forward, placed the arrow in her right hand, and nudged her bow in place.

"I think you will do splendidly, my dear. Just aim high. One ought never aim low in archery—or in life, either."

She caught his sidelong glance at Mr. Milburn. The two evidently considered they were rivals. What a bit of folly that was!

Chapter Nine

When Nympha returned to her room, feeling slightly breathless and certainly confused, she found Mrs. Rankin awaiting her. A handsome gown of a pleasing shade of blue had replaced the simple costume Nympha had envisioned. She slipped it over her head, then watched in the looking glass as Mrs. Rankin laced up the back. The thin linen fabric clung to her like a second skin.

"Now, this is how the gown is to be laced. It must be tight, so there will be no gaps," the mantua maker explained to Annie.

Nympha studied her reflection, swallowing with care. If this was an example of how Maid Marian looked, it was a wonder every man in the county hadn't attempted to toss her over his saddle and ride off with her. "It is, er, very revealing in a way, isn't it?"

"That they were, miss. If you study the gowns worn by the effigies on all those old tombstones and in the stained-glass images, that's the way they were."

"Oh, mercy."

"You will have a sheer veil for your head, and your hair *ought* to be in braids."

"A wig! Just the thing," Nympha declared. Wearing a wig would make it seem like a play, that it wasn't her in this garb. Because what she saw in the looking glass was more than a trifle disturbing.

She slipped from the gown to try on the lilac-sprigged

muslin. It certainly was more decorous. Tiny lilac flowers were so close together that the fabric almost appeared all lilac at a distance. The high neck had a treble ruff of lace, and there were scallops of lace on the bodice as well as the lower edge of the long sleeves.

"I intend to add more scallops of lace around the lower part of the skirt as well, but I wished to see if the fit was right first." Mrs. Rankin poked and pinned until content.

Nympha almost said that the lace might be left off the skirt until she recalled that she was now the inheritor of a lace manufactory. Not only was it stylish to use the lace, but it was also a good advertisement. Although, precisely who was to see her in the wilds of Nottinghamshire was beyond her. Even if this area was called the Dukeries because of the large number of dukes here, it didn't mean they did all that much socializing.

The cherry-striped percale she tried next had been designed with a low neckline, but it had such a ravishing ruffle around it that Nympha swallowed all objections. Puffed sleeves peeped out from beneath the wide ruffle, and a deep flounce was trimmed with a self-fabric cord and truly looked stylish. It was the prettiest afternoon dress she had seen. When she told this to Mrs. Rankin, the good lady blushed and curtsied.

To don her simple cream muslin, sewn in the rectory drawing room, was not easy to do. What a difference fabric of the first quality made in a gown—not to mention superior sewing and fit.

She left her room, intent upon reaching the drawing room where she thought to find her great-aunt, when she was stopped by her great-aunt's abigail, Talbot.

"Would you come with me, miss? Mrs. Coxmoor wishes to see you in her room."

Curious, Nympha obediently followed in the wake of the abigail. Her great-aunt must toss garments away often, as the maid was garbed in the highest fashion. The silvery gray favored by Great-Aunt Letitia looked well on her.

"Come in. Come in," her great-aunt demanded. "I want your opinion. My late husband favored red, but I am becoming weary of it. What do you think of a different paper in here?"

Nympha stared at the red walls. The vibrant color overwhelmed the classic lines of the walnut four-poster bed, not to mention the beautifully designed chests and the writing desk with its delicate chair.

"What about a Chinese style of paper?" Nympha slowly pivoted, inspecting the furnishings. "We read that it is all the style now, since Brighton is turning oriental. A cream background with flowers and birds would be charming in here. Then you could have cream draperies bordered with green, perhaps," Nympha concluded, quite carried away by the mental image of how the room might appear.

"The very thing. Langley in Mansfield claims to have a vast assortment of paper hangings. He won't, of course, have any Chinese-style paper, and I will enjoy twitting him about it. Thinks he is so smart and fashionable. Humph. He advertises that he can have a room papered on the shortest notice. I will wager you it is impossible." The elderly lady assumed a pixyish smile, her eyes twinkling with mischief.

"Indeed, ma'am, it will be interesting to see what he has in stock." Nympha waited to see what would be next.

"Good. You can set out now. You have plenty of time before you need to be home for dinner. Select the paper. I can order the draperies from London, using a scrap of it for color. Tell him I want it done at once."

She nodded emphatically, shooing Nympha from her room with more energy than Nympha had at the thought of dashing into Mansfield to search for paper hangings to be put on the bedroom walls.

"Ah, Miss Herbert," Lord Nicholas cried when he spotted her crossing the entryway, dressed for her jaunt.

"Good afternoon, my lord. I am off to Mansfield."

He glanced at the longcase clock that stood in the corner of the entry. "Rather late, don't you think?"

"Great-Aunt wishes me to select new bedroom wallpaper for her. I suggested the oriental sort, and she now declares that is the very thing to have."

"I'll go with you. It is not right for you to go on such an errand all alone."

Since Nympha had intended to take Annie with her, she shook her head. To no avail. "I insist, dear girl. Can't have you taking any chances." Since it hadn't bothered him in the least to have Nympha trotting behind him all over the golf course, she found this hard to believe.

A footman fetched his lordship's hat and gloves. In minutes Lord Nicholas was escorting Nympha out of the house to the waiting coach.

"I must say, your great-aunt certainly has excellent servants. They anticipate her wishes better than mine do."

"She must have sent instructions when I went to put on my pelisse. Mrs. Rankin had a few questions, and by the time I met you in the entry at least twenty minutes must have elapsed."

She was quite certain his lordship noticed her trembling reaction to him when he assisted her into the coach. How could he not? He was a man who seemed to observe the slightest thing. Could he guess how his merest touch affected her? Oh, she hoped not!

This time he sat next to her, and in a way that was better. She didn't have to wonder why he stared at her so, as if she had a bit of smut on her nose. On the other hand, when the coach swayed from side to side on the less-than-smooth road, she could feel his body against hers—all the way from thigh to shoulder.

The drive to town was too slow. By the time they arrived, she was totally out of innocuous conversation, and her nerves were on the point of shattering. They drew up before Langley's none too soon.

"This is where I found my sketching paper." Lord Nicholas moved from his seat, holding out his hand for hers. "The fellow has a little of everything in here."

"Smaller towns are like that. Only in London do I fancy you can have a shop that has nothing but wallpaper. If there is an errand you wish to tend to, or something else you want to do, please feel free to go." Once he had set her down on the pavement, she edged from his side.

"Miss Herbert—are you trying to get rid of me?"

He assumed such a stricken expression Nympha didn't know whether she should laugh or assure him that *that* was the least of her desires. She gave him no reply to his bit of nonsense, which was no more than he deserved. They entered the shop to find Mr. Langley himself coming to serve them.

Nympha explained what her great-aunt wanted in the way of wallpapers. If she had hoped to perturb him, she failed, not even when she offered the room dimensions.

"I have just the paper. I am told it is much like a paper in a room at Chatsworth, Miss Herbert. Oriental is the very latest thing."

Nympha could hardly complain on any score as the paper was utterly gorgeous and precisely what she had envisioned, perhaps better. There were butterflies and birds flitting among the fantastic plants and flowers. It would definitely call for a book on oriental plants.

"The paper was hand painted in China. I was so fortunate to obtain it on my last trip to London. I had thought the Duke of Portland might like it." He cleared his throat, as though he wished to stress his client.

"Mrs. Coxmoor desires to have her bedroom papered as soon as is possible," Lord Nicholas declared in his most pretentious manner.

It worked. Mr. Langley assured them he would be there in the morning with the paper in hand.

"Are you always so forceful?" Nympha queried after the shop door closed behind them.

"When it is necessary. There are times when gentleness and soft persuasion are needed instead."

She chanced to glance up at him, only to encounter an expression that in a woman might be called wistful. Were men ever wistful? Her father never seemed to be, always a decided gentleman with strong opinions no one ventured to challenge.

"And when is that, may I ask?" she dared to inquire.

"I may explain to you in detail someday—but not at the moment while walking across the marketplace. Do you wish to return home immediately? Or will you join me in a cup of tea?"

"Tea would be lovely." Annie had been left behind again. It seemed that whenever Nympha went off with his lordship, he contrived for them to be alone. Or was it merely a happenstance?

They had the same room as before, and as before he saw to it that the door was left open. The rosy-cheeked maid who brought them the tray holding the teapot, cups, and all the other things necessary, flirted with his lordship in a shameful manner. Nympha longed to give her a poke and tell her to mind her business.

She poured out tea for him, handing it to him with care.

"You have been kept busy since you arrived," Lord Nicholas said. "Not a moment to yourself, if I make no mistake." He peered at her over the rim of his cup, and she was reminded of their last private tea here.

"I'd not have it any other way. I far prefer to be kept occupied. A daughter in the rectory has no idle moments, sir." Not that she wouldn't enjoy them; they merely never came her way.

"Harriet—my brother's wife—told me that you tend the sale of the exotic hens your mother raises. Is that true?"

"Mama raises them. I handle the sale of the eggs and keep her books. You would be amazed how many people there are who desire fancy fowl strutting about their chicken yard." She smiled at the memory of a few of those people.

"Clever girl." At her look of inquiry, he added, "To keep books and handle sales. It cannot be easy for you."

"Papa taught us our sums and numbers. I can write and calculate as well as anyone, I imagine."

"Good. You won't be cheated by a conniving shopkeeper in that event."

She bit into a crisp lemon biscuit. It crunched loudly in the silence of the room, sounding like bombarding rocks.

A door slammed. Conversation could be heard again. She glanced up and was thankful she had swallowed the last crumb. "Mr. Milburn, what a surprise."

"May I join you?" He tossed Lord Nicholas what Nympha thought was a challenging glower.

"By all means. I'll call for more tea."

"Do not bother, old man. I requested a mug of their fine home brew." He sauntered across the room to stand by their table. At a gesture from Nympha, he pulled out a chair and sat down.

"You were very certain of your welcome, old chap," Lord Nicholas countered.

"I knew our softhearted Miss Herbert would not deny me her company—even if you might wish me elsewhere." His smile bordered on smug.

Nympha again knew the feeling of being a bone about to become the contention between two dogs.

Nick watched the faint color creep across Nympha's cheeks. The color enhanced her already attractive complexion and brought a sparkle to her eyes.

When they first traveled north he had thought inviting her to join him was merely a kind gesture to a neighbor. As time went on, he had found himself drawn to her in many ways. She possessed a quick wit, a very nice figure, showed a kind heart to her great-aunt, and had quite captured his. He doubted if she had the slightest notion of how he felt. For one thing, she would believe he must look higher for a wife.

A wife. The very thought of marriage shook him, yet

his brother had wed last year, and seemed very happy. Nick supposed that most men met that fate sooner or later. For some years he had kept the thought in the back of his mind, particularly when he'd attended balls or evening parties while in London. That was where one went to find a wife. One didn't search in the wilds of Nottinghamshire.

Money! He wished he had thought to ask for her hand before he knew she was to inherit a vast fortune. In any event if she fell in love with him, there should be no problem. But he wished he had told her before. Would she now believe he was after her eventual fortune? For that matter, could she fall in love with him? He had the idea that she would marry only for love.

"I was surprised to see the Coxmoor coach out behind. A special errand?" Milburn regarded Nympha, then Nick.

"Mrs. Coxmoor wanted some new wallpaper for her bedroom, and nothing would do but that it be found at once." Nick wondered if having a vast fortune made a person like that—wanting instant satisfaction. Yet the old girl was so agreeable that it was impossible to take umbrage at her requests.

Milburn focused his attention on Nympha again. "Have you indulged in a stop at Sherwood Forest? I fancy you must see the great oak under which Robin Hood is said to have met his merry men." He drank his ale as though he'd been in a desert.

"Yes," she replied, glancing at Nick, "I did see it. 'Tis an amazing tree."

"And Friar Tuck's walk?"

"No, I didn't see that," she said slowly, as though she was recalling her insistence upon going right home.

"Someday you must allow me to show it to you. A very romantic walk, so I am told, with ferns and spreading trees over the walk to form an archway."

"It sounds nice," she replied politely.

Nick hoped Milburn noticed the lack of interest in her courteous answers. Drat it all, the fellow was fawning all over her, and he was dressed as fine as fivepence today. Nick wondered anew where Milburn had been spending his hours and how he financed his trip.

"I trust you are enjoying your time here in Mansfield, Milburn. You never did say if you have been able to visit with your . . . uncle, I believe it was?" Nick set his cup on the saucer and then leaned back to study the man he thought of as his opponent. Could he trip him up, confuse him?

"I had hoped to stay with him, but he has been quite ill. The doctor has advised that the house be kept quiet—so I may visit him for brief times, but that is all." Milburn spoke in a bland, subdued manner.

Nick cynically wondered just how genuine that long face Milburn pulled might be. His story remained the same.

"I am sorry your uncle is still ill," Nympha said. "No wonder you prefer to stay with my great-aunt. How long do you plan to be in this area?" Nympha ran her eyes over Milburn, quite as though she were assessing him.

Nick leaned forward to see what the fellow had to say.

"I really do not know," Milburn replied with seeming frankness. "You see, I could go, but since I am likely to be his heir as his son has disappeared, I feel it urgent for me to remain close by so in the event he fails further, or heaven forbid, dies, I'll be here."

"I can see where you are in a bit of a fix." Nick studied Milburn, and wondered if this was the means of his "coming into money" he had mentioned before. It would stand to reason that he would want to remain just in case he was wanted one way or the other. He wondered what had happened to the son.

"I appreciate your great-aunt's hospitality very much." Milburn bowed with exquisite courtesy.

Nick took out his watch to check the time. "I fear we had better return to the Hall. We will just have time to change before dinner. You will excuse us, Milburn?"

"Aye. I'll be right behind you."

* * *

That evening was a strain as far as Nympha was concerned. The two gentlemen seemed to vie for her attention, in a mannerly way, to be sure. But she *was* coming to feel being the object of rivalry unpleasant.

Her great-aunt sat on her favored sofa, garbed in another of her silvery gray gowns, and looked as though she watched a raree-show, her eyes sparkling.

When Nympha had quite enough of it all, she rose with the intent of fleeing to her room.

She paused by the doorway to address her great-aunt. "Do not forget they will come to paper your bedroom in the morning."

"I intend to visit a neighbor. What shall you do, my dear?"

"Mrs. Rankin may require me for a fitting."

Mr. Milburn gave what Nympha thought was a very sly grin. "What say we have a few games of skill on the morrow, Nick?"

"What did you have in mind?"

Nympha had not heard his lordship called Nick before, and thought it suited him, but wondered if he appreciated having Milburn call him by so familiar an address.

"Another match of archery. I noticed there is a setup for quoits and a lane for a game of bowls. Or tennis again. Pity there aren't enough for us to have a game of cricket."

"I notice you didn't mention a fistfight." Lord Nicholas propped his chin on his hand, leaning on the arm of the wingback chair in which he lounged.

"I do enjoy a bit of sport, but you forget—I have seen you spar at Gentleman Jackson's. I wish to survive a bit longer, my lord."

Lord Nicholas raised a polite eyebrow at that bit of flattery. "It's a shame we've no golf links nearby. I think I could beat you on the seventh green."

Mr. Milburn paled, muttered something about retiring early, and shortly left the room.

Nympha had made the connection. "Was that quite wise, my lord? He is bound to assume you know more than you do. There is no way you could pin the blame on Mr. Milburn. Is there? Was that merely a wild guess because I said I had seen him talking to that man?"

"Yes," Lord Nicholas admitted. "But I must say his reaction was curious, was it not?" He rose from the chair where he had been chatting with Mrs. Coxmoor and crossed to where Nympha stood, irresolute and curious.

"Will you play those games tomorrow, sir?"

"Perhaps. At the moment, I wish to escort you upstairs to your room. I believe we all need an early night."

Mrs. Coxmoor rose to follow them, murmuring something about telling Foley to let in that paperhanger when he arrived in the morning. "Goodness knows what time he will arrive—some ungodly hour, I am sure."

"Well, it is what you wanted, after all. Perhaps he will make short work of the job," Nympha said.

"He'd better, or he will not work here again!"

"She is rather determined, I think. But delightful, nonetheless," Nympha murmured to Lord Nicholas once they had quit the room.

They made short work of the stairs and were at Nympha's door before she wished.

His lazy smile should have warned her. It didn't. He bent to gently take her lips captive in a kiss that would give her enchanting dreams all the night.

She gave him a misty smile before fumbling with the doorknob. She slipped inside to float to her looking glass, amazed she looked just the same when inwardly she was so transformed.

Mr. Langley and his minions arrived as Nympha left the breakfast room. Rolls of paper and a large pot of paste, plus assorted other items went sailing past her up the stairs toward her great-aunt's bedroom in the arms of the workmen. Mr. Langley informed them that he had personally come to supervise the work.

"I do not believe it," Great-Aunt Letitia muttered. "I lose my wager."

"Since we did not actually wager anything, as far as I can see you are in the clear." Nympha offered a cheerful smile to her irrepressible great-aunt.

Nympha decided to go with the men on their games. She would watch, taking care to be out of the way of stray balls and the like. Not that she actually thought she could be hit again. Surely that previous time was a chance thing?

She was standing in the entry hall when there was a knock at the front door. Foley promptly went to open it, revealing two ladies and a gentleman, all young, and all in the latest mode of dress. One woman was a petite brunette, the other a slightly taller brunette. Both were remarkably polished. The gentleman bore all the earmarks of a dandy, with shirt points so high and sharp Nympha marveled he hadn't stabbed himself. They all held themselves with the sort of assurance that comes with wealth and a title.

Nympha was extremely thankful she had donned the new lilac-sprigged muslin dress this morning.

Her great-aunt left her library just at that moment, greeting the newcomers with cries of welcome.

"Mrs. Coxmoor, rumor has it that you have two gentlemen as well as your grandniece staying with you. You are very naughty not to let us know," cried the petite brunette. "We are here to become acquainted."

Her great-aunt touched Nympha's arm. "Dearest, I would have you meet our neighbors. Lady Anne Nelthorpe, Lady Jane Nelthorpe, and Lord Henry Nelthorpe. This is my grandniece, Miss Nympha Herbert. I would not be surprised if Lord Henry would enjoy joining in the games proposed for today."

"Games?" the dandy echoed faintly.

"What was decided upon, Nympha?" A mischievous light gleamed in her great-aunt's eyes.

Nympha was hard put to keep a properly demure expression after seeing those eyes. "I believe they settled on archery, quoits, and tennis if they have time."

"Well, we can all do quoits, and I'm a dab hand at archery, if I do say so," young Lord Henry declared.

Lady Anne and Lady Jane exchanged looks, but they did not deflate their brother's opinion of his skills.

Milburn came clattering down the stairs at this point, followed more leisurely by Lord Nicholas, who seemed to be sizing up the guests. Both gentlemen were garbed in appropriate breeches, coats, and shining boots.

Introductions followed. Nympha had the dubious pleasure of watching Lord Nicholas charm the Nelthorpe ladies. Milburn poured on the charm as well, but it didn't bother Nympha as much. It was obvious to her that these two young women were gifted with poise and a knowledge of society that she lacked.

"What is this we hear about games?" Lady Anne demanded, taking hold of Lord Nicholas's arm to propel him into the drawing room. Lady Jane promptly latched on to Mr. Milburn, leaving Nympha with the dandy, Lord Henry.

"Well, you cannot say my sister allows any moss to grow under her feet. When she sees something she wants, she does tend to go after it—or him, as the case may be."

Nympha wanted to inform this boy that Lord Nicholas was not for the taking. She wished she might. What a pity she had to do the civil thing, and be all politeness.

"We shall begin the day with archery, I believe." Lord Nicholas detached himself from the clinging Lady Anne to walk over so that he could give Foley a few instructions. That done, he beckoned all to follow him, and somehow he ended up next to Nympha, with Lady Anne on his other side.

Nympha admired his ability to avoid being monopolized by the tenacious Lady Anne and yet give the impression that he was enormously pleased to meet her.

"I believe I have seen you in London, Lord Nicholas," Lady Anne declared. Her vivacious face beamed a smile, in spite of his avoidance of her claim on his arm.

"It is possible, although I spend much time at my country home—near where Nympha lives."

Nympha wondered if it was a slip of the tongue, or if he deliberately used her first name, indicating that they had a more than casual relationship. She waited to see what reaction, if any, followed.

"And where is that, pray tell?"

Lord Nicholas chose not to reply.

Nympha decided that archness was not a desirable trait. She accepted a container of arrows from Foley before leaving the house. Lord Nicholas and Mr. Milburn each carried several bows, and strolled down the front steps behind her. The Nelthorpes were right beside them.

Lady Anne lingered near Lord Nicholas when he tossed a coin and won the right to shoot first.

"Perhaps you would like to go first, Lady Anne?"

"Never. I am not a great strapping girl to be able to use a bow like Miss Herbert. Jane is delicate as well, I fear." She dimpled up at the men, much like sugar candy.

Nympha took a good look at both young women and decided they were very clever. Would the men see through that ploy? She'd wager they were as sturdy as oaks.

"Perhaps we can watch while the gentlemen impress us with their skill?" Nympha led the two Nelthorpe women to an attractive stone bench not far from where the target was set up.

"Have you been here very long?" Lady Anne inquired.

"Not very. There has been much to do since we arrived." Nympha gave Lady Anne a melting smile.

"You traveled all together?" Lady Jane wanted to know with an arch of a brow.

"Lord Nicholas and I shared a coach after the one my great-aunt sent for me met with an accident. I have known him since childhood, you see. My father thinks highly of him." She paused. "Mr. Milburn met us at the first inn and henceforth we joined up for meals and the evening." Nympha wasn't sure she had put that right.

She wanted to give the impression that Lord Nicholas was not quite as free as they seemed to think.

"I see." Lady Anne didn't reveal what she saw. Instead she shifted her attention to the contest taking place.

It was soon evident that Lord Nicholas could beat the other men to flinders. He had none of the mannerisms possessed by Mr. Milburn, nor the irresolute attempts by Lord Henry. However, Lord Henry—after a few quiet comments from Lord Nicholas—improved his shooting dramatically.

In the end it was Lord Nicholas who walked off with the honors.

"Quoits!" Mr. Milburn declared, not discouraged by his poor showing in archery.

The dandy, Lord Henry, surprised them all by being a dab hand at quoits. He picked up the iron ring, letting it sail from his hand in the most effortless of ways. And always his ring encircled the peg stuck in the ground, bringing a win to his credit.

Nympha thought the peg should protrude more than an inch, but said nothing. After all, these people had been at this for years. She was a novice—and at more things than games.

From the area where they had played quoits, the group wandered over to the tennis court.

Nympha sought a position where she would be least apt to be hit by a stray ball. Lady Anne and Lady Jane seated themselves on a center bench, while Lord Henry chose to join Nympha.

"I can see this is a contest between those two. I wonder why," he mused thoughtfully.

Nympha had a few notions, but she wasn't about to reveal them to a stranger. When Lord Nicholas won after a skillfully fought battle, Mr. Milburn flashed a look of ill will at him, but otherwise was a good loser.

Chapter Ten

"Oh, ma'am, I cannot believe the change in this room with the new wallpaper in place. How fine the furniture appears. Even the cream bed covering goes well with it. I must say, I am very impressed with the results. Who would have thought Mr. Langley could actually achieve so much in such a short time!" Nympha slowly revolved, absorbing the delightful aspect of exotic plants, birds, and flowers on the wall.

"Well, he did have help, you know," Great-Aunt Letitia replied with her dry manner.

"Well, I think the results splendid."

"Fine! Now I want you to inspect the ballroom. I ordered what I wanted to be done, and it should be finished by now. Foley knows just how I like things to be. Come."

Nympha gave the invaluable Foley a smile of approval when she saw him. She followed in her great-aunt's wake as she marched off down a hall that Nympha had yet to explore. They paused before a tall set of double doors.

If fairyland ever existed it must be like this room, Nympha decided when she entered to gaze about with awe. Cream walls had tall windows interspersed with equally tall pier glasses. Above these arched branches of greenery and silk flowers. Potted trees served to soften the corners of the room and added the feeling of being in a forest. Overhead, more greenery was draped from the chandeliers that held hundreds of beeswax candles. She could imagine the dancers whirling about to the music, colorful costumes lending to the magical atmosphere.

"Oh, my. It is overwhelming. I have never seen the like of it." Along with the greenery the subtle scent of moss and primroses drifted in the air. Nympha discovered there were pots of primroses here and there in corners by the potted trees.

"I attended the Nelthorpe ball last year. It was spectacular, of course. I desired this ball to be just as impressive. You will have the opportunity to meet everyone of interest or importance in our little area. All those I invited have accepted." Great-Aunt Letitia walked along the length of the vast room, examining the arches of greenery at length. "So, what did you think of the Nelthorpe girls? I won't inquire about Lord Henry, for he couldn't hold a candle to Lord Nicholas, but is a good lad for all that." She paused to study her young relative.

"Lady Anne is vivacious and I think would be great fun to know. Lady Jane is quiet, but seems equally nice. And as to Lord Henry, well, he played a splendid game of quoits." Nympha's golden curls bounced as she nodded with emphasis at her last words.

What her real feelings were regarding Lady Anne had best be kept to herself. How could she explain her suspicions that that young lady was making a dead set at Lord Nicholas? With her sparkling looks and vivacity, her title and family background, who could resist her? And Lord Nicholas did not appear to make too much of an attempt. He had permitted her to latch on to his arm as though it belonged to her alone. Although, to be fair, he did distance himself shortly. And his smile? Well, some might call it teasing, but Nympha called it nauseating.

"Never underestimate a man's ability to play games," Great-Aunt Letitia cautioned. "Much strategy is learned on cricket fields, not to mention bonds of friendships that last a lifetime. Lord Henry has a good future in hand unless he makes a botch of things. He might be second in line to the dukedom, but it is no bad position for all that. You never know what the future may hold," she concluded.

Great-Aunt Latitia resumed her walking, chatting about nothing in particular as she inspected all that had been done to decorate the ballroom. At last satisfied with the arrangements, she headed toward the door, with Nympha in tow. "I think all is in readiness. Your costume is as well, I take it?"

"It is beyond what I expected. Mrs. Rankin is quite remarkable." A sound at the door brought her head around, her eyes widening as she saw who it was.

"Here you are," Lord Nicholas exclaimed as he crossed the floor to meet them. "Foley was so good as to direct me here." Words ceased as he looked around the room. "Superb!"

"I'll warrant you have seen a fair number of ballrooms even as young as you are." Great-Aunt Letitia planted herself in his way. She appeared to be ready to settle for a long conversation.

"Indeed, I have ma'am . . . but none more admirable than this one," he said with a gracious bow. "I was hunting for Miss Herbert with the hope that she would join me for a walk since the sun is unusually warm today." His dark eyes caught Nympha's gaze seductively for a moment. She felt the intensity in his eyes clear down to her toes.

He was particularly admirable today, his dark green coat contrasting nicely with biscuit breeches. She doubted it was possible to have boots shine brighter than his did, and his waistcoat appeared to her a wonder of elegance. Her assessment ignored his handsome face. Nympha couldn't imagine how her great-aunt could deny him anything.

Indeed, she did not deny his request. She nodded. "If Nympha is agreeable, you both might as well enjoy a good bit of weather. Do you walk here or elsewhere?"

"I discovered a curricle in the stables. After a bit of cleaning up, it is ready to take us for a little jaunt, if that is agreeable with you, ma'am."

With the smile he bestowed on her great-aunt, Nympha knew he would easily overcome any resistance her relative might offer.

"Clever of you to have nosed that out. My late husband ordered it, but I never use it. By all means, enjoy the sights hereabout. Newstead Abby stands empty; don't bother to go over there. Try the Friar Tuck walk instead. Used to be a pretty area."

After fetching her bonnet and sky blue pelisse, Nympha joined Lord Nicholas in the entryway where he stood chatting with her great-aunt. Nympha wondered what they had discussed. He seemed far too smug to suit her.

"I told him that since he was such a good friend of your parents you might dispense with your maid this once. I believe a groom up in back will suffice." Her great-aunt shot Lord Nicholas a look that told Nympha there was little she didn't know or suspect about the behavior of a young gentleman when with a young lady. Her brother, Adam, would have said that Great-Aunt Letitia was awake on all suits!

Nympha pulled on her gloves and adjusted her bonnet again. Lord Nicholas had a way of flustering her. It was disconcerting to feel so under a spell from this man she had known most of her life.

Nicholas bowed. He offered Nympha his arm with his customary charm.

How satisfying to feel the leashed strength in that arm, to shiver with delight when he picked her up to place her in the curricle. Quivery, that's how she felt inside—but oddly enough, only with Lord Nicholas.

"Milburn was summoned to Mansfield by his uncle's groom. Seems the old chap has had a reversal, for which I am sorry. But it leaves me free to be with you, without Milburn making an unwanted third. I enjoy your company and want no others." He grinned at her, and Nympha's insides melted a little. It was difficult to be vexed with Lord Nicholas for any length of time.

Nympha tried not to grin, but succeeded only in sputtering with laughter. "You are a dreadful man, Lord

Nicholas. I had no idea you were like this when I was home. Everything seems so different here. You—I—seem changed. I hope it is not the aspect of my inheritance that is causing me to feel this way."

He joined her in the vehicle, cocking his head as he studied her. "Somehow I doubt the essential *you* will be altered." He picked up the reins, waited for his groom to scramble up behind, and set off down the avenue to the main road. "Your parents saw fit to instill some common sense in your head."

Nympha thought that common sense did not sound the least romantical. Aware of the elderly groom that perched up behind them, she resolved to keep her comments to the minimum. Evidently Lord Nicholas had no such reservations.

"I think it would be a good day in which to take that walk your great-aunt mentioned. Someone remarked there is an abundance of ferns along the path. Perhaps a few primroses as well? You seem to enjoy them."

"I do. They burst forth in early spring with such joyous abandon, poking blooms into the world from along the road or in the fields for our enjoyment. In addition to a bright spot of color, they offer such a lovely scent."

He was silent following this torrent of speech. Nympha scolded herself for her enthusiasm. She could not picture Lady Anne, much less the quiet Lady Jane, behaving with such *esprit*.

In short order they arrived at the point where the Friar Tuck path began. The groom leaped to the road, promptly taking the reins in hand.

Lord Nicholas came around to lift Nympha from the carriage. She again felt the strange tingling at his touch when he held her perhaps a few moments longer than quite necessary. His lazy smile touched her heart, but also cautioned her to be wary.

"Lord Nicholas," she scolded when they had walked a short distance from the curricle and groom, "I believe you are a tease."

To her surprise, he didn't deny the charge. Instead he

said, "Would you believe me if I said I am sincere in my regard?"

She thought back to her worry concerning the inheritance she was supposed to receive. Could she believe him to be sincere? She knew she wanted to have no doubt that he was honest with her. He did not *need* the money, but on the other hand, money was such a useful thing.

Mr. Milburn flirted with her, seemed genuine in his regard, yet she felt as though it was a surface emotion. But her father had once remarked that some people had difficulty in revealing their inmost feelings. That might be the case with Mr. Milburn. And then again, it might not. She didn't know a thing about his finances, he was remarkably close about them. Lord Nicholas was not the sort to gossip about the man, either.

From what she knew of Lord Nicholas, he seemed a trustworthy man, certainly a man of whom her father had always spoken highly. Even his folly of a golf course did not bring forth condemnation from Papa, and that was saying a great deal. Papa took a dim view of a number of sports. Apparently hitting a little ball from hole to hole appeared to be an innocuous pastime. As long as it did not interfere with church, a sport might pass scrutiny. She certainly couldn't imagine such a simple game would ever interfere with Sunday worship.

The graveled path wandered along past large rocks around which ferns had taken root. Now the ferns cascaded over the rocks, a green serrated froth. Overhead tender young leaves had burst forth to offer shade that was welcome on the warm day. The path was sheltered, weaving as it did between the bowers of low trees and shrubbery and the banks of ferns.

"Papa would say this is an appropriate walk for a friar, peaceful and offering great inspiration."

"And so close to where your great-aunt lives," Lord Nicholas reminded.

They walked on for a time, admiring the varieties of ferns and the newly leafed trees. As he had suggested, there were a few spots of primroses, although Nympha suspected they had been planted. "It is like being in a green world, certainly one far removed from our everyday life."

"Something like that paper your great-aunt ordered, in a way. Quite different from what one usually sees in a bedroom, isn't it?"

"True, but quite charming. I should like to have a paper like this, a green bower, for my bedroom someday," Nympha said, sweeping an arm about to encompass the green.

"I fancy she will enjoy the new paper. It seems in the best of taste." Nick drew her closer to his side when the path narrowed. She was such a dainty thing, so fetching in her blue pelisse the very blue of her eyes and the little chip bonnet tied with matching ribands. Why had he never before noticed what a delectable creature she was? Did a removal from familiar surroundings make a difference? he wondered.

The path was not smooth. When Miss Herbert stumbled, Nick put a protective arm about her. Overhead a bird was warbling, but all he could think of was the soft skin that begged to be touched, the sweet lips that invited a kiss, and the bewitching enticement of a body that fit so perfectly in his arms.

"Miss Herbert? Nympha?" When she looked up at him, her trust clear in her eyes, Nick wondered if he dared to do as he longed. He bent his head to lightly touch her lips, deepening his kiss when he felt her innocent response.

"Hello there!" From around the bend could be heard the chattering of several people.

Nick hastily withdrew from Nympha, tucking her arm close to his side while he thanked heaven for the protection offered by the wandering path with the trees that arched so gracefully over it. There was little likelihood that the kiss had been observed. He wanted no scandal to taint his little love.

"Your great-aunt said you likely had taken this path,"

Lady Anne cried when she came around the last of the bends in the path. "How providential we were able to find you. And we found Mr. Milburn as well!"

Lady Jane walked at the side of Mr. Milburn, who wore a sly little smile when his eyes met Nick's. Lady Anne rushed forward to enthusiastically greet Nympha. Her dark curls peeped from a velvet bonnet that fairly screamed London. And her ermine-edged pelisse was a shade of crimson that reflected color into her pretty face.

Somehow, and Nick could never figure quite how, she took his arm, and suddenly Nympha was walking with the estimable Lord Henry.

Nick bent his head so he might hear Lady Anne's artless chatter about the coming masquerade and what she intended to wear. He would have to have patience if what he wanted was to come about.

"Good morning, Lord Henry," Nympha said, trying to return to earth following the wonderful kiss bestowed on her by Lord Nicholas. "Have you decided on your costume for the masquerade?" She thought that a safe, if rather dull, topic. She would not have to listen to his answer with her full attention.

"Won't go as Robin Hood or Friar Tuck. Too many of those. Milburn said he will be King John. I might try for the sheriff of Nottingham. I've a soft spot for villains. They have such interesting roles to play."

"But only in plays! I would wager that in true life they find matters somewhat different. It cannot be a simple matter to deceive and deceive forever. Sooner or later the villain is caught." Nympha watched as Lady Anne chatted with vivacious sparkle, laughing up at Lord Nicholas with such charm. Behind them Lady Jane spoke quietly with Mr. Milburn, discussing the masquerade as well.

Well, it seemed the ball her great-aunt proposed had captured the interest of some of the local people, if Lady Anne and Lady Jane were examples.

"Do be careful, Miss Herbert. The ground here is a bit uneven," Lord Henry cautioned.

Nympha was glad that he didn't seek to take her arm

or draw her close to him, as Lord Nicholas had. She didn't think she could cope with Lord Henry's attentions after enjoying her moments with Lord Nicholas.

"I suppose you will be Maid Marian," Lady Anne cried to Nympha. "And you, Lord Nicholas, will you be Robin Hood?" Without waiting for his reply, she caroled on, "I intend to be something vastly different, like Cleopatra, or perhaps Queen Elizabeth."

"She will probably end up a shepherdess," confided Lord Henry with a gleeful grin. "She usually does. One year she took a live lamb with her. What a disaster! The lamb was anything but lamblike and made a dreadful to-do."

Nympha chuckled as she was likely intended. "I shall be on the lookout for a shepherdess, you may be sure. Especially one with a live lamb."

"Nice to have a ball coming up. At times the country can be dashed dull. M'father goes to London, but expects us to stay here, forever, most likely. I am probably one of the few chaps glad to return to Oxford. This is my last year. I shall have to decide whether to choose the church or the army."

"Couldn't you opt for the law if you wanted to? Surely there must be something else if you don't feel drawn to the church or army. My father is a rector and quite enjoys it, but not every gentleman in that calling does. If you think country life is boring, well . . ."

"M'father offered to get me a fairly good living. But still—as you say, I do not feel called to serve in either capacity."

"What would you *like* to do?" She glanced up at him, thinking there was more to this young man than she had first suspected.

"Manage an estate in the country, but one of my own. Dashed if that will ever happen." His usually cheerful face wore the deepest dejection.

"Perhaps you could persuade your father to allow you to manage one of his lesser estates?"

He gave her an arrested stare. "Might try at that."

She wasn't the slightest unhappy when they decided to go back to the carriages.

From what Nympha could tell, Lady Anne was determined to cut her out with Lord Nicholas. Of course, it was far more appropriate that he wed someone from such an exalted family, a girl with a title such as she had. Little Nympha Herbert might be in line to inherit a fortune. She, however, did not possess a fine pedigree, although her father came from the cadet branch of an illustrious family who was mentioned in the Domesday Book.

"I say, Anne said she figures you are to inherit the estate from your great-aunt. That true?" Lord Henry intruded on Nympha's reflections with a query she wasn't sure how to handle. Such nosiness was difficult to deal with tactfully. It was none of his business, even if he would eventually learn all about it—if it came to be. "I'm afraid I couldn't say, my lord."

The scent of primroses teased her nose, but it was a bittersweet perfume now. Mingled with the damp fragrance of the woods, it served to remind her of the precious walk with Lord Nicholas before the Nelthorpes interrupted. Mr. Milburn as well, although she figured that he was likely intercepted and dragooned along with the others. Lady Anne had a way about her that drew others into her wake, regardless of what they seemed to wish.

Would it be that way with Lord Nicholas? Would he fall into her clutches like the others? While it was difficult to truly dislike her, Nympha was fast coming to wish she would direct her attention elsewhere.

When they reached the carriages, Nympha wondered how the clever Lady Anne would connive to remain by his lordship's side. She could have saved herself the effort.

"La, I am certain Jane will enjoy a drive in Mr. Milburn's carriage, for it is quite admirable. And Miss Herbert must see how well my brother handles the ribbons. *I* shall like very much to watch Lord Nicholas."

Nympha watched as Lord Nicholas obediently handed Lady Anne into the curricle. Annoyed, and vowing to somehow overrule this young woman's effrontery, Nympha entered the Nelthorpe vehicle utterly seething with frustration. Mr. Milburn dashed past the Nelthorpe gig with a certain panache, with Lady Jane beaming an admiring smile at him.

Nympha wondered where he had found his Stanhope gig. It was not one of her great-aunt's carriages. Perhaps it was one that belonged to his mysterious uncle?

Lord Henry seemed to guess that Nympha was less than pleased to be fobbed off on him, although she tried her best to conceal it. He had ridden alongside his sisters, while Lady Anne had tooled their gig. He transferred his horse to the groom from Coxmoor Hall, then joined Nympha in the gig with manners that did him credit.

They trotted along behind the others, hanging back to avoid much of the dust. Lord Henry proved to be a fine whip. He did not pretend to be a top sawyer, but he handled the horse well, feathered his corners neatly, and in general exhibited a sensible attitude toward driving. It was a surprise, given his dandylike attire.

"I should think that your father would be very pleased with you, if what I have observed of your character is true," Nympha said impulsively. "You do not seem to be a man who would be irresponsible, given an estate to manage. I think you must plead with him to allow you the opportunity. He can only say no, and he might say yes."

"Have you ever met my father, Miss Herbert? He dotes on my older brother and cannot see the rest of us for dust." There was a dry acknowledgment in his voice that wrung her tender heart.

"And your brother? Would he help you to attain what you wish?" A cloud passed overhead, and Nympha shivered with the sudden chill.

The gig slowed as he slackened his hold on the reins. He turned to meet her gaze, a puzzled expression on his kind face. "I might try. Hadn't thought of going through him. George isn't such a bad sort, but being the spoiled heir does have an effect on one."

"Which is likely how you chanced to be so fine."

His light chuckle was all the reply he made to her bit of flattery.

When they entered the stable yard at Coxmoor Hall it was to find the others gathered around, chatting and laughing.

"See!" exclaimed Lady Anne to Nympha as she was helped from the Nelthorpe gig. "Did I not tell you what a good driver my brother is?"

"I would say your brother could take honors for many things, including his driving," Nympha replied with far more civility than she felt.

Lady Anne did not seem to know how to reply to this comment. She frowned slightly, but only for the moment. "Perhaps we could have another round of quoits today. I venture to say we could make teams with six of us here."

"First you must join us for a bit of lunch." Nympha asserted her position as grandniece of the house, with a wave of her arm to encompass all. If she knew Foley, he would have observed the arrival of the group, and had an excellent lunch on the way.

This suggestion was met with universal agreement. They six ambled along the neat graveled sweep to the front steps. Within minutes they were in the entry hall to be met by Mrs. Coxmoor at her most gracious. Foley moved to stand behind Nympha.

Nympha turned to meet his gaze, her eyes questioning.

Foley nodded ever so discreetly.

"I have invited everyone to partake of lunch with us, dear Great-Aunt Letitia."

"How nice. Foley will help you with your pelisses and hats. We can chat a bit in the drawing room while lunch is put on the table."

A maid appeared to assist the ladies while Foley accepted the gentlemen's hats and gloves. Once again, Nympha marveled at how well her great-aunt's house was run. Could she ever learn to do as well?

Lady Anne dominated the scene with her energetic chatter, drawing everyone into her conversation, skillfully luring Lord Nicholas to her side.

There was utterly nothing Nympha could do to combat her charm. She wasn't nasty, just determined. Never had Nympha felt so helpless, so lacking in social skills. This was not the sort of situation she had encountered at the rectory!

In a blessedly brief time Foley summoned them to the dining room where an abundant array of food graced the sideboard. Footmen stood ready to serve, and one would have thought the luncheon was a long-planned affair.

Mrs. Coxmoor took over the direction from the purposeful hands of Lady Anne. First of all, she seated Lord Nicholas between Lady Jane and Nympha. She sweetly placed the others to either side of her and opposite. There wasn't a word Lady Anne could say to the arrangements.

The conversation centered on what game might be enjoyed by all after they finished eating.

"What about bowls?" Lord Henry suggested. "I noticed you have a neatly clipped alley not far from the quoits pegs."

"My husband was very fond of bowls. You have enough people to set up triplets." Great-Aunt Letitia gave them all a benign smile, and the matter appeared settled.

Nympha wondered if her elderly relative, so suave and knowing, would also settle who would be on each team.

Lady Anne took no notice of Mrs. Coxmoor's intention. She ate lightly, then commenced an across-the-table dialogue with Lord Nicholas, inquiring whether he knew this one or that person in London. Had he been to this rout or that ball, and surely he had attended the balloon ascension in Green Park?

Nick studied the pretty face across the table from him. He knew her sort, had encountered them often in his time while in London. Usually they focused on his older brother. But he had not escaped the matrimonial bazaar either—being deemed a fine catch. Wary covered his mood at the moment, but it would accelerate to watchful and cautious within minutes if she kept up in her attack.

Perhaps she was too aggressive, and that was why in her early twenties she was still unwed. He'd noticed that women tended to become a trifle desperate at that age, especially if they longed to leave home. And he was positive she craved freedom from her overpowering father. From all Nick had heard, the duke was a despot, ruling his entire family with an iron hand.

Mrs. Coxmoor rose from the table to escort them into the hall before they realized they were being led. Once again she marshaled the maid and Foley to assist the guests.

There was no particular order when they left the house after donning their outdoor apparel. Nympha briefly found herself next to Lord Nicholas. Lord Henry ambled along at her other side, offering suggestions on who ought to make up the teams.

Lady Anne fetched up before the neatly positioned bowling green, beaming a smile of goodwill at everyone, organizing with determination. "Lord Nicholas and Jane will be with me. Miss Herbert can champion Henry and Mr. Milburn. If things get too lopsided, we can always make a change later on."

Nympha had played with Adam any number of times, and she well recalled his strictures on rolling the bowl toward the little white jack at the far end, making allowances for the odd bias of the bowl. It took skill and cunning. Nympha noted Lord Nicholas was good, but Lord Henry and Mr. Milburn were equally good, and she was a dab hand as well.

Lady Anne was so-so, but Lady Jane was wretched. She spent more time admiring Mr. Milburn than perfecting her own game. Lady Anne flirted with Lord Nicholas, her delightful charm odiously evident to Nympha. She apparently did not care to concentrate on her game either. It was impossible for Lord Nicholas to compensate for both of them. He bore the disparity with good-natured humor that earned him respect from Nympha and Lord Henry as well, oddly enough.

When the game was over—due more to the increasing clouds overhead than the scores—Lady Anne smiled as though she had won, and clung to Lord Nicholas on the way to the house.

Nympha's heart sank as she realized who had won the day. It wasn't her team, although they had the higher score. It was Lady Anne Nelthorpe, who had walked off with her prize, Lord Nicholas Stanhope. The sight of him laughing down at that pretty face, framed with dark curls and possessing hazel eyes that fastened on his lordship with particular intensity, was chilling.

Nympha felt distinctly ill.

Chapter Eleven

Lord Nicholas had driven Lady Anne home to Nelthorpe Castle, leaving Lord Henry to tool Lady Jane in their carriage, with his horse trotting amiably behind.

Mr. Milburn escorted a suddenly frozen Nympha into the Hall with comforting sympathy. His consideration was a balm to her wounded self.

"Perhaps we could enjoy a cup of strong tea? The weather is becoming decidedly nasty out there." He spoke a few words to the ever-hovering Foley before guiding Nympha into the drawing room with the tenderest regard.

Foley brought a tray to the drawing room in short order. It held everything one could want. For tea, that is.

As she began to thaw she slipped off her pelisse and dropped her bonnet beside her on the sofa. Mr. Milburn poured her a cup of tea, nudging it into her fingers. He murmured soothing words designed to make her feel better.

Nympha wrapped her icy hands around the cup and took a sip. She raised her eyes to meet his gaze. "Thank you. That was very kind of you to do. I had not realized how chilled I had become."

She said nothing about the slight from Lady Anne, for she felt that was what had happened. What a fool she was to think she might mix in this elevated company.

"I am not such a bad sort, you know."

At that bit of nonsense Nympha had to smile, and

searched for something to say. "How is your uncle, sir?" Since Mr. Milburn appeared to spend much of his days at his uncle's home, he ought to know.

"I fear he will not live long. I try to rouse him, even brought his favorite liqueur for him to sip. There seems little the doctor can do for him."

"Has any sign of his heir been found? I should think it would be imperative for him to present himself at this time." Nympha shook off the hollow feeling in her chest, trying to offer intelligent conversation and sympathy.

"As to that, it is feared he met with an accident. He was last seen in London some weeks ago, but not since. He has apparently disappeared." He drained his cup, set it on the tray, then rose to pace back and forth before the fireplace. The fire offered warmth, but Nympha shivered just the same.

"What a pity. Do you know who is next in line?" She inquired more from politeness than real curiosity. She felt numb, if truth be told. She couldn't have imagined such pain she had felt as when she saw Lord Nicholas disappear down the drive with Lady Anne smiling so coquettishly up at him. It had stabbed her right in her heart.

"I am. Our family has always been a bit short of male heirs. So, that leaves me as the heir presumptive." His narrowed gaze was intent as he studied her where she sat huddled on the sofa.

"I forgot you mentioned that before." Something niggled at the back of Nympha's mind. She impatiently shook it off to offer felicitations of a sort. "I am very sorry your uncle has been so ill, but it will be good for you, I daresay. You will be Sir Jared Milburn, if I make no mistake."

"What a nice memory you have, dear Miss Herbert. This is quite remarkable, that you should remember my first name. Dare I hope that you made a point of fixing my name in your mind?" He paused in his pacing to study her, standing closer than she deemed necessary.

Nympha clasped her teacup before her mouth as

though it would offer protection from the predatory gleam in his eyes. But was it predatory? Or was he simply admiring, perhaps flirting a little? What a poor honey she was, not to recognize flirting!

"My memory is likely no better than any other woman's ability to recall names and places." She glanced to the open door, pleased to note that Foley had taken up a position just outside it. Mr. Milburn might be the next baronet, but it didn't mean she wanted to be Lady Milburn! And that meant being chaperoned at all times when with Mr. Milburn.

"I cannot deny I will like a title, minor though it is. The estate is a lucrative one. I'll welcome the administration of it. I have always enjoyed a challenge."

And the income, Nympha thought privately. Money again. No one ever seemed to have sufficient. She made no reply to his remark, not feeling equal to the topic.

"You will face a challenge as well, unless I miss my guess. Since you are heiress to your aunt, you will certainly wish to learn something of administration. It is a vast responsibility for so young a woman." His voice held warm sympathy and something else Nympha couldn't identify. However, it served to raise misgivings.

"I trust that will be years away, sir. I would like to know my great-aunt much better. She is such a delightful lady." The thought of that dear person brought forth a smile.

"Indeed, she is all of that. But I fancy you will marry, and your husband will assist you in all that must be done. It will require a man who is willing to study management of an enterprise." He took another perambulation before the fireplace before pausing again to ask, "Your costume is ready? The ball is soon."

"Yes, although I wonder just how many Maid Marians there will be in attendance." She stretched out her hand to set the teacup on the saucer, making a loud clink in the stillness of the room. His comment on marriage as solving all her problems rankled. Did he imply that she was not intelligent enough to administer the estate?

Likely with the help of the excellent managers her aunt had told her all about, it should be possible.

If she couldn't wed the man she loved, she would simply remain a spinster and devote her life to worthy projects and the running of her enterprises. Could there be anything more dreadful than to marry a man you could not love, and having him assume total control of your life? She had no illusions on this score. She had observed too many tyrannized wives to be unaware of the pitfalls in marriage. Her mother had offered comfort to many such women in the rectory drawing room while Nympha had tiptoed about doing her tasks.

"And Robin Hoods as well. I doubt there will be many King Johns in attendance." He placed his hands behind his back, standing before the fire, and in so doing blocking its warmth from reaching Nympha. She shivered again, wishing she might feel warm once more.

"Lord Henry said something about coming as the sheriff of Nottingham. I imagine that costume will be totally imaginary?" She debated whether to pour another cup of tea and decided against it.

"Well, as to that, it is a legend, you know. No proof exists that Robin Hood and his men, Maid Marian and Friar Tuck really lived."

"That is like so many things—an illusion."

"There you are, my dear." Great-Aunt Letitia walked into the room her gaze darting from Mr. Milburn to Nympha. "I thought you might have gone with the others to Nelthorpe Castle. You decided to remain at home?"

"I was cold. Mr. Milburn suggested a cup of hot tea would be beneficial." Although it had become brisk, Nympha knew her chill came from her heart, not the weather.

"That fire wants stirring up. Would you be so kind, Mr. Milburn? I shall ask Foley to have more coal brought immediately." She returned to the hall for a moment, coming back to settle on her favorite sofa.

While Mr. Milburn stirred the fire, Nympha had a chance to gather her pelisse and bonnet to bring to her room and thus escape the interrogation she sensed coming.

"I shall take these up and refresh myself at the same time." She waved gaily on her way from the room, not giving anyone time to offer comment.

The front door opened just as she crossed to the stairway that wound up to the first floor. She paused to see who it was, and was trapped in the cool stare of the man framed there.

"Lord Nicholas! I trust you had a pleasant drive. Is the castle as impressive as I have heard?" Her voice sounded strained to her ears.

"Why did you not join us and see for yourself? Lord Henry could have ridden his horse. You are more than capable of handling the gig from the castle." He stalked across to where she stood frozen in place.

"If you must know, I was not invited to join you. I make it a practice never to go where I am not wanted."

"What gave you the cork-brained notion you were not wanted?" He closed the gap between them, and she eased toward the stairs a few steps.

"I thought it quite clear, as a matter of fact. But then when one is wrapped up in another, it is sometimes difficult to see what is under one's nose." She flashed him a false smile, intent upon making her escape up the stairs.

She did not get very far. They were alone in the entry, Foley seeing to the matter of more coal for the drawing room fireplace. For some odd reason, he had not returned as yet.

Lord Nicholas grabbed her arms, looking absolutely furious. His hand clamped tightly, not allowing her to flee from him again. He had brought the freshness of the outdoors with him, and his hair was tousled from the wind, creating a style many a dandy would spend hours to achieve. His voice was rough, however, and his eyes threatened punishment, she thought.

"Never again, do you hear? If a situation like this arises again, you *will* join us."

"I am unaware that you have so much power over me, my lord. If I choose to remain at home with congenial company, I will do so." She peered behind him to the drawing room doorway. "Mr. Milburn was most kind, seeing to my comfort. Tea is an excellent restorative when one is chilled."

"Tea? That is all Milburn offered you?"

"I should think it quite enough, my lord."

He checked the drawing room doorway, taking note no doubt, of what she had observed. They were unseen by those close to the fire.

With her hands full of pelisse and bonnet, there was little Nympha could do to fend off anything—even if she had wanted to ward way this seething man. He was angry, but not truly frightening.

He scooped her close to him, kissing her with a fierceness that totally did away with any chill that might have lingered. The bonnet fell to the floor, the pelisse slithering after it when Nympha let them go to wrap her arms about him. This more than made up for his drive with Lady Anne. Didn't it? When he released her mouth, he remained close, so close his slightest whisper was loud and clear to her.

"That is what I would have offered you, my dear. Nothing less."

"I think I preferred the tea, my lord." If her mother could have heard her utter such a whopping lie, Nympha would have been relegated to her room for a week.

Instead of becoming angry again, he chuckled down at her, his dark eyes dancing with teasing lights. "And you the daughter of a rector. For shame."

She wrenched herself from his clasp, retrieved her pelisse and bonnet from the floor, and hoped her heightened color would be blamed on that, not the kiss and his taunting remark. "And I thought you a gentleman!" she whispered before dashing up the stairs as fast as she could.

"I am, dear heart, but I am first of all a man."

Nympha whirled around the corner and along the hall to her room, his words echoing in her mind. A man first, a gentleman second? He certainly had proved that!

Annie was putting one of her new dresses away when Nympha burst into the room. After a startled exclamation, the maid assisted Nympha into one of the new gowns that had come from Mrs. Rankin.

The blue spotted muslin had made up beautifully into a round dress suitable for morning wear. She liked the loose sleeves that fastened tightly at the wrist. A vandyked lace edging somewhat covered her hand and she admired that as well. The treble ruff of pointed lace was becoming, she thought as she fingered it. Mrs. Rankin evidently intended to trim all Nympha's garments with yards of lace. How appropriate. She hoped her sisters enjoyed the large package of lace she sent home for them.

Annie fetched little blue kid slippers. She stood back to admire the effect. "What your sisters would say to see you now."

"When I am able, I intend to have new dresses for them as well. Surely Great-Aunt Letitia will give me a generous allowance so I can do that?" Nympha twisted a bit so as to view in her looking glass the small covered buttons that trimmed the back of the dress. They were simply for show, the dress fastening with clever tapes.

"That Lady Anne will have nothing on you now, miss."

"Why do you mention Lady Anne, pray tell?" Nympha dropped her hand, moving away from her reflection.

"Talk is that she fixed her eyes on Lord Nicholas. Miss Talbot saw her when you were all playing bowls earlier. Said as how Lady Anne was flirting with his lordship something disgraceful."

"I see. Well, if she is what he prefers, who am I to argue with him?" Nympha grimaced.

Annie bowed her head, compressing her lips as though there was a deal more she would have liked to utter.

"At least I have some pretty gowns now. And my costume is vastly delightful. I doubt anyone will have a costume half as pretty." Nympha walked over to where the Gothic gown was draped across a chair, waiting to be worn for the momentous masquerade ball.

She almost felt guilty that she had done so little to prepare for it. But on the other hand, all her great-aunt had done was issue orders to the servants. All had been accomplished with amazing ease.

Fortified with her new gown, Nympha sped from her room to the staircase. She paused at the top, listening.

"You may as well go down. Milburn awaits you there—in the drawing room with your great-aunt."

The words coming so close to her, and so equally unexpected, startled her. Nympha clutched at the stair rail to keep from tumbling headfirst down the stairs. "Don't *do* that," she scolded Lord Nicholas. "I had no idea you were behind me. I could have been killed, or at the very least, hurt."

"I would have caught you."

"I give leave to doubt that, sirrah. And as to Mr. Milburn, I doubt that he awaits me in particular." She went down a few steps, then added, "His uncle is in a bad way, not expected to live. Poor man."

Nick wondered if she meant Milburn or his uncle.

He was still furious that she had been left behind when Lady Anne assured him that she would be with Lady Jane. The ploy hadn't worked, for as soon as they arrived at the castle and he had found that Nympha was not with the others, he had spun on his heels to depart. He hoped he gave the impression he was displeased, for that was mild compared to what he wanted to do to that smug Lady Anne.

She deserved a good scold. However, it was beyond him to administer it, and he doubted anyone else would give it either. Daughters of rich dukes were more likely to be spoiled and pampered than not.

He took a step forward, tucked Nympha's arm in his to walk down the stairs at her side. He paused at the door to the drawing room, keeping Nympha beside him while enjoying the effect on Milburn. A glance at Mrs. Coxmoor also pleased him. She approved; he could see that at once.

"Have you any success with the sketch you distributed in Mansfield, Lord Nicholas?" Mrs. Coxmoor inquired.

"None. Several said the face was familiar. I suppose my sketching ability is not good enough."

"Perhaps you should take some into Nottingham? It would be a pity if you could not discover the identity of this man." Mrs. Coxmoor reclined on her favorite sofa. Her soft gray lustring gown trimmed with yards of lace was most becoming, as was her cap fashioned entirely of lace. He wondered why she had never made a splash in London. She should have been a great success.

"You never spent time in London, ma'am?" Nick released Nympha, but made a point of seeing that she was comfortably seated. His stare at Milburn as challenging, to say the least. But Milburn evinced no interest in Nick's drawings even though he had glanced at one. He turned his attention back to his hostess, his stare becoming a smile.

"Too busy here to bother with the nonsense in London. I get the papers sent up, the latest periodicals in the mail every week. I keep up with what is going on, my lord. When I want something, I order it."

"I should think it delightful to wander along Bond Street to see the displays in the windows," Nympha said thoughtfully.

They discussed the topic at some length. Before Nick realized it, Foley appeared to announce dinner.

"I told Foley not to bother with a dressing bell when we all look respectable and it is a waste of time to change." Mrs. Coxmoor rose to take the hand offered by Nick, as was proper. He glanced at Milburn just long enough to send him a discreet warning. He intended to be understood that Nympha was to be hands-off as far as Milburn was concerned.

"You remind me of my mother, ma'am," Nympha said with a chuckle. "I can see you are related!"

Nick observed that she did not seem to mind being escorted by Milburn. Not in the least.

The next day dawned uncommonly mild, with the spring sun shining gently on the land. After such a frigid winter, mildness was particularly welcome.

Nympha opened her eyes to find Annie standing by her bed with a tray containing rolls and steaming chocolate.

"Best rise, miss. It will be a busy day for you, what with the ball this evening and all." The maid adjusted the tray just so, then walked to open the draperies a bit wider.

"The sun blesses the day for you, miss. 'Tis a good omen, I'm thinking." Annie gave Nympha a shy smile. "We all hope you will have a good time tonight. That ballroom is as fine as fivepence. Never thought to see anything so grand."

Nympha agreed. She made short work of the dainty rolls and chocolate. Once Annie had removed the tray, Nympha was free to toss back the covers and slip from her bed.

From her window she spotted Lord Nicholas returning from an early-morning ride. She glanced to the clock that sat on the fireplace mantel, realizing that he must have risen very early. He chanced to look up in her direction and waved his whip in recognition.

Mortified that he should see her while she was still in her bedgown, Nympha hurriedly stepped away, anxious to dress. She begged Annie to hurry with a suitable dress for the day. The lilac India muslin she declared acceptable. Within a brief time, she was properly dressed and on her way, lilac leather slippers speeding her to the stairs.

Just why she wanted to hasten to the breakfast table, she refused to admit.

To say she was disappointed to find Mr. Milburn at the table was putting it lightly. How silly to think that the attentions paid her last evening compensated for his lordship's earlier neglect. Although to be fair, he had insisted he wished her to join the party and had departed immediately when he learned she had been left behind.

Without a confidant in whom she might share her bewilderment, Nympha was unsure of herself. If only she had Priscilla here. While she often stuck her head in books of Greek myths, she had a sensible streak that was greatly comforting. She would have gone to the heart of Nympha's worries.

"Good morning, sir. I trust you slept well?"

"Excellently, Miss Herbert. This is an important day for you, I should think."

"But, of course." Nympha seated herself after indicating what she would like for her breakfast. She was in the process of tucking into a light-as-air scone when Lord Nicholas entered.

"Ah, Miss Herbert! Milburn. I trust I find you both in high spirits?"

"You were up bright and early," Milburn said with a curious note in his voice.

"I saw you return." Nympha hoped her cheeks didn't flame with the memory of what he had seen when he looked up to her window. "Did you have a good ride?"

"Actually I rode into Nottingham with some sketches. I took Mrs. Coxmoor's suggestion to heart. The shops open early there, and it was an easy matter to distribute the rest of my drawings."

"Did you have any reaction to them?" Nympha caught a frozen expression on Mr. Milburn's face. He offered no comment.

"As a matter of fact, I did."

When he said nothing beyond that, Nympha decided it was best not to pry. Had he wanted to tell them what he had learned, he would have.

"Anything of interest?" Milburn asked.

"Yes." Lord Nicholas helped himself to coffee and a plate of scones and jam.

If Mr. Milburn wanted to know more he was to be disappointed. He obviously was not an inquisitive person.

For the rest of the day there were many last-minute tasks for Nympha to do. She wondered if her aunt kept her busy to prevent a fine case of nerves from developing. If such was the case, it failed. By the time she was to dress for the ball, she was a bundle of nerves.

On her way to her room she encountered Lord Nicholas, who apparently was intent upon the same purpose—to change for the evening. They met at the bottom of the stairs.

"Your great-aunt has kept you going from pillar to post all day. I trust you are not too tired to enjoy your ball?" He flicked a glance over her that brought a hint of color to her cheeks.

"They were light tasks, little things like checking the candles, making certain none of the floral arrangements drooped, that the screen for the musicians was properly in place. It kept me occupied."

"But I daresay your mind was in a whirl."

"Indeed, it was. I suppose that is not unnatural for a young woman about to attend her first ball." She didn't like to reveal her lack of polish, but he likely knew it.

"Yes, it would be, wouldn't it? I doubt if the rectory leans towards balls for its daughters." The dry note in his voice brought a smile to her lips.

"No room," Nympha replied with a laugh. Suddenly she didn't care a jot about the effect she might have on the local citizens. Her great-aunt would only have invited those people she wanted to have Nympha meet. It was to be an evening of fun, full of pleasure.

They parted at the top of the stairs. He went his way, whistling as though he anticipated a splendid party.

Nympha swallowed her fears, entering her room with high hopes.

It took some time for Annie to remove the lilac India muslin and replaced it with the blue linen costume. Lacing up the back was not as simple a matter as Mrs. Rankin had said. Annie persisted while Nympha tried not to fidget.

"Lucky for you madam had a wig in one of those attic trunks. There must have been costume balls held here in past days," Annie muttered as she tied the last of the lacing. She picked up the wig to settle it on Nympha's head with a flourish.

"Oh, dear! I am another person." Nympha stared at the woman in the looking glass with curiosity. What a difference the gown and wig had made. She could easily see how a disguise could make it possible to fool people. Why, she doubted even Priscilla would know her in this apparel.

She wondered what Lord Nicholas would think of her costume.

"Will be a wonder if some gentleman doesn't make off with you this evening, lookin' the way you do, miss. My, you are that nice." Annie stood back to admire her handiwork.

Nympha adjusted the gold circlet set with precious stones that held in place the very sheer linen serving as a veil. The veil was like gauze, it was so gossamer. She took one last inspection of the image she saw in the looking glass, then left the room to search for her great-aunt.

The house hummed with subdued activity. Sounds of last-minute additions in the dining room, the arrival of the musicians, and the voices of early guests who were to join them for dinner mingled to create an atmosphere of anticipation—at least for Nympha.

There were strangers in the drawing room as well as Mr. Milburn and Lord Nicholas. For a moment Nympha worried that she was late for dinner.

Lord Nicholas stepped forward, his costume fitting amazingly well for something pulled from a trunk. He bowed over her hand. His gaze met hers. "Very nice, indeed, my dear girl."

Mr. Milburn edged his way forward, his long, simple velvet robe quite right for King John. "May I say that I think the legend needs a different ending? I believe the king ought to have the fairest lady of all."

She flashed a delighted smile at both gentlemen. "I believe I shall enjoy this evening very much." She hurried to her great-aunt's side, anticipating introductions to the strangers.

"Mr. and Mrs. Popham, Sir Mark and Lady Ollerton, Mr. and Mrs. Endcliff and their daughter, Penelope." A gentleman dressed as a knight stepped forward. "And Sir Giles Arnold."

Penelope Endcliff made a charming shepherdess. Nympha hoped that Lady Anne decided to wear something else tonight. It would be confusing to have more than one shepherdess—although Penelope had soft brown curls of a lighter shade than Lady Anne's.

Foley appeared to announce dinner before much conversation could get underway.

Nympha found herself seated between Sir Giles and Lord Nicholas, with Mr. Milburn seated next to Penelope Endcliff. She was too nervous to eat, yet with Lord Nicholas urging her to sample this and taste that, she discovered she ate a very good meal. Of course she couldn't have said what she ate, but that was all right.

Once dinner finally ended, they all wandered toward the ballroom. Those invited to dinner naturally felt precedence to those who came later. Nympha stifled a strong urge to grin as she observed a bit of preening on the part of Lady Ollerton and Mrs. Popham as the remaining guests began to enter the room.

Great-Aunt Letitia introduced each person as they came forward, taking care to speak clearly so Nympha might recall them later.

The room was well filled when the contingent from Nelthorpe Castle arrived. Lady Jane fancied herself as a shepardess—another one—complete with crook, with her brother dressed as a knight. Lady Anne followed, pausing to greet someone she knew. When she came to make her curtsy to her hostess, Nympha froze.

It was like peering into the looking glass, right to the

blond wig that gleamed beneath the sheer linen veil. Her bosom was fuller, her gown cut lower, and altogether she cut a more dashing figure than Nympha.

What a nasty thing to do!

"How charming, Lady Anne. You might be Nympha's twin." Mrs. Coxmoor gave her a disdainful perusal.

Chapter Twelve

"How very clever of you, Lady Anne," Nympha said clearly, with far more composure than might be expected of so young a woman. "I am flattered beyond belief that you would wish to copy my costume."

"Indeed, my dear. Mrs. Rankin devised Nympha's costume a week ago," Mrs. Coxmoor said, her voice and manner cool. "You were extremely inventive to match it so precisely—and in such a brief time. Isn't that so, Lord Nicholas?"

"Inventive, indeed." It was his frostiest tone, reserved for depressing toads.

Lady Anne looked as though she would suddenly like to be elsewhere. She glanced back at her parents, presumably to see if they paid the slightest attention to the conversation.

Lord Henry gave his sister a disgusted glance, then turned to Nick. "Told her not to do it. Bribed the sewing woman's helper, silly female." He spoke in an undertone just loud enough for Nick to hear.

The Duke and Duchess of Nelthorpe followed, but seemed to notice nothing amiss with their daughter's costume, or the fact that it was identical to Nympha's.

Nick suspected they rarely paid the slightest attention to their children, and admitted surprise that they had deigned to attend so mundane an affair as a masquerade ball at Coxmoor Hall.

The duchess paused before moving on to offer a cool

smile at Mrs. Coxmoor. "It was so thoughtful of you to send me a sample of that latest pattern of lace. You may be certain that I shall inform my friends where it is made. What a beautiful design." Her fluting tones could be heard a fair distance away.

Nick suppressed a grin. Another bit of bribery, perhaps? He shot a knowing look at Mrs. Coxmoor, which she returned with a limpid gaze.

The musicians began playing a sprightly tune. Nick immediately turned to Nympha. "Miss Herbert, I believe this is our dance."

Lady Anne had lingered close by, giving Nick a pert smile, quite as though she hadn't done something stupidly outrageous. If she thought Nick was going to invite her to be his partner, she could think a long time.

Nick led Nympha out to the center of the ballroom floor, bowing to her with old-fashioned courtesy. How Lady Anne thought she might compare to Nympha Herbert was beyond him. It was not merely Nympha's sweetness of expression that had captured his heart. Her voice was pleasing to the ear, her smile dazzled, and her instant concern when trouble brewed appealed to him greatly.

He recalled how she helped him with his golfing project. While she might have wished to see his brother, she had been a good sport about trudging around the links, jotting down figures and the like for him.

How had her figure escaped him then? Had he suffered from temporary blindness? Nympha possessed a sylphlike figure. When he had carried her in his arms, he had relished her slim, yet soft roundness, her inviting curves.

In the candlelight Nympha's porcelain skin had the allure of a rose petal. And hazel eyes couldn't begin to compare with her dazzling blue. When he drew close to her, a light scent of lavender teased his nose. There was little not to adore in his chosen young lady, his goddess.

Mrs. Coxmoor had requested a minuet to begin the ball, so Nick guided Nympha through the various patterns of the dance. The minuet was going out of style, indeed, no longer performed at many balls, but it was a graceful dance, and Miss Herbert performed it with éclat, her eyes flashing with transparent delight when he held her hand just so. If she was upset with Lady Anne's treachery, she hid it well.

What always surprised him was the sensuality that could be conveyed in this dance. It was quite possible to flirt, send tender messages with the eyes, and press the hand in such a way. It served a gentleman far better than romping through a reel.

Miss Herbert possessed a very fine pair of blue eyes, eyes that now cast a flirtatious glance at him, a tempting look. He knew great reluctance to leave her enticing side when the dance concluded. The ball was not so large a group that he would find it impossible to dance with her again—although she looked so delicious in her Maid Marian attire, he was tempted to keep her all to himself. Surely he might beg three dances, and the gossips could simply have a grand time.

Nympha fanned herself when Lord Nicholas escorted her to the side of the room. Never mind that the minuet was supposed to be a stately dance. Whoever said that had never observed Lord Nicholas—or danced with him. She thought she could have melted merely from the heat in one of his searing looks. Why had she never seen this side of him at home? She had merely considered him one of the Stanhope family up at Lanstone Hall, a person she might sit by at a dinner without any expectations. Of course, when she had dined there, she had paid a bit more attention to his older brother. And now all she could do was think of Lord Nicholas. What a fickle creature she must be!

As to what she thought of Lady Anne copying her costume, she seethed with a healthy dose of un-Christian anger. Papa would be shocked, but so was she. It was all very maddening. Surely Lady Anne would not have any trouble devising a costume on her own. What did she have in her devious mind? Many of those in attendance had given her and Lady Anne puzzled looks. Well, as her mother always said, it was better to ignore something like this than to make an issue of it. For all the others knew, it had been planned.

Lord Nicholas walked along with her, nodding to people they had met, while obviously admiring the interesting and amazingly varied costumes. She rather liked the Old King Cole outfit one gentleman wore. A matron had donned a Columbine costume that ill suited her stout form. And Lady Jane wore a confection of a French shepherdess—but without the lamb her sister supposedly took with her in the past.

"My lord," one of the footmen said, offering a folded paper to his lordship, "this arrived a short time ago from Nottingham. Mr. Foley thought perhaps it might be of importance."

Once the servant had left, with an apology to Nympha Lord Nicholas broke the seal on the paper, unfolded it, and began to read. His expression was exceedingly interesting, if one read faces.

"I trust it is not bad news, my lord?" Nympha stood quietly at his side, not seeking another partner. Somehow she thought it better to linger, at least for the moment.

"Well, it is a curious bit of information for us, but perhaps not so good for Milburn. I wonder how he will react? Come with me."

He held out his arm, and she placed her hand on it. Since Nympha brimmed with curiosity, she was not about to be left out of whatever was going to happen next—regardless of what it might be.

Mr. Milburn was dancing with Lady Anne at the moment, flirting smoothly in a practiced manner. Nympha was surprised that the polished Lady Anne would succumb to such obvious flattery. Simple country girl that Nympha was, she could recognize a dumped butter boat when she saw it.

"I believe we shall wait here," Lord Nicholas said, gesturing to the area where the couple was likely to end up at the conclusion of the country dance.

"What has happened?" Nympha didn't think she could

wait until the country dance finished to know what was so momentous in the letter from Nottingham.

"Recall the sketches I took to Nottingham? Someone recognized the man." He gave her a meaningful look, then watched Mr. Milburn with a narrow gaze. Nympha decided she would not like to be the recipient of such a look. "I shall explain all to you later, but I think it best if I confront him with my knowledge alone."

At long last, the dance over, the couple promenaded along the side of the ballroom a short distance before Lord Nicholas stepped forward to block their path.

"A word, Milburn, if you please."

With an uncertain glance at Nympha, Mr. Milburn bowed to Lady Anne, excused himself, then walked off with Lord Nicholas, leaving Lady Anne and Nympha Herbert staring after them.

Lady Anne immediately sought her sister.

Once they were somewhat apart from the others, Nick drew forth the missive, unfolded it again, and held it up to show Milburn. "I had a response to my inquiries regarding that sketch. Someone in Nottingham recognized my poor likeness of the fellow who was killed at the seventh green of my links. You ought to have known the chap, dear fellow. It was your cousin—the heir! Yet you made no comment."

Milburn gave Nick a steady look. "And? Other than to tell me for certain that I shall inherit the title and estate, I see no complication. Are you expecting one, perhaps? I must confess that I did not recognize him in your sketch—I saw him so rarely, and he was wearing his hair differently when I last saw him."

"Perhaps you were observed that day at the links when you were arguing with your cousin." Nick flicked the paper against his other hand, frustrated by Milburn's calm demeanor. Egad, the chap was a cool one. Nick felt in his bones that Milburn had done in his cousin. After all, he had everything to gain by his cousin's death, and little to lose—unless someone could identify him. What a pity that Nympha had not observed him trounce his cousin on the head with that golf club. Not that he would wish a gently bred female to witness a murder, but it would cinch the matter of the culprit.

"I did happen to see him that day. He wanted to borrow some money from me—I had to deny him funds," Milburn said without apology. "He wasn't a bad fellow, just improvident. Apparently Miss Herbert saw us together, but that is that. There is no proof one way or the other as to how he was killed or by whom, is there?" Milburn folded his arms before him, looking rather kingly in his borrowed velvet finery, particularly with the fake crown on his head.

"That is partly true," Nick admitted. "We do know how he was killed. But as to who perpetrated the crime, that is the mystery." But hadn't Milburn said he had *not* seen the dead man? What precisely had he said when the death had been brought up? Nick was sorry he hadn't taken notes at the time. It was too late now, and as Milburn said, there was no proof one way or the other.

"I would say that it will remain an unsolved case for you." Milburn's gaze seemed sly and secretly amused.

"Someday I trust there will be a means of proving by whom a crime is committed." Nick crumpled up the paper he had hoped would help solve the crime. Perhaps had he been more skilled he would have found a means of forcing a confession from Milburn. However, he would wager that the man had covered his tracks well, leaving no evidence behind, other than the golf club that was linked to Nick and no one else.

Milburn gave Nick a half smile. He added nothing more to what he had said before he sauntered off to speak to Miss Herbert.

Nick would have given a pound or two to know what he was going to say to her. He forced himself to look about. Spotting Lady Jane not far away he walked to her side to request the next dance. Although it was supposed to be a masquerade ball, he found it relatively easy to identify those he had met, and Mrs. Coxmoor had tipped him off as to which young ladies he might deem agreeable partners.

Not that he would expect Mrs. Coxmoor to invite less than the cream of local society; far from it. By this point he had ascertained that despite her position as the owner of mills and a coal mine, she was not shunned by society as were most people termed cits. Perhaps she was simply too wealthy, or maybe it had to do with her impeccable taste and sweet nature. It also might have something to do with her paying bills promptly, patronizing the local merchants whenever possible, and supporting local causes with generosity.

He had learned that she was a prominent contributor to the relief of the poor in the parish. The vicar, Reverend Bowerbank, had importantly listed her as an employer who was assisting those poor who were without jobs. No less than the Duke of Portland also had an interest in the scheme. Neither did it do any harm that she offered samples of lace to people like the duchess.

No matter, he was grateful for her position as Miss Nympha Herbert's great-aunt. He intended to take advantage of her kind offer for him to remain as long as he pleased.

His present problem was how to converse with Lady Jane and the other young things at the ball until he deemed it time he might invite Nympha to be his partner again.

"Robin Hood—such a mystical, magical hero," Lady Jane said with a sweet smile peeping from beneath her half mask. With her mask, it seemed she shed some of her shyness.

"I doubt the sheriff or others in power thought that of him. You admire heroes of, er, mystical, magical qualities?" He tilted his head to smile at her, admiring the way she managed her full-skirted shepherdess gown and the crook she carried.

"Oh, certainly, my lord."

He laughed. "In spite of this being a masquerade, it would seem that everyone knows who the rest are."

"A few of the costumes are quite familiar—like Old King Cole. We all know he is the vicar."

"I see. Well, it is a change for him, as a jolly old king, that is." He glanced to the far side of the room to spot the vicar in an animated conversation with the plump matron wearing the Columbine costume.

"Miss Herbert told me that Mrs. Coxmoor had her bedroom newly papered and that the design is utterly heavenly." Lady Jane peered up at him, the eyeholes in her half mask not in the least concealing her curiosity.

"I chanced to be there when the paper was bought and can say it is of the first style. Something like a paper used at Chatsworth and the Brighton Pavilion, I believe."

"I must know—is it red? Her late husband had a great fondness for red," she concluded with a gurgle of laughter.

"No." Nick laughed. "It is Chinese in appearance, with plants, birds, and butterflies in abundance on it. Quite refined, not a bit of red in sight. Do you admire red?"

"No, but I do like Chinese paper. If Mrs. Coxmoor has some, Mama will allow me to order some as well."

Her remark served to reinforce Nick's opinion of Mrs. Coxmoor as one who had admirable taste that others flocked to emulate.

A supper had been promised, and Nick sought Nympha so he might enjoy her company while they ate. He gave Milburn a narrow look when he discovered him fawning over the girl. Pity the fellow didn't learn to read expressions. Nick would swear that Nympha did not admire the gentleman in the least. Her taste was as good as her great-aunt's.

"Miss Herbert, you promised me the supper dance." She had done no such thing, but Nick hoped that she would agree now. At her slow smile, he could almost guess what went on in her mind.

Milburn wandered off. When Nick next saw him, he partnered Lady Anne once again. The lady flirted with him, but then, she seemed to flirt with every partner she had.

"I thank you for this dance, Miss Herbert. I admit to a little falsehood, and hope you would be so kind as not to deny me your hand."

"Never, good sir. How could I when you saved me from Mr. Milburn? He gives me the oddest feeling when he stands close—most uncomfortable, I assure you. When he looks at me in such a manner, I could swear I have an insect crawling on my arm."

Nick shook his head with amusement, but he thought he knew how she felt.

It seemed, however, that they were fated to have Milburn and Lady Anne in their set. He fancied Lady Anne wangled that.

If Nympha had ogled him in the same fashion as the very forward Lady Anne, he would have been more than delighted. He would have whisked her around some dark corner to indulge in a number of kisses and perhaps more. With Lady Anne, he just longed to paddle her—or send her back to her nanny to learn better manners.

"La, my lord, what a prude you are. I vow I thought you had London polish!" she whispered loudly as they met in the pattern of the dance. Her eyes mocked him for his lack of flirtatious ways.

"Oh, but I believe I do. Have you been there?" he inquired with a dulcet tone and bland manner. As a set down, it was admirable. Lady Anne had proclaimed her marvelous come-out in London Society a number of times, and his memory was not so bad that he didn't recall a few of the details. She was behaving like a trollop, and deserved far worse than he had given her.

Sharp anger flashed in her eyes for a few moments before she offered an indifferent smile. It was the sort that made him wonder if his set down had been wise. Was there anything more spiteful than a woman scorned?

When the country dance concluded, he swept Nympha along with him to where an elaborate supper had been set out on a long table. After filling plates for them both, he found her seated at a small table somewhat secluded from the others. Ah, she was a girl after his own heart.

"I fear we were vastly rude to Lady Anne and Mr. Milburn." Nympha's eyes twinkled with mischief.

"Why do I have the firm belief that we truly do not care?" he countered.

"You are naughty. And how Lady Anne can allege that you do not have Town Bronze is more than I can imagine. In fact, I should say you not only have Town Bronze, but a very nice country manner as well. I have not missed your kind attentions to my great-aunt, dear sir. There are many lords who would turn up their nose at a woman who not only owns, but supervises, her mills."

"More fools they, in that instance. Anyone who cannot admire such a nice lady is an idiot."

Nympha beamed back at him, thinking she was a most fortunate young woman to be his chosen companion for supper. Beyond that, she didn't dwell.

She scarce knew what food she consumed. The conversation was witty, diverting, quite fascinating. She might never have made a London come-out, but she could listen with the best of them—and she believed that gentlemen enjoyed a good listener. Her father certainly did. Nympha had learned from watching her mother.

They finished the light meal. On their way back to the ballroom they passed Lady Anne. Nympha wasn't sure how it happened, but in some manner, Lady Anne trod on the hem of Nympha's gown, tearing something possibly vital. A sudden touch of cool air on her back near the lacing was not a good omen.

Lady Anne made no sign she noticed anything wrong.

"Excuse me, Lord Nicholas, I fear I *must* make a repair to my gown." Nympha stood as tall and straight as she could, hoping that whatever the damage, it would be less visible that way. She sent him a look of appeal.

"She deliberately stepped on your hem. It was not possible to miss her intention." Nick looked at the back of the gown to see a tantalizing sliver of pale skin on her lower back. "Come, I shall walk behind you close enough so that others cannot see the rip."

"But you can?" Her horror at this simple matter was almost amusing. Lady Anne's intent was not.

"There isn't that much damage. Your maid can likely whip it together in no time." He escorted her from the ballroom along the hall to the bottom of the stairs. He watched while she hurried up to her room.

He was killing time strolling about in the hall, studying the portraits of long-dead ancestors, thinking one of them appeared not only regal, but somewhat familiar, when the footman approached him with a note.

Politely thanking the servant, Nick unfolded the paper and scanned the message. What intriguing nerve! Lady Anne begged him to attend her in the little anteroom off the ballroom. She had something to tell him.

Flicking the note with a finger, Nick paused before one particularly stern portrait to think. Had she wished to apologize for her unseemly conduct she had merely to offer a few words while in the ballroom. It did not require the utmost privacy. The instincts he had learned during his London Season told him this had all the earmarks of a trap, something a bachelor learns fast to avoid.

He thought a bit longer, then summoned the footman stationed near the ballroom door. Nick gave him his instructions and Lady Anne's note. He returned to the bottom of the stairs again to wait for Miss Nympha Herbert of the estimable Herbert family he knew could be traced to the time of William the Conqueror. Compared to that family, Lady Anne Nelthorpe was an upstart.

On the far side of the ballroom, Mr. Jared Milburn received the note from the footman with a puzzled frown. Not bothering to thank the servant for the courtesy or service, he opened the missive and read it. Moments later he sauntered from the ballroom to the door leading to a little anteroom he had noticed earlier. He had thought it an ideal place for a bit of dalliance. It seemed another had the same thought.

When he opened the door, leaving it ajar a tiny bit, he saw a figure standing by a window, her back to him, the blond braids unmistakable. A sly smile hovered over his mouth. He hastened to her side. Spinning her around, he lost no time in kissing her.

She yielded in a manner that would please any man, clinging to him with abandon.

"What's this!" a voice cried. Milburn sprang from the embrace to see the Duchess of Nelthorpe in the doorway, a note in one hand, her other hand clinging to the doorknob. Behind her a cluster of curious souls peeped in at the scene. There was no way it would go unreported, discussed, and tittered over by every gossip in the county. The Nelthorpes were well-known, but they were not particularly admired.

Lady Anne looked up at him with dismay. He gazed at her with all his considerable charm in evidence. He turned to face her mother, one arm snaking around his now soon-to-be-betrothed wife. It was certain he observed the sum of people pressing in behind the duchess.

"My dear Duchess, I have the felicity to proclaim your daughter as my future wife. She has done me the honor of accepting my offer."

Lady Anne's gasp was lost in her mother's swift evaluation of the circumstances, and an equally fast awareness of the inevitable conclusion. Since Lady Anne was a handful, and had not taken during her London Season, a mother would be quite justified in accepting a reasonable proposition. Mr. Jared Milburn would likely become the very rich Sir Jared according to gossip. Her daughter could have done worse.

"How lovely," the duchess replied. She sailed across the room to bestow an arid kiss on her daughter's cheek. "It is a surprise, but surprises are so lovely. Just lovely." She glanced behind her to note how the scene was being received. "We must go to your father, my dear. He will be so pleased, I know."

If the duchess had hoped for a different suitor for her older daughter's hand she gave not a hint of it now.

In the hallway Nick was rewarded for his patience

when Nympha came floating down the stairs into his arms. Well, at least one of them. She cast him a demure look, then tucked one hand in his.

"It took longer than I expected. I truly did not believe you would wait here. How exceedingly kind of you, my lord." She gave a little skip, then walked at his side while they returned to the ballroom.

The first person they encountered was Mrs. Coxmoor.

"What is afoot, dear lady?" Nick inquired.

"You will not believe it. Mr. Milburn asked Lady Anne to marry him and she accepted!" Mrs. Coxmoor had a highly skeptical expression on her face.

"You doubt the announcement? Pray tell, why?" Nick tilted his head, his shock of relief and amusement raging in full force within.

"I saw him accept a note from my footman, James. Within moments Milburn marched from the room to enter the little anteroom just off the entrance. He left the door ajar, but apparently that was not sufficient. I was right behind the duchess when she pushed the door open to discover the pair . . . Lady Anne and Mr. Milburn locked in a torrid embrace!"

"How shocking," Miss Herbert exclaimed with a distinct hint of mirth in her voice.

"Lord Nicholas, you do not seem at all surprised," Mrs. Coxmoor said. "I wonder why? James confided that the note Milburn received had first gone to you, but that after you read it, you informed him it was truly intended for Mr. Milburn. Is that true?"

"Precisely as you were told. When a bachelor is in London, and possesses a title—even one such as mine—he learns rapidly to avoid certain situations. Being closeted with Lady Anne reeked of a trap." He exchanged a look with the older woman before turning to Nympha.

"You thought she was trying to trap you into marriage?" This time the note of alarm in Nympha's voice sounded genuine.

"I am quite certain of it," Nick responded.

"How intriguing." Mrs. Coxmoor walked between them into the ballroom where a goodly amount of talk centered on the choice bit of gossip.

Not every day does the duchess get such a son-in-law for her wayward daughter. Not a few mothers savored the set down for the hoyden who all too often had been cruel to their own daughters.

"Now, we will chat agreeably with the duchess and her family; then you two will dance as though nothing unusual had occurred."

They did precisely that.

Chapter Thirteen

The duchess was all graciousness. In spite of the many whispers and circumspect glances, she carried on as though all was rosy and just as she wished.

Lady Jane was the one who appeared subdued. She edged up to Nympha during a lull in the dancing. "I confess I am perplexed. I was so certain she meant to have Lord Nicholas. And now to find her betrothed to Mr. Milburn is far too much for my poor head to absorb!"

Nympha gave her a cautious smile. "Well, it does take two people to agree—most of the time. Perhaps she found Lord Nicholas had other plans that did not include her?"

"I suspect he did." Lady Jane glanced to where her sister, supported by Mr. Milburn, held court. "I told her that her scheme wouldn't work."

"She had a scheme?"

"There is no harm in telling you now. She thought it would be great fun to have a costume just like yours, then lure Lord Nicholas into a side room to cadge a kiss. At least, that is what she told me."

Lady Anne had plotted far more than a kiss. She had intended to snare the catch of the evening in her net, and she had captured a minnow instead. There was no way Nympha could keep a smile from creeping over her face. She realized that Lady Anne suspected Lord Nicholas would kiss *her*—Nympha. How curiously amusing.

Fortunately, Lady Jane was watching her sister and not Nympha. "I won't miss her. Nor, I fancy, will Mother. Anne has always been the rebel. If there is anything Mother deplores it is a woman who goes against society's decrees. But Anne did catch a husband after all." She fiddled with her shepherdess crook.

Thinking back to all she had learned about Mr. Milburn, Nympha decided they well deserved each other.

The vicar, so colorful as Old King Cole, presented himself as a partner. Nympha gladly accepted his offer, whisking off to the dance floor with gratitude. While she was not unwilling to learn of the plot against Lord Nicholas by the scheming Lady Anne, she did not wish to hear any other gossip from her younger sister.

The vicar was a lively dancer, cavorting down the line of a country dance with ease and grace. Nympha had to mind her steps, and thus switched her attention from the newly betrothed pair with appreciation.

When the dance at long last concluded, the vicar mopped his brow. "I declare I need a cooling drink. Would you join me in some lemonade, dear Miss Herbert?"

The vicar was single. Nympha was learning to be wary of every male within the marriageable age. "I should like to sit over there for a few moments. Perhaps you could simply take two glasses from the footman with that tray." She gestured to James, now bearing a tray with glasses of what appeared to be lemonade. She sank down on the lone chair set against the wall near the windows that led to the terrace. She had already enjoyed two glasses of champagne. Lemonade would be good.

The vicar needed no urging. Perhaps he had no ulterior motive and had not intended to improve his situation by an alliance with a rich heiress. She found the thought depressing. Would she now have to judge all men by how she perceived their intentions?

When the vicar returned with two glasses in hand, he handed her one, then sipped from his with appreciation.

"Ah, champagne. How like dear Mrs. Coxmoor to have the finest of everything—right down to her grandniece."

Nympha's warning bells rang again. She took a generous swallow of her drink and nearly choked.

"My dear girl," Lord Nicholas said as he joined them and proceeded to not so gently pound her on her back, "sip it slowly so as to savor the delicate flavor." He ignored her annoyed glare. He plucked another glass of champagne from a tray and offered it to her. "Drink this more slowly, my sweet."

"I was warm. Do you not think it is warm in here? It is most definitely warm." Yet the drink was delicious, and she *was* warm. She took another gulp of the cool liquid with appreciation, smiling at the bubbles that teased her nose. Nympha opened her lace fan to waft it back and forth with more vigor than was likely seemly. Never mind that it didn't particularly go with her costume. She had guessed how it might be with all these people, and brought a defense—her fan. Her energetic use didn't go unnoticed.

"May I suggest a walk along the terrace?" Lord Nicholas proposed smoothly, just as the vicar put himself forward.

"I was about to offer my arm to dear Miss Herbert myself," the vicar said, darting an annoyed glance at his lordship. His Old King Cole crown was tipped to one side, and he stared owlishly through gold-rimmed spectacles.

"I have known Miss Herbert since the cradle, so by way of being an old family friend, I claim first rights." Lord Nicholas placed a proprietary hand on her shoulder.

Nympha wondered what on earth his being a family friend had to do with walking her on the terrace. And since when had he been an *old* family friend?

However, she was not about to deny herself the pleasure of cooling air, or the company of a gentleman of the first stare of elegance. She rose, downed the last sip of champagne, and then placed her hand on his arm after handing the vicar her empty glass.

That last dance must have been more tiring than she had thought, for she felt a bit awkward on her feet.

"Come," Lord Nicholas said, sounding amused at something, perhaps the annoyed vicar in his King Cole costume looking like a frustrated owl.

Little bubbles seemed to be floating through her, and her feet wanted to dance rather than walk. Happiness did odd things to one.

The fresh air felt good, if bracing. Lord Nicholas had grabbed a wrap from somewhere and now draped it around her shoulders. They alone braved the chill of the terrace.

"We won't stay here long. If you prefer we will remain by the door."

"Let's walk." She tucked her arm close to his side, relishing the warmth and strength she found there.

He chuckled for some odd reason. They set off at an ambling walk, his hand on top of hers to keep it warm.

"You are a *very* thoughtful gentleman," she said with a very faint hiccup. "Oh, dear. I suppose that is the result of drinking that delightful champagne?" Her brain was now bubbling with the strangest joy. She wasn't accustomed to drinking champagne.

"It has been known to happen to others."

"And I am a *very* silly girl, I suspect. Yet I am here with you and not the vicar."

He seemed to understand her reasoning, for he replied, "I should say you were clever, not silly. Unless you desire to trap me, as Lady Anne trapped Milburn?"

"No," she said, followed by a long sigh.

"You don't want me?" Now he sounded like he was laughing inside.

"You dare laugh because I said I don't want to trap you? I would not like to snabble a husband that way, thank you very much. I would far rather be wooed with kisses."

"That I can handle with ease, dear girl."

"I wish you would not call me your dear girl, because I am not. Your dear girl, that is. Am I?" She gave the stone balustrade a considering perusal.

"You are."

He put one gloved finger under her chin, tilted her face up, and placed a delicate kiss on lips that had been hungry for his touch ever since the last time he had kissed her. It was amazing how she had learned to enjoy kisses so rapidly. He was the only gentleman who had kissed her, true. But he must do it extremely well, for she decided it had to be the nicest feeling in the world—along with being held in his arms.

She stepped closer to him, wanting his warmth, but unconsciously wishing for something more as well, only she didn't know quite what.

"Nympha," he murmured in a warning voice. Although what he might be warning her against she didn't know. Hadn't he told the vicar he was an old family friend?

And then his lordship really kissed her, just as she had been wishing he might. He was fiercely tender, wrapping her tightly in his arms. When at last he lifted his face from hers, he spun her about and marched her back to the door. They were inside the ballroom before she could begin to complain.

"You do tend to court disaster, dear girl."

"I wouldn't with the vicar." She was *quite* certain that she wouldn't walk with him at all, much less kiss him.

"Thank heaven for small mercies, in that event." He handed the borrowed wrap to a footman.

"I do have some sense, you know. In fact, I am reckoned to be a very sensible girl."

"I wonder . . . ?" He led her along the wall to an open space where people waited for the next dance to commence. "Come. We will try the waltz. You ought to be able to manage if I support you."

"I could support you, too, I suppose."

"We are not talking about the same things. I suggest you curb your tongue before you really fall into trouble."

She became silent, for he took her into his arms, first placing her hands just so, then drawing her close. It was not the least like dancing with her sister. Not at all. One must practice, of course, but a scandalous dance is not permitted at the local country assembly.

"I like this," she said at last.

"So do I, if truth be known. I shall be very sad to see the evening end."

"Umm," she murmured into his shirtfront.

"I suspect we are dancing too close, but since all of us have enjoyed a taste of champagne, others are dancing close as well."

"I think the room is whirling."

"Not in the least; it is you."

"I like it. I think." She smiled at him and closed her eyes as he twirled her about again, slowly, delightfully. She hoped this dance lasted longer than the one with the vicar. Being in his lordship's arms felt very right and good.

Nick smiled down at the exquisite face smiling up at him. Oh, she tempted a man. That dreamy expression said far too much. He hoped that no one else paid the slightest bit of attention to them, and in particular to her. It had been a touch of madness to take her out on the terrace. March nights were still far too cool, and since no one else dared the elements, they had been just as alone as Milburn with Lady Anne. The main difference was that he would welcome an alliance with Nympha. He thought she might be receptive to him as well, although a man could never be sure of such a thing until the knot was tied. Perhaps not even then.

When the dance ended, he walked with her until they encountered Mrs. Coxmoor. That dear lady sized up the situation in a trice.

"Strong tea, I believe. Come along children." She tucked Nympha's hand close to her side and strolled with a purposefulness that belied her casual air.

In the room set aside for supper, they found the tea

they sought. James poured out a cup for each of them and bowed before prudently leaving.

"I am not cold," Nympha protested as the heat from the tea seeped into her hands.

"I can attest to that," Nick murmured naughtily.

"I trust you are the honorable man I judged you?" Mrs. Coxmoor said in an aside.

"Indeed, ma'am. I would never do a thing to harm those I cherish." Nick cast his gaze down at Nympha. The pins holding the veil had slipped, and her blond wig was a tiny bit askew. She still looked wonderful to him.

"Lord Nicholas is from an excellent family, Great-Aunt Letitia. His father is a fine patron of our church. His mother paints beautiful watercolors and is the dearest person you could imagine. His brother married a nice lady, Lady Harriet. I believe they expect the birth of their first child before too long."

"How illuminating," Mrs. Coxmoor said. "Drink your tea, dear."

Nympha obediently drank her strong black tea. When she finished she gave Nick a sapient look that told him he wasn't going to hear any more delightful, if somewhat indiscreet, words this evening.

"What is the reaction to the coming marriage of Lady Anne to Mr. Milburn?" Nick noted the family still grouped closely about the couple.

"I think them well suited," Nympha observed.

"And so they are," Mrs. Coxmoor observed. "The duke seems amenable. He talks about buying a viscountcy for the new son-in-law. Mr. Milburn may have been compromised into a fine marriage from his point of view. I heard his uncle is at death's door. Even if he does not achieve the title of viscount, he will have his baronetcy to fall back upon."

Nick thought back, for some reason recalling Milburn's reference to offering his uncle his favorite cordial. Would he be so bold as to assist his uncle to his final resting place? They would never know. But he'd put nothing past him. He did not envy Milburn his future wife. Imagine being married to that hoyden!

"I think I shall sit down now." Mrs. Coxmoor left them abruptly to walk to where a comfortable chair awaited her.

"One forgets her age. She doesn't seem that old, you know." Nympha placed her hand trustingly on his arm. They slowly walked from that room to stand not far from her aunt. "It is all so beautiful, isn't it?"

"Truly, is it." But Nick wasn't admiring the room, or the couples so gracefully dancing. Instead, he gazed down at Nympha, wondering how he would overcome a problem he saw looming on the near horizon.

She thought *she* would support *him*. She had said as much when that champagne took over her tongue. *In vino veritas* was most apt on occasions. In wine comes truth, and sometimes the truth is not palatable.

All good things eventually must come to an end. He claimed the final waltz with her, not in the least caring what the locals thought about his monopolizing the heiress.

After the dance ended, having constituted of a companionable silence for the most part, they joined Mrs. Coxmoor to bid the guests a good night.

Few had very far to travel, and there had been no highwaymen around these parts for a long time. All felt safe to remain to enjoy themselves without worry about being stopped on the way home.

When the last person had left, Nick ushered Mrs. Coxmoor and Nympha up the stairs, pausing at Nympha's door first to say a hasty good night when he longed to kiss her senseless. He escorted Mrs. Coxmoor to her door instead.

She pushed the door open, permitting Nick a glimpse of the beautiful wallpaper that had been hung.

"You like the new paper in your room?"

"I do, for I was very tired of red. You must remember that—never overdo a good thing." With those words she entered her room, leaving Nick to wander along to his.

* * *

Nympha slept late the next morning. Upon arising she went to the window to inspect the day.

"How be you this morning, miss?" Annie brought in a tray loaded with hot chocolate and rolls. It also had a note folded neatly and tucked beside one plate. Curious, she hurriedly went to the little table where she indicated she would sit to eat. Before so much as pouring out a cup of hot chocolate, she unfolded the note and read.

"What do you wish to wear, miss?"

"Hmm? Oh, the white muslin, I suppose." Lord Nicholas begged the honor of her company for a drive to Nottingham. Why? He didn't reveal a thing in the note.

Her mind was occupied while she consumed her chocolate and rolls. Contrary to what others indicated might be the case, she remembered all that had occurred last evening, even her injudicious remarks after downing the glasses of champagne too hastily.

How had he taken her comment to support him? She had not meant to say it, even though it was the truth. She had no knowledge of his finances. Second sons were not known for their affluence, unless they had another source of income. Or they married an heiress.

She allowed Annie to help her into the white muslin while she considered the oddity of the second-eldest girl at the rectory worrying about being married for her wealth.

Once Annie had done the tiny buttons at her wrist and tied the complicated tapes at her high waist, Nympha pinned a pretty cameo where the neckline dipped in the front. It was a daring bodice opening, going all the way to the point where the skirt met the bodice. Nympha thought it prudent to have that pin in place!

Still undecided as to what she ought to do, she went down the stairs only to confront Lord Nicholas when she reached the bottom.

"Your great-aunt wishes to see you in her library. I believe her lawyer is with her."

"You may as well come along. I might need a supporting hand—or sympathy." Nympha flashed a teasing smile at him.

"I am not certain my presence is desired."

"As you wish." She'd not dragoon anyone into doing anything.

Like any perverse male, he elected to join her anyway, pausing at the door of the library. He bowed to Mrs. Coxmoor with the correct degree of hesitancy. "Miss Herbert suggested I might attend?"

"You may as well. Nottingham will be there tomorrow, or even later today." Mrs. Coxmoor gave them an amused look, while the lawyer frowned over his spectacles.

"This young man, Mr. Smedley, has some papers you are to sign, Nympha." Great-Aunt Letitia gestured to the gentleman at the desk. "I have made a final disposition of my estate—signed, witnessed, and sealed. All is to be yours, dearest girl. I trust you to use it wisely. I believe you will never mismanage it, nor throw away the money foolishly. I have observed in you the traits of honesty and frugality, both of which I admire."

Nympha was glad of his lordship's surprisingly soothing closeness. As stimulating as he often proved to be, he could also lend a sympathetic ear or countenance.

Nympha read over the papers handed to her, then went to the desk to sign where indicated. When all was completed, she again sat down, very thankful for a solid chair beneath her. Her altered station in life was almost too much to comprehend. This house was to be hers, along with the factories, the coal mine, everything. She glanced at Lord Nicholas, wondering what went on in his mind.

"That does it, Miss Herbert. All is in order here," Mr. Smedley said while bundling up the papers. Some copies were placed aside, likely for the safe that hid behind the oil painting hanging above the fireplace mantel. "I trust that if there is ever any manner in which I might serve you, you will not hesitate to call upon me?"

"Thank you. I will remember that." Nympha curtsied to her great-aunt and the lawyer before leaving the room.

"Do you wish to take the drive to Nottingham now?" Lord Nicholas inquired.

"I think that would be nice." She sent a maid up to her room for a pelisse, reticule, and bonnet. She felt oddly reluctant to leave Lord Nicholas. They walked to the entry hall, waiting there for the required items.

"The papers cover my possible marriage," she said at last into the silence of the hall. They stood alone, Foley having been summoned to the library.

"That is a good thing, to have all eventualities covered." Lord Nicholas stood at her side drawing on his York tan gloves.

"Even though my husband can manage everything, most of the money and this house are in my hands, but I share the rest. I suspect it is an unusual circumstance. I can't say I have ever given much thought to settlements." She gave him a wan smile, her mind returning to the simple statement that she could support him.

"Settlements can be the very devil, I imagine, depending on what is involved."

He had said nothing of his own circumstances, leading Nympha to wonder what they might be. Hadn't her father said something about Lord Nicholas being the recipient of a bequest from an aunt or grandmother? Her memory failed her when she most wanted to recall the words.

Annie bustled down the stairs at that point, doubtless horrified if anyone else should help her mistress into her pelisse. Within minutes Nympha was ready to depart.

"The curricle ought to be here by now. I trust you will find that agreeable? We could have taken the coach, but I thought since the day was fine and there is little wind, the curricle would be acceptable."

"I think it would be good."

Garbed in a silvery gray dress of finest kerseymere and trimmed with a lace ruff, her aunt along with the lawyer, joined them in the hall.

Lord Nicholas greeted the lawyer with a polite expression. "We are traveling to Nottingham as well, sir."

"You take the coach or the curricle?" Mrs. Coxmoor studied Nympha's pelisse likely with an eye to its warmth.

"Lord Nicholas thought the weather so fine that a drive in the curricle would be nice." Nympha sought to assure her relative that she agreed with the vehicle choice.

"Nice spring day," Mr. Smedley concurred.

In short order Mr. Smedley departed in his equipage, a shiny black coach of high respectability.

Nympha and Lord Nicholas followed in his wake.

They spoke of common things while traveling. The ball was discussed at length, the coming marriage as well.

"Mr. Milburn left this morning, did you know?" Lord Nicholas glanced at Nympha. "The duchess invited him to the castle, and you may well imagine he lost no time in packing his gear. Your great-aunt offered the loan of the coach so he might arrive in style."

"I will not miss him. But he does not deserve such fine treatment." Nympha fixed her eyes on the distant spire of the larger church in Nottingham.

"It has been my observation that too often that is the case. We can only hope that the guilty will reap their just rewards eventually."

"His will be having to live with Lady Anne." Nympha couldn't stifle a chuckle at the thought.

"You know, I'd not be surprised if he went to London by himself. Actually, it might be safer for Lady Anne."

Nympha sobered at once. "I'd not considered that aspect. Surely you do not believe he would harm her? I would suspect that the duke is wise to his sort and would put something in the settlements that restricts Mr. Milburn's access to her income."

"I doubt it. It is customary for a wife's fortune to be in the hands of her husband. He may do with it as he pleases." He fell silent at those words. They seemed to hang in the air between them.

There it was—the custom and law of giving over everything to the husband upon marriage. Her mother had remarked on a widow she thought unlikely to remarry, as she enjoyed her freedom to spend as she pleased. Yet, if a girl trusted her husband to do what was right with the money, why not? It was a worrisome thing. Perhaps she would simply not wed, thus avoiding the entire dilemma.

It wasn't long before they entered the town.

"This is the old Bar Gate, once the restricted entry to the town. Ahead is the Market Place, and there is the Market Cross."

"What a nice name, Angel Row. Do you suppose a row of angels were ever there?" Nympha gazed at the neat row of houses on her right.

"Down here is St. Peter's Church, just beyond Wheeler Gate."

"Papa said the word 'gate' comes from the Danes when they occupied so much of the country."

Lord Nicholas skillfully guided his team down the narrow street to an inn where they might leave the curricle while they explored the town and all it had to offer.

He insisted upon tea and a nuncheon before they set out, and Nympha readily agreed. If she did decide never to marry it would be nice to have some happy memories, of which this would be one.

The nuncheon was ample and tasty. Nick watched as Nympha ate of everything, if a bit sparingly.

Thinking back to the words exchanged while on their way, he wished unsaid his comments regarding the fortune of a woman when she married. Not only had Nympha remained silent, a chill had descended over the carriage that had nothing to do with the weather.

As is so often the case, there was little he might say to offset words once spoken. If he assured Nympha that he didn't care about her fortune, or would not seek to control it once married, he was being premature. He had yet to ask her. Now he wondered if he dared.

Without any vanity, he knew that her father would be pleased to welcome him as a son-in-law. They could spend part of the year in Nottingham, with a visit to his home when they pleased. He'd not give up the house and links he'd worked so hard to obtain, but he had grown to love the home Nympha was to inherit.

"You are deep in thought. I'd not expect scones to merit such contemplation." Her smile was tentative, her eyes guarded.

"I'll confess I was thinking about our prior conversation." Nick decided to be bold. "Are you so afraid of having a husband who might be given control of the vast inheritance you are to receive eventually?"

"It may be some years away, you know. As to my fortune, I doubt I am equipped to deal with it. Perhaps I will be so fortunate as to acquire a husband who will be my partner in all things—the family as well as business."

He thought her pink cheeks delightful. It had likely been difficult for her to give voice to her thoughts.

"Time will tell." It was a trite phrase to offer, and he wished he could think of something more appropriate to say.

They left the inn to wander along Wheeler Gate up to Market Place. The shops here were finer than the ones in Mansfield, offering goods direct from London, or so the signs in the windows insisted. They paused before a millinery shop window.

"I believe there is a bonnet that would look good on you."

Nympha allowed herself to be enticed into trying on a bonnet that went well with her blue pelisse, having blue ribands with cornflowers tucked in the top of a bow. She objected to his buying it, however. With inspired logic Nick claimed it was in appreciation of her company.

He tried to cheer her, pointed out things to amuse, and in general exerted himself as a genial host. He didn't think he had made much progress, however. She was too quiet. She was polite, laughed at his jokes, but nevertheless had an inner quiet he could not pierce.

It was not going to be an easy courtship! But, slow and steady wins the race.

Chapter Fourteen

The next morning Nick looked out of the window to see a rain-washed scene. There was no wind; the rain simply fell in torrents, blotting out the landscape. It was enough to give one a fit of the dismals. He leaned against the window surround, staring off into the liquid gray curtain with a frown.

He wasn't in too good a frame of mind to begin with. The previous day had not gone well. He thought back on the trip to Nottingham, devised with such hope. If he had expected to make any progress in wooing Miss Herbert, he would have done better to stay in bed! While not a total disaster, it had not been well done.

The bonnet was a success, and she promised she would wear it to church this Sunday. He didn't know if that meant she wanted to show it to the vicar and those from the castle, or if she wished to please him. He had insisted upon buying the bonnet for her, although he knew full well it was not proper for a gentleman to buy a bonnet for a young lady. Hang the proprieties. If he wished to please her with a bonnet, he would. Besides, he wanted to show her he had funds enough to live well, if not lavishly.

It had been the matter of her inheritance that dealt the worst blow to his hopes. As far as he could tell, she now viewed him as a fortune hunter. What a touch of irony that was—with him the son of the marquess from Lanstone Hall. All the years he had known her she had been nothing more than the second daughter of the rector. Reverend Herbert was a kind gentleman, given to overlong sermons and absentminded conversation. His wife was the practical mistress of the rectory, and guide for the children. While they might be a cadet branch of an old and highly respected family—and he thought there might be an earl in there somewhere—their rank was nothing compared to his.

Not that he judged people by their rank. He didn't. But he knew others did. Was money coming to have greater importance in Society than rank? It appeared to locally.

Miss Nympha Herbert needed a lesson, but what or how it might be given was more than he could imagine. He would simply have to be his natural self and see what developed.

At least he no longer had to deal with Milburn and his flirting with Nympha. Nick guessed Milburn wanted distance from the one man who connected him to a murder. Come to think of it, just his suspicion was enough to make Milburn wish to dispose of him. Distance was a good thing for both of them! It had been a frustrating experience to sense so strongly that Milburn was guilty and not be able to prove it. Someday . . .

Once dressed, he proceeded to the breakfast room. It was good not to see Milburn's smug face over his coffee cup. On the other hand, the room was ghostly quiet, with the soft-footed ministrations of Foley and James to interrupt his total peace.

Blast it all, he didn't wish for peace right now. All he did was ruminate on his failure of yesterday.

"Good morning."

He twisted around in surprise to find Nympha standing in the doorway, her greeting finding him at a loss. "Good morning, although quite what is good about it is more than I can see. It is pouring outside." He gestured to the window, beyond which could be seen the gray veil of rain.

"I noticed." She walked to the sideboard where she

selected a scone and a sliver of gammon. She paused by the table, looking at him, then the chair, then him again.

"I promise not to bite," he assured her with a perfectly straight face.

"I did not think you would."

He couldn't help the chuckle that escaped. When he recalled all the years of evading matchmaking mothers and their precious daughters who were intent on a good marriage, it was amusing to discover the one woman he wanted did not want him. Or if she did, didn't wish to admit it.

She gave him an uncertain look before settling on a chair not too close but not at the other end of the table, either. She set about buttering her scone with purposeful intent.

"What do you propose to do today?" he queried. "Read, I suppose? The light is too dim for needlework." He sent her a quizzing glance, but didn't push for a reply.

"I believe I was very rude to you yesterday," she said after a time, when Foley had again departed from the room.

"How so?" Nick studied her down-bent head. Her curls were more pronounced today, possibly because of the rain. She wore a blue-spotted muslin that emphasized the blue of her eyes—when she looked at him, which she was *not* doing at the moment.

"I cast aspersions on your character. I do not know why. You have not given me reason to believe ill of you. Please," she choked out, "accept my apologies."

"Dear girl, there is nothing for which you need apologize. I cannot recall a thing—unless you are referring to my having to talk you into accepting that attractive bonnet that so well becomes you." He hoped that by giving a positive answer he might discover her reasoning.

"Well, I as much as called you a fortune hunter. That was dreadful of me. I cannot think what maggoty notion got into my mind. As if you would marry someone of my status when you could have any peer's daughter in the realm."

He admired the color that crept over her face when she finally met his gaze. There was something about the pale rose that went so well with blond hair, although he suspected that she hated her tendency to blush.

"You have an exalted opinion of my standing, I assure you." He quirked one brow at her that had the effect of her blush deepening in embarrassment. "And I find the notion of marrying you rather appealing."

He tossed that out, hoping for a positive response. He toyed with his cup while she stared at him—in shock?

She was definitely skeptical. "No. It's not possible." Perhaps she thought he jested?

He was no coward, but decided to let his words be absorbed before venturing further. If she considered it a bit, the idea of marriage to him might take root in her mind and be acceptable.

"What say we find something entertaining to do today, since you won't agree to anything truly interesting? If it weren't raining what would you suggest?" He set his cup on its saucer with a clink, thinking of a number of things *he* would enjoy doing with his fair nymph.

"A rousing game of battledore and shuttlecock?" She gave him an amused look. She polished off her slice of gammon, then put the final bite of scone into her mouth.

Nick watched.

"Well, have you any ideas?"

If he told her, she would truly mistrust him—and then perhaps not. After all, she had returned his kiss.

"Why not play a game indoors? Surely we could use the ballroom now that all the decorations have been removed. It is not such a violent game."

"You mean *not* like Lord Byron shooting holes in the walls when he is bored?" Her expression was somewhat amused, but nonetheless cautious.

"Precisely." He wondered if it would work. Surely they could hit that dab of cork and feathers back and forth without doing any damage?

She took a final sip of her tea, pushing back her chair

to rise from the table. "I shall ask Great-Aunt Letitia. If she approves I will meet you in the ballroom."

Nick also rose from the table, but too slowly to walk with her. Instead he found Foley, explained what Miss Herbert wished to do, going along with him to collect the small battledore rackets and the shuttlecocks.

He leaned against the ballroom door, tossing a shuttlecock in one hand while he waited. He fancied Mrs. Coxmoor would give her permission for the game. She doted on her grandniece, would probably allow her to do as she pleased with anything.

If her doubtful smile was anything to go by, Mrs. Coxmoor had given consent to the game, yet Nympha still wasn't sure of the scheme.

"Come, we shall have a fine time."

And they did for a while. Now the color in her cheeks was from natural exertion. She proved to be a dab hand with the racket, sending the feathered cork high in the air, requiring Nick to dash madly after it. He wondered how good she was at tennis.

"Miss Herbert, Lord Nicholas, madam requests you join her in the drawing room. There are visitors." Foley's face revealed precisely what he thought of such early callers.

Nick pulled out his pocket watch to check the time. Around noon? Who on earth came at this hour of the day?

"It will be people calling after the ball. I imagine even here in the wilds of Nottingham they observe such proprieties." Nympha tossed him an arch glance from eyes no longer an arctic blue.

Nick turned to Foley. "We are both disheveled from the game. We will join madam in the drawing room once we have repaired ourselves."

"Am I so dreadfully mussed?" Nympha asked when Foley had gone.

"Delightfully so, dear girl." Nick found the situation irresistible. He swiftly stepped to her side, tilted up her face, and lightly kissed her. It was like food for a starving man. Could a hungry chap stop at one nibble of sustenance? Nick decided that since she had not slapped his face, nor rushed from his side, he dared to try again. He did so with great success. The rackets and shuttlecocks tumbled to the floor as he took her in his arms and really kissed her. And, by heaven, she kissed him back!

When he released her he wondered if she expected an apology. He wouldn't.

"That ought not to have happened, sirrah," she finally declared once she had pulled herself together. However, her words lacked fury.

"I know," Nick admitted. "That, my dear girl, is what you get for being so thoroughly delectable. Now, we had best restore our appearance before Foley comes to hunt for us again. Your great-aunt will not be pleased if we delay."

"Oh, dear. I tend to forget things when I am around you." She spun away from him, rushing from the ballroom in her haste to please her great-aunt.

Nick sauntered slowly after her, elated with what had happened, but especially what she had just said. So, she tended to forget things when around him, did she? Promising, to be sure.

A short time later Nympha paused at the door to the drawing room before gliding in to greet the guests, her blush sarcenet gown swishing about her.

"Nympha, my dear. Sir Mark and Lady Ollerton and Sir Giles Arnold are here." To them Mrs. Coxmoor added, "We are so delighted to see you."

They all looked at the door as though expecting to see another person. Nympha guessed they wanted to see Lord Nicholas—second son of the Marquess of Lanstone.

The subject of her thoughts entered shortly, and Nympha's heart sank to her toes. He looked every inch of his rank from his carefully tousled hair and pristine cravat to his superbly cut bottle-green coat and biscuit breeches molded to fine legs that needed no padding. That his boots had a shine to rival the candles her great-aunt had ordered lit was almost too much. He strode across the room to bow to Great-Aunt Letitia before turning to face the callers.

"Sir Mark and Lady Ollerton, what a pleasure to be sure. And Sir Giles, it is good to see you again." He shook the men's hands and bowed low over Lady Ollerton's outstretched and ungloved hand. Nympha managed not to giggle at that. And the lady was old enough to be her mother! She simpered and preened like she was sixteen.

How did he do it? In two short sentences he had totally captured them. Of course, the handshaking and bowing had helped. He ought to stand for the Commons. He would be good at all that was required there, from what her papa said when discussing the politics of the day. Perhaps he might consider it if he was to meet the local gentleman who was also in the same position of being a younger son, and destined for the House of Commons.

"Nympha." Her great-aunt recalled Nympha to her duty. When Foley brought in a tray laden with tea, a bottle of fine canary wine, and slices of delicious fruitcake, she became busy. Lord Nicholas endeared himself to the guests by insisting on helping Nympha. He took plates of cake, glasses of wine, and the tea for Mrs. Ollerton with a charming grace that was so natural one could only view him with admiration.

He quite definitely should stand for the Commons. The House needed a man of his integrity. His handsome looks wouldn't count there, but it wouldn't hurt on the hustings, the temporary platform from which the nomination of candidates for Parliament was made, and on which these men stood while addressing the electors.

Under the general chatter, Nympha edged close to her great-aunt to verify what she thought she knew. "Lord William Bentinck is standing for the Commons here, is he not?"

"And likely to be approved for the by-election when it comes around. I imagine he will win. Why?"

Nympha glanced at Lord Nicholas, then back to her great-aunt. "I think he would do well."

"Hmm. And so he would. Do you intend to challenge him to it?" Great-Aunt's eyes gleamed with impishness.

"That would be a worthy objective, indeed." Nympha made a slow assessment of her projected candidate. Why could he not stand in his home district?

"Does he have a dog? The public likes a man with a dog. Makes him seem more down to earth."

"Lord Nicholas, you have a dog, do you not?" Nympha dared to inquire, knowing she possibly interrupted some banal exchange with Lady Ollerton, who then glared at Nympha with indignant eyes. But it seemed important that she know right now.

He looked justly startled at her query. "As matter of fact, I do. A terrier named Rags. Why?" he gave her a curious gaze.

"I just, er, wondered. I thought I recalled him tagging along after you on the links."

Her mention of his golf links brought eager questions from the gentlemen. Lady Ollerton, seeing she was outnumbered, moved to sit by Mrs. Coxmoor.

"So many men want their dogs, do they not?" She ogled Lord Nicholas with a speculative eye.

"True. I suspect they somehow deem it manly." Nympha darted a glance at Lord Nicholas. He didn't need a dog to look manly. What a pity women did not vote; he would win so easily.

Country calls might be a little longer than Town calls, but they all came to an end eventually. Nympha bade her aunt remain seated, escorting the callers to the door with as much grace as she might muster. Sir Giles was a trifle obsequious in his manner to her. She chalked it up to her inheritance. Then she wondered at her blasé attitude. She was not the same girl she had been when she left the rectory! Once the door closed behind them, she went back to the drawing room.

"That was nicely done, Nympha." Her great-aunt

beamed a smile of approval that made Nympha glow with pleasure.

Lord Nicholas leaned against the fireplace mantel. He had been talking with her great-aunt, and she could see he was not pleased with what had been said. "Whose idea is this? I stand for the Commons? How preposterous!"

Nympha regarded her great-aunt and saw at once there would be little help there. "I did, if you must know. You do have a certain way about you. And you get along so admirably with people. Look at Lord Ollerton and Sir Giles—you had them in the palm of your hand in moments—not to mention Lady Ollerton. I thought she just might cart you off with her." She flashed a defiant glower at him, wondering what his next argument would be. She didn't have long to wait.

"The money. I might be comfortably set, but I don't run to those sort of expenses." He gave her a stubborn stare from beneath frowning brows.

"Rubbish, you find a patron, someone who believes in you, who supports your positions. I know you have them, for I have often heard you spouting off on some government folly or other. I imagine the gentlemen in the Commons raise funds in many ways. I doubt many can afford to finance their elections out of their own pocket."

"I already have one folly—yes, I know that is what people call my golf links. I hardly need another." His dark eyes had a hard glint in them, obstinate in his refusal to even consider her suggestion.

"What about Lord William Bentinck? He is a younger son who intends to carve out a career for himself in the Commons. He will represent this district if he wins the next by-election." Nympha took a step closer, determined he at least consider her proposition.

"He'll be nominated I am certain," Great-Aunt Letitia inserted. "You might call on him, sound him out as to the support required. I hardly think you will need to go to the length of having Nympha offer kisses for sale, as did the Duchess of Devonshire in one election."

"I'd not do it!" Nympha stared at her great-aunt with disbelieving eyes. "I do not care if a duchess did such a thing, it is not proper. Is it?" Nympha looked to Lord Nicholas who had an unholy gleam in his eyes and a sly grin forming on that well-shaped mouth.

"I should think it would bring in any amount of cash, not to mention win votes from young and old gentleman alike. I vow—that is almost enough to persuade me. Would you sell kisses for me if I stood?" His grin, lop-sided and dazzling, threatened to overcome her scruples.

Nympha backed away a few steps. She didn't care for the direction her idea was taking. Selling kisses, indeed.

"What suggestion do you have for raising money—just supposing I did decide to take this mad start you propose?" He folded his arms over his chest, crossed one leg before the other, and looked the consummate skeptic.

Mrs. Coxmoor cleared her throat, then offered in the mildest of voices, "Nympha will have a considerable amount of money at her disposal. Once I am gone, it will be vast, indeed."

Nympha switched her gaze from her aunt to Lord Nicholas. That was unfair, to dangle her wealth before his eyes. Did her great-aunt think he would marry her to get at her money? That was not what she wanted. Whatever happened to love? Not to mention happily ever after? "Perhaps," she began, then took courage. "Perhaps I could sponsor you? Would you accept money from a woman?"

"Why not," he sneered. "Everyone will wonder what I had to do to obtain it. You will be pilloried, for certain, with the men eyeing you and wondering. And you, a rector's daughter? I don't think so."

"You could, Great-Aunt. No one would say a thing if you decided to finance a campaign for Lord Nicholas. Think how wonderful it would be for him to serve in our government. He truly is a fine man." Nympha gave her great-aunt a pleading look.

"If we are getting into such personal matters, I think you may as well call me Nick, Nympha. And I haven't decided one way or another on this matter. I'm not even sure which party I would enter. I lean to the notion it is a harebrained idea, frankly. I have never in my life considered sitting in the House of Commons. My father has never attended Lords."

"Well," Nympha said, "he has his birds." She could see she would have to explain this later to her great-aunt who positively oozed curiosity at this peculiar remark.

"How true." Lord Nicholas stiffly turned to Mrs. Coxmoor. "My esteemed father collects birds—stuffed or painted. He and my mother presently live in Italy where she paints and he collects."

"How interesting," Mrs. Coxmoor said, looking as though she longed to laugh. "I have always thought it good to have a minor obsession. I ought to think of one."

"Enough." Lord Nicholas slashed the air with his hand. "I suggest we change the topic to something less fruitless."

"I won't give up, you know," Nympha said with determination her mother would instantly recognize and take precautions against. "First you decide on your party affiliation. Papa said the Whigs lean toward the merchant and progress, and Tories lean toward the land and the church. They are the more traditional. Are you for progress or tradition?"

"Both. Where does that put me?" He assumed a devious expression she didn't trust in the least.

"Wanting," she promptly shot back at him. "You must have some idea regarding your beliefs."

"I said enough, and I meant it. My beliefs, wanting or otherwise, are not up for discussion. Is that clear?"

Chastised, Nympha nodded. She walked to the window to stare out. "The rain has stopped. I do believe the sun will shine before too long."

"How English we all are. From politics to weather in a trice."

"Well, what would you do?"

Nick knew what he would like to do and couldn't. She stood silhouetted against the light of the window, her blond curls rioting about her head in spite of an attempt to tame them. Her eyes flashed at him with fire. But her person was poised, sweetly delineated in the blush sarcenet gown she had worn to greet the callers. Oh, he knew precisely what he would like to do.

Had he his way at this moment, he would gather her in his arms and forget all about the world. Her kisses would be his food and drink. There would be no discussion about money or political parties or government service.

"And why dogs, pray tell?" he wondered a moment later when the earlier question came back to him.

"Men are inclined to trust a man who has a dog. That's the way things go." Mrs. Coxmoor regarded him with amusement glimmering in her blue eyes.

Nick thought for a moment. "I'll give you that. I noticed Milburn had no dog, and it did make me wary of him."

"You see! Rags is an asset."

"You do recall what he looks like, do you not?"

"He is a sweet doggy," Nympha insisted.

"I think I'd need a bloodhound instead.

"Why?" Nympha frowned at him.

"Why to sniff out support and funding!" He gave her a sly, tongue-in-cheek grin.

"May I suggest you take a turn in the garden while it is still light? You never know but what it might rain tomorrow. Although one can always hope," Mrs. Coxmoor interjected.

"Yes, Great-Aunt. That is a fine idea." Nympha flashed him a look that dared him to argue.

He was tempted, but decided to meekly go along with the notion. After all, he might be able to talk her into playing a game of tennis—or some other sport far more interesting.

In short order the pair went out the front door. Behind them came Annie, muffled to her nose against the chill. Nympha wore her blue pelisse.

"You are sure this isn't too much for you?" He

watched Nympha march along the walk toward the tulip beds with the same sort of determination she had shown earlier when talking about his standing for the Commons.

"Not in the least. Papa always says there is nothing better than a good constitutional."

Considering how the rector appeared as though he didn't walk farther than from his desk to the dining table, Nick decided to allow that to pass.

"Whatever gave you the idea that I ought to opt for the House of Commons?" He really was curious about that. Her remark had seemingly come out of the blue, and Mrs. Coxmoor had appeared to support it.

"Well . . ." She paused in her walking.

"Come now . . . It cannot be that difficult?"

"As I believe I said, you are natural with people. You can put them at ease instantly. And you have integrity. Great-Aunt Letitia agreed with me on that. Besides, you have a dog."

"I do enjoy being with people, although I far prefer being on my own."

"With your dog," she reminded.

"But integrity? I thought you were angry with me." She fascinated him. Her mind seemed to work contrary to all he might expect of a woman.

"Well, it has to do with a number of things, actually."

She was hedging, and that made him even more curious. "Such as?" He would probe until he got an answer.

"Well, if you must know, it is that you came north determined to find the identity of the man murdered on the seventh green—even though it was nothing to you personally. You had not been charged with a crime. You wanted to see justice done. And when my carriage broke down, you offered your help without conditions, and you never once made advances—at least not then." She made a self-conscious little gesture. "You have been wonderfully kind to my aunt"—she turned to look him in the face—"and to me. And you were tolerant of Mr. Milburn in spite of your suspicions. Just think," she added artlessly, "were you in the Commons you might have a chance to do something about unsolved murders—or something."

"Forget the House of Commons, will you? I shall." But he knew he wouldn't. She had planted a seed, and he was finding the idea curiously intriguing.

"I meant what I said about financing you."

"I could not accept money from a spinster." He knew that would annoy her, being called a spinster. Yet that was what she was in the eyes of the law, as were all unmarried women of age.

"That was not nice, Nick. Not nice at all. What a pity Mr. Milburn seeks a peerage; he would not be so finicky about money, I'll wager."

He observed the stubborn tilt of her chin, and smiled to himself. So she thought to rile him by a comparison with that man?

"Well, I'll give you this much—I will consider what you have said. Fair enough?"

"I suppose I must be satisfied with that. I should think your father would be proud of you, should you venture into politics." Her voice sounded wistful. He knew he ought to compensate for her disappointment in some way, but he wasn't certain how.

Annie had wisely huddled in the warmth of what sun there was, leaving Nick virtually alone with Nympha. If he were such a virtuous man he wouldn't even think about kissing Nympha Herbert. That just showed how wrong a person might be.

"Nympha? I still do not completely understand why you think I ought to stand for the House of Commons. But I said I would think about it and I will. Shall we seal that bargain?" Behind them beds of tulips were in bud, on the verge of bursting forth in glorious color.

Clearly puzzled, she lifted her face to his. The sun-gilded skin that was already blessed with fine texture and healthy color. He'd had no choice, when he came to think on it later. So he kissed her, and quite thoroughly at that.

Chapter Fifteen

Dinner was a quiet affair. Nympha wore her blue silk. Lord Nicholas was extravagant in his compliments. Great-Aunt Letitia said, "You'll do nicely, girl," when she observed her grandniece enter the drawing room prior to dinner.

Nympha thought that considering how the kitchen staff must have worked yesterday it was only proper they not have something elaborate.

Once they had consumed the sweet, they retired to the drawing room to talk. Lord Nicholas brought a glass of port with him at Mrs. Coxmoor's suggestion. Just because he was alone was no reason to deny him her late husband's excellent port, nor should he be required to drink by himself.

"I truly believe you ought to consider standing for the Commons," Mrs. Coxmoor insisted, returning to the earlier topic. "You show great common sense, and that is certainly needed in the House. Surely you might stand from your home borough? You should be well-known there. I would wager you could connect with the Tory party leaders—or the Whigs, if you lean that way—and have support. Does your father have any influence?"

"The seat is in my father's gift. I merely have never had any inclination in that direction." He stared at the rich wine in his glass, turning it back and forth as though to study the color in the candlelight. "It is possible the fellow who holds it now would be willing to vacate his seat in exchange for some favor."

"Well, then," Nympha declared, "I should say that it is your duty to take the seat in the Commons!" She stared at her friend. He was merely her friend, was he not? She dared not consider him more than that. Their differences were considerable. If his father held the giving of a seat—it would be Lord Nicholas's for the asking. He scarcely needed her money.

But *she* needed him. She hadn't realized how much until now, when she recognized how little was her chance of ever having him as hers.

Her great-aunt allowed the matter of Lord Nicholas standing for the House of Commons to rest, and went on to other subjects.

Foley entered with a letter, handing it to Lord Nicholas with polite courtesy. "This was just brought from Nelthorpe Castle for you, my lord."

Excusing himself, he broke the seal, then unfolded the page. "It is a note from Milburn, requesting a match of tennis tomorrow. How curious. I would have thought he wanted nothing more to do with us once he left here. I really did not expect to see him again—except at a distance—before I left."

Nympha studied him a moment. There truly was no reason for him to remain in Nottingham now. Although he felt he knew the identity of the murderer, there was nothing he could do about it, frustrating as that might be. He probably was anxious to see his home—yet he remained.

"Perhaps he wants one last game before you head south again." Mrs. Coxmoor subjected him to a searching inspection. "I suppose you feel drawn to inspect your new home. It might be completed by the time you get there. Not that we wish you to leave, mind you. But I *am* aware you must have many demands on your time. It was most kind of you to escort Nympha north. We have enjoyed having you here as our guest—and you know that you are welcome to remain with us as long as you please."

She nodded when Foley brought in the tea tray, placing it before Nympha so she might pour.

"I imagine your dog misses you very much," Nympha said, then added mentally, *Not to mention all the women.* He must have them littering the landscape down there, as handsome as he was and with a lovely new home just waiting for the proper wife. A knot settled in her chest at the very thought of Nicholas with a beautiful woman—for of course she would be breathtakingly lovely. She couldn't imagine him with anyone ordinary.

She poured out tea for her great-aunt. When Lord Nicholas nodded in reply to her raised brows, she poured for him as well, adding the sugar he preferred. Lastly she poured a cup for herself, taking a restoring sip at once. The thought that Lord Nicholas Stanhope would disappear from her life forever stabbed her heart with anguish. She very much doubted another could ever replace him in her affections.

Conversation was the trivia one expected over a late-evening tea tray, with Nympha more than a little absent-minded. The weather always drew comments, possible plans for the morrow.

"I believe I shall retire early," her great-aunt announced once she had finished her tea. "That ball took more out of me than I realized. You two young people needn't go up just yet. With Nympha a rector's daughter, and Lord Nicholas as fine a man as he is, I need not worry in the least about propriety. Besides, Foley is around the corner," she added dryly.

She could be heard in the hallway—speaking to Foley, a soft laugh, then her steps on the stairs.

When she had gone, Nympha poured more tea. She met his lordship's gaze, and chuckled. "That assuredly put us on our honor, did it not?"

"Hmm, there is nothing like high praise to make one likely to behave." He finished the last of his tea, placing his cup down with deliberation. His gaze was intense, she thought, uneasy with the notion he might read her mind. Could he? Never. She hoped.

She sipped, studying him over the rim of her cup. Dare she remain? It was testing her willpower as well as his if she did. She set her teacup on its saucer with a note of finality, and rose. "I believe it might be wise if I also retired."

"I am flattered if you think me a temptation to stray." The wry, half smile he assumed brought an answering smile to her lips.

"Actually, it is drawing late. I had a short night last eve. Perhaps it is sensible to follow my great-aunt."

He rose when she did, trailing her to the door.

In the entry, Foley pretended not to see or hear anything. But he was there.

She glanced at Lord Nicholas, suddenly a bit nervous, although why, she was not quite certain. He had never stepped *too* far out of line before. He walked at her side, but not overly close.

"Does your great-aunt wish me gone?" He picked up a night candle from the hall table, lit it, offering it to her when they reached the bottom of the stairs.

He was nothing if not direct. "I do not believe she does—she has said nothing to me on the subject. Tonight she indicated you are welcome to remain as long as you please. Perhaps she thinks you would wish to leave us?" She accepted the candle, staring at the flame in an effort to avoid meeting his eyes again.

"And do you? Wish me gone?" He leaned against the beautifully carved newel post, crossing his arms before him. Nympha had the oddest notion he held them in place lest he do something else. It was as though he restrained himself.

What a dreadful question to put before her. She had been raised to be truthful. One did not ever tell lies, and his query had been very pointed.

"I have enjoyed your company very much," she replied, intent on telling the truth as far as she needed to go.

"Should I remain for a time?" His eyes studied her with an intentness she found disconcerting. She discovered it easier to look at the understated elegance of the pin placed in his cravat.

"I would miss you," she confessed, although she had not meant to utter those words.

His smile lit his eyes as though capturing the flame from her candle. Reaching out one hand, he picked up hers where it rested on the handrail. Holding her hand as though something precious, he brought it to his lips and kissed it. She had never thought of a hand kiss as a sensuous matter. Lord Nicholas changed the simple gesture into something to melt one's bones, send shivers up and down the spine, and send a shock of longing through one.

"Good night, dear girl." His low voice sent tremors through her from end to end.

Her answering good night sounded a bit squeaky to her ears. She rushed up the stairs to her room, intent upon reaching it before she begged him to allow her to be his dear girl in all ways.

Saturday morning was clear, with a somewhat watery sun beaming through the windows. Nympha checked the view below to note that more of the tulips were opening. Spring was most assuredly here. She could almost feel it.

How glad she was that Lord Nicholas decided to remain a little longer. How he could, when his new home was likely finished and awaiting his inspection, was beyond her. She wasn't likely to quibble about it, though.

With a light heart and a smile, she jauntily marched down to the breakfast room to find Lord Nicholas seated with the *Nottingham Review* and his cup of coffee in hand. He rose, bowed to her, and resumed his seat when she waved her hand at him.

After selecting a plate of nourishment from the sideboard, she seated herself not too close to him. He drew her like a magnet, and she decided she had best use prudence.

"You have the tennis match with Mr. Milburn today? Did he suggest a time?" She didn't gaze at him, studiously examining her roll as though it held great secrets. She applied butter with a judicious hand.

Nick put the newspaper aside and set down his coffee cup with a gesture to Foley to refill it. "Late this morning, I should imagine. Somehow I doubt the castle encourages early risers."

"So, he will truly marry Lady Anne?" Nympha seemed skeptical, as well she ought.

"Unless one of them calls it off, or the duchess finds a gentleman she prefers who is willing to accept Lady Anne. I suspect she will be a handful for any man." Nick grinned at his table companion, who plunked her teacup down at his words.

Nympha's eyes grew round. "You think that might happen? That she might fix her attention elsewhere? Mercy me."

"It has happened before in other cases. You are not married until the knot is tied, all official, and the register signed." He watched her with amusement.

"No bride wants to leave the church until that is done," Nympha stated. "The wedding certainly wouldn't be legal." She looked adorably prim.

"What does your father do about special licenses?" Nick had toyed with the idea of obtaining a special license, but suspected Nympha—if she agreed to marry him—would want her father to perform the wedding ceremony.

"The couple still has to have the information entered in the register of the home parish. I suppose you well know that if two parishes are involved, both must be notified. Why are we discussing this boring topic?"

"You find the subject of marriage boring?"

She blushed. He so enjoyed provoking her.

"Not really," she replied. "It is just that it is not *normally* a matter for discussion at the breakfast table."

"I will remember that, and never discuss it other than

at lunch or dinner." He grinned at her, watching her blush deepen to a tantalizing rose.

"You, sir, are utterly impossible!" She nibbled at her roll. A bit of butter clung to her upper lip.

Nick wished he might have the right to lick it off.

"Do you mind if I watch your tennis match with Mr. Milburn?"

"I thought you were not eager to see him again," Nick replied with a frown at the thought that Nympha might again be hit with a tennis ball.

"Well, I am not, of course. But I admire your playing and thought it would be fun to see you play once more."

Was there a hint of "before you are gone" in her voice and manner? he wondered, for the first time in his life, unsure of how his advances were being accepted. "What if I suggested you might see me play tennis more often?" He couched his query in a casual manner. He would like to be more direct, but still hesitated to put her to the test. She had considered his previous mention of marriage a joke! No man likes to be rejected.

"You intend to build a tennis court at your new home? In addition to your golfing links?"

"If you are here, you wouldn't be able to see it." He imagined she seemed a mite dejected at that thought.

"True. Perhaps when I come to visit my family. I do not intend to break all contact with them, you know. How could I be so unfeeling?"

"I could never believe it of you."

Mrs. Coxmoor swept into the room at that moment. She glanced at Nick, then her grandniece. "Lovely morning, is it not? Perhaps you would like to hit a few tennis balls before Mr. Milburn comes? I daresay Nympha could partner you in a pinch?"

Nick had risen when Mrs. Coxmoor entered. He glanced to where Nympha sat, her eyes shining with delight at the thought of hitting a tennis ball with him. Hmm. She had been very good at the battledore, hitting the shuttlecocks with wild abandon. "Would you like a try? I could use a bit of practice, you know. Milburn has a vicious serve."

"I will be ready when you are," she declared, jumping up from the table to plant a kiss on her relative's creamy cheek.

Blue eyes only a little lighter than her grandniece's gazed up at Nick with what he would swear was mischief in them. He bowed slightly, joining Nympha as they left the room in favor of the tennis court.

Neither of them took long to change to suitable clothing. Nympha found one of her old gowns, the skirt of which was shorter than her others.

Nick waited at the bottom of the stairs. His patience was rewarded with the sight that greeted him when Nympha lightly scampered down to join him.

"That appears to be an excellent choice for an active game," he said, taking note of the shorter skirt and the loose fit of the garment. It didn't hide much of her figure, he decided with thanks.

The efficient Foley had the racquets and balls set out for them, a light cloak for her as well.

"I trust you will have a good game, sir, miss," he said when ushering them from the house.

"Would you say Foley is a romantic?" Nick queried.

"Never!" Nympha said with an endearing little chuckle.

"I might be wrong, but I think him happy to see us off on our own."

A shadow crossed her face, making Nick wonder what it was that saddened her at the mention of them together. Was she so set against him? She had apologized for implying he was a fortune hunter. That didn't mean she did not think it, however. Yet she had called him a man of integrity. So why was she so against his suit?

"Now, I want you to play the best game you can. Do not spare me!" Nick laughed at her grimace.

"If you think I can compete while wearing these skirts and you in breeches, think again." She swatted him lightly on his behind with her racquet.

"Madam! You are the most shocking flirt." Nick swatted her back—just as lightly.

"Never say so! Ah, well, I will do my best to make you a worthy opponent. I must say, I think I could do better at archery. My skirts would not hamper me nearly as much."

"Pity you cannot play in breeches." At her scandalized expression, he added, "I didn't say you ought; I said merely that it was a pity." But with her slim legs and slender shape, she would appear very enticing in a pair of his breeches. Perhaps? . . .

They settled down to a lively session of tennis once in the tennis court. However Nympha might have felt hampered by her skirts, she did a creditable job of returning his shots. Of course, he more or less directed them to her, but still, she did well, hitting the ball square and hard.

Nympha was fatigued by the time Mr. Milburn was supposed to appear. She suggested they take a break and enjoy the lemonade brought for them by James.

"Pour me a tall glass. I could drink the pitcher dry, I do believe." Nick sank down on the bench, closing his eyes a moment while he waited.

She poured out for both of them, before taking a seat in an area she thought safe from harm, yet where she could see well. "You are to play at the other end of the court?"

"You think to sit behind Milburn, and thus be safe from one of his bullet balls?" Lord Nicholas frowned. He nodded. "It might be a good notion." He downed the contents of his glass, then poured another.

Whatever Nympha might have said in reply was not to be known. The door opened and Mr. Milburn entered, attired in a coat that he promptly removed to expose a loose-fitting shirt of fine linen such as Lord Nicholas wore. He exchanged a few comments on the weather, living at the castle, and their tennis game.

She suspected that it was not to be a tame match.

It wasn't.

It was not a game, but more like a battle. Nick served the ball so it went just over the net. Mr. Milburn raced up to hit it back, dropping it equally close just over the net. With a beginning like this, it was easy to see that not only were the two men well matched, but Mr. Milburn for some reason wanted to beat Lord Nicholas into the ground, so to speak.

The ball flew back and forth at great speed. Nympha thought her neck would wear out with swiveling to and fro as she watched so intently. The score mounted up, seesawing just as the ball had gone back and forth.

At last the first set was done. The two men, both of whom had been sweating profusely, wiped off with the towels James had brought out along with another pitcher of lemonade.

"You are tied," Nympha observed.

Mr. Milburn shot her a glance of surprise, as though he had forgotten she was there. He accepted the drink she poured for him and retired to study Lord Nicholas. He said nothing, as though he saved energy that way.

Pleased that she had been so unobtrusive, Nympha poured out the last of the lemonade for them. She found a place to sit that would be well out of any direction that Mr. Milburn might send the ball. He might forget she was there, but she did not trust him in the least—not after that last time.

The game continued just as hard fought. Nympha wondered if it had been a good idea for Nick to "warm up" as he had put it. She couldn't call him Nick to his face, but she noticed he didn't object when Mr. Milburn used it.

Of a sudden, the ball burst! Possibly it wasn't made to withstand such vehement pounding. Nympha saw there was another ball near where the tray sat. She nimbly hopped down, tossing it to Nick, to whom Mr. Milburn had shot the ball. She signaled she would retrieve the remains of the battered ball, lest she be caught in the crossfire and be hurt again.

The leather had split, the firm wool packing oozing out of the ruptured ball. She set it aside, retreating to watch again.

Mr. Milburn attacked Nick with as fervent a return as she had ever seen. Nick wasn't prepared, and the ball hit him on the shoulder, much as it had hit her head.

Nympha had been watching Mr. Milburn. She was horrified to see he seemed disgusted rather than shaken or sorry when Nick dropped his racket to clutch his shoulder.

"I think that ends this game," Nympha insisted. She ran over to where Nick still had his hand against his wounded shoulder.

"That was one wicked shot, Milburn."

"It was, wasn't it?" He sneered at Nick, ignoring Nympha completely. "I fancy you have done with this game—at least for today?"

"Not quite," Nick replied quietly. He massaged his right shoulder before bending to pick up his racquet. "I believe we have a final game to play in this set."

Nympha was as disbelieving as Mr. Milburn appeared to be. Surely he couldn't play with that shoulder so injured? And his right shoulder at that!

It seemed he not only could, but he obviously intended to whip Mr. Milburn within an inch of his life—tennis wise, that is.

Nick delivered a shot as wicked as the one Mr. Milburn had aimed at his shoulder. It went deep into the backcourt. Mr. Milburn almost fell trying to return it.

Nick's next stroke was amazingly powerful, and went just inside the baseline on the far side of where the last shot had gone. Mr. Milburn apparently hadn't expected the ball to go so deep again. This time he did fall, his breeches ripping as he tumbled to the floor.

He crouched, still, unmoving. Then he massaged his shoulder, wincing as he did. There was a spot of blood on his breeches where his knee stuck through the ripped fabric. He really appeared done in.

Nympha hoped he was hurt as badly as she sensed Nick had been. Mr. Milburn made a Gothic villain seem like a milksop.

"Pity," Nick said, breathing hard as he walked around the side of the court to where Mr. Milburn remained. "I thought we might have been able to complete that game. It shows you must never underestimate your opponent. Isn't that right?"

Mr. Milburn slowly rose to his feet, gave Nick a glare of pure loathing, then without saying a word limped to where he had tossed his coat and shrugged into it. He left the court in silence, slamming the door behind him.

Nympha dashed up to where Nick now leaned against the wall. Pale and appearing drained, he looked as though he might collapse.

"I insist you lean on me while we go back to the house. You look utterly dreadful!"

"My thanks, dear girl. That is such a comfort to know." His voice sounded strained. He closed his eyes, tilting his head back, breathing shallowly but even.

"Sarcasm does not become you, particularly when you are in pain—I can see it in your eyes. Now, do you come peacefully?"

He half-smiled, nodding at her. "Take me away. I can see you will whether I want it or not."

James met them at the door, taking over from Nympha, who was very glad. Nick might be light on his feet, but at the moment he felt like a ton of wet bricks.

Mrs. Coxmoor was horrified when the trio entered the house. She insisted upon examining the injured shoulder at once.

Nympha gulped as James eased the shirt over Nick's head, revealing a decidedly well-muscled chest and a rapidly purpling shoulder. She ought not stare, but wild horses couldn't tear her eyes from his form at this moment.

"I gather this was not an ordinary game of tennis?" her great-aunt inquired.

"No, ma'am. If you don't mind, I should like to get to

my room. Simpson has a magic salve he puts on injuries that cuts pain and helps heal. I could use that about now."

Nympha suspected Nick hated to have others see him feeling so weak. She also suspected that he had better get flat on his back before he really did collapse.

Mrs. Coxmoor stepped back, murmured something comforting, and urged James to assist Nick to his room.

"That man!" she snarled when the men had gone.

"Well, if it is any comfort to you, Mr. Milburn was worse off than Nick, that is, Lord Nicholas. His knee came through his breeches when he fell, and he was decidedly whipped when they stopped."

"The score?"

"Thirty-love on the last game, although it was not completed. I couldn't say what all the games totaled. Perhaps Lord Nicholas kept track?"

"I am glad he soundly beat Mr. Milburn. One can't help but wonder why the man was so insistent on playing, and so hard at that."

"I suspect he wanted to hurt Lord Nicholas."

"Possibly." Her great-aunt stalked off to the drawing room, motioning Nympha to follow her.

The remainder of the day went extremely quietly. The servants tiptoed about their duties.

Lady Anne came, demanding to see Lord Nicholas. Foley firmly declined the prospect of her seeing the injured man. Since Nympha was in the act of crossing the entry when Lady Anne came, she stepped forward to greet the unwelcome caller.

"Perhaps I may be of help, my lady? I fear Lord Nicholas is in his room at present. None of us wishes to disturb him."

"Well, I think him despicable. I could not believe how battered my dear Sir Jared was when he came back from playing a mere game of tennis."

"Sir Jared?" Nympha immediately pounced on the vital words in the sentence. "His uncle has gone aloft?"

"You had not heard? Yesterday, as matter of fact."

His uncle had died yesterday? Why had he said nothing? And to attend the ball when he should have been in mourning was shocking, to say the least. On the other hand, it was no less than one might expect of such a man.

Lady Anne was not appeased, leaving the house in a huff in spite of Nympha's attempts to smooth matters over.

The remaining hours of the day were without intrusions of any sort, for which Nympha was profoundly thankful.

Nick joined them at dinner, wincing only slightly when he ate. "I intend to go to church with you come morning. You will attend?"

"By all means. I fancy the vicar may have a few words to say regarding the demise of the late Sir Cosmo Milburn."

"So Milburn now has his title, such as it is?" Nick's voice reflected his doubts.

"Yes. Although now he has the wealth in hand, he may be off to London at once." Mrs. Coxmoor raised her glass in a toast. "To the departure of a most unpleasant man."

Chapter Sixteen

Nick groaned when Simpson touched him lightly to awaken him. He ached in spite of the liniment Simpson had gently rubbed into his shoulder before he slept last night. He carefully stretched out the many kinks in his body. Perhaps the day would not be too trying after all. He could always hope.

"Forgive me, my lord, but you did say you wished to attend divine services this morning." Simpson withdrew to begin preparations for the day's events. Fine biscuit-colored pantaloons, a discreet waistcoat of quality cassimere in a pale cream, and a dark blue coat of the best Bath cloth were reverently placed on a nearby chair. His best shoes, polished to a blinding shine, sat on the floor beside these garments.

"So I did. I seem to have one folly after another, don't I?" Nick eased himself from the bed, gingerly moving his shoulders, relieved that the aching seemed less.

"As to that, my lord, I'd not say you commit follies."

"What would you say?" Nick wondered aloud.

"Things seem to happen when you are around. You *are* an active gentleman. It is a pity that you should have become involved with Mr. Milburn." The valet set out the shaving gear, shaking his head when his master shaved himself instead of properly allowing Simpson to do it.

"Oh, he is Sir Jared now. Uncle popped off the day of the ball." Nick cocked a knowing eye at his shrewd valet.

"Indeed? And he attended anyway? Shocking behavior, if I may say so." Simpson tenderly assisted his master into his shirt, then set about changing him into the premier gentleman he was.

When Nick joined the others at the breakfast table he felt as though he could tolerate sitting in the straight-back pew for an hour. Unless the vicar, the Reverend Mr. Bowerbank, was one of those prosy preachers who wished to impress the listeners with the quality of his voice and the erudite wanderings of his mind.

They left the house in Mrs. Coxmoor's coach. Nick had to admire its comfort. Small wonder that Nympha was reluctant to travel in his when she had experienced such luxury.

Nympha wore the stylish bonnet he had bought her in Nottingham. It sat nicely on her head, with blue ribands and flowers draped around its brim. With it she wore her elegantly cut white muslin. She'd pinned a cameo to the front of the dress, closing up what must be a very low neckline. She looked wonderful.

The church service proved to be well attended. A small organ provided the music. It was not what he heard in London, but was quite agreeable, mostly because he was sitting beside Nympha.

The reverend had reached what he obviously felt was a telling point in his homily when a loud noise was heard.

The entire building shook sharply as though some demon was objecting to what the reverend had to say. Nick felt a rolling shock, like a wave on dry ground. To say it was disconcerting was far too mild. He felt dizzy for a few moments. A glance at Nympha revealed wide-eyed fright.

People screamed, chairs tumbled over, some books fell off a shelf in the back of the church, and the chandelier swayed. Nick glanced up to see dust and lime falling everywhere. It was like he had imagined the end of the world, with chaos reigning. Mrs. Coxmoor coughed, dust all about her.

"Let's get out of here. I think a beam may have given

way." He grabbed Nympha's hand, pulled Mrs. Coxmoor to her feet, and attempted to lead them from the building to the street. He could hear a roaring, rumbling noise, as though the army decided to fire off a number of cannon at once. He knew there was no army anywhere near here, not even a small militia.

Everyone else immediately attempted to leave too, people instantly rushing to make their escape. They pushed and shoved, and Nick could almost smell their fear of being trapped inside a collapsing building.

"Nick," Nympha screamed as she was pulled from his clasp and knocked to the floor. A burly man with his thin, acidulated wife trampled over Nympha, anxious to flee and not caring whom they trod on.

"Run while you can!" Nick cried to Mrs. Coxmoor. He fought to rescue his darling girl. "Stand aside!" Nympha was down, possibly hurt, and he wasn't going to allow anyone else to trample on her! He knelt and quickly grabbed her up in his arms. No time to assess her injuries.

He forged his way through the thinning throng. Several had been hurt. Nympha was not the only one who had been thrown down. While he felt sorry for them, his only true concern was for Nympha and Mrs. Coxmoor.

At last they made it through the door of the church to the fresh air outside. People thronged about the street, bewildered expressions on numb faces. A mother counted heads. A man whose pregnant wife had fainted begged for a doctor. The Reverend Mr. Bowerbank displayed heretofore-unknown heroic qualities by administering to those injured.

Nick placed Nympha against a fallen gravestone not far from the street, his concern for her almost choking him. Mrs. Coxmoor slumped against another. He glanced about to see the people calming down, talking in shaken voices, leaning against one another, dazed, confused.

Nick gently brushed dust and lime from Nympha's hair, figuring her new bonnet must be a squashed blob on the church floor. "Where does it hurt the most?"

"Oh, here and there. It's not too bad. What a dreadful mess I must be. I'm so glad I don't have a looking glass to hand." Her gown would never be the same again. Being trampled on doesn't lend itself to improvement.

He half-smiled in spite of the situation's severity.

Mrs. Coxmoor had managed to cling to her bonnet. Now she brushed down her dress, then looked about to assess the damage. "Won't be able to hold services in there for a time to come. The place is a shambles."

A bloodcurdling scream rent the air from close to the west side of the church. Nick craned his neck to see what had happened. "A stone fell on someone—came from the roof," he was told by an onlooker.

"Nick, see what happened," Mrs. Coxmoor commanded. "I shall watch over Nympha. Please?"

Obediently, Nick wound his way through the throng to find Lady Anne in hysterics, kneeling beside an ominously still Sir Jared Milburn. Beside his head was a stone gargoyle, one of many that served as waterspouts for the roof gutters.

"Oh, is he? He can't be! Oh, I fear he must be!" she cried to Nick as he neared the spot.

Nick knelt to check the still figure, finding precisely what he expected. "He's dead, Lady Anne." It was a blunt speech, but he had no time for gentle words now. "I expect your parents will see to matters for you."

Nick rose, paused a moment to look at the face of the man he suspected of murder as well as an attempt on Nympha's life. He could feel no regret at his passing, other than sorrow for a life misspent.

Lady Anne ran back to the duchess, who offered comfort and an arm on which to lean. Behind her Lord Henry helped Lady Jane to the family carriage, his tall, lean figure standing out above the crowd. The Reverend Mr. Bowerbank dealt with Sir Jared.

Nick went back to the women and explained what had occurred. Both expressed horror at the accident, but it was muted with the knowledge of what sort of man had been killed.

"We must leave here. I am certain our coachman will bring our carriage. Can you see it, Lord Nicholas?" Mrs. Coxmoor fanned herself with a lace handkerchief.

Nick craned his neck to see the familiar vehicle slowly making its way through the milling crowd. He didn't ask, he scooped Mrs. Coxmoor up in his arms. "Sirrah," she cried indignantly, "Nympha is the one hurt." Nick ignored her.

"I'll be back for you in seconds," he cried to Nympha. "Don't move!" He hated to part from her for a moment, but as the coach drew closer, he knew it would be brief.

Again he forged his way through the throng of people, only this time they were more willing to ease aside. Many were heading for home, no doubt wondering what they would find when they got there.

When he reached the coach, the footman had the door open for him. Nick gently deposited the lady inside, saw to her comfort, before whirling to run back. There was no proof that the strange occurrence might not recur. He wanted to be away from here if it did. He dashed back to Nympha.

She was precisely where he left her, leaning against the headstone as though a carved adornment. He drew her to her feet, and uncaring of those around, kissed her soundly. "If anything had happened to you . . ." He cradled her close to him, nestling her in his arms.

"I shall be fine. I think." She leaned back in his arms to give him a misty smile, somewhat marred by the dust and lime streaked across her face.

He gathered her up carefully, walking back to the coach as though he carried a priceless object. She was priceless, to him. He placed her in the coach as well, tucking her up with care next to her great-aunt.

Before he entered the vehicle, he stepped forward to speak to the coachman. "How bad is the town?"

"Seems as though there is scarcely a street that doesn't have chimneys thrown down from what I saw and heard." The man shook his head in amazement. "I saw houses with cracks across 'em, windows split, plaster trim knocked off. Never saw nothing like it in all my born days. Hope to heaven I never do again." He nodded at the horses, adding, "They were jittery just afore the shakin' began. Still a mite bit frightened."

Nick nodded in understanding. "Best try to head for Coxmoor Hall at once. Who knows what we will find when we get there." With that sobering thought, Nick left him, entering the coach to sit opposite the two women.

"I do believe that is a church service I will never forget," Mrs. Coxmoor vowed, sounding more shaken than she looked. "Bowerbank will likely declare it a divine warning. He might be right at that."

"There is Sir Giles Arnold, also heading out of town," Nympha observed as she leaned forward to look out of the window.

"I would imagine he also wonders what he will find when he gets home." Nick looked at the departing carriage, tearing along the road as though the hounds of hell were after him.

"What about the castle?" Nympha wondered.

"Those thick walls should withstand more than we experienced today." Nick broached the subject that really worried him now that they were safe. "What do you think about your house, ma'am?" Nick decided it might be well to prepare the elderly lady for a shock. He had no idea what condition the house might be in when they reached it.

"My husband wanted it built with thick walls to insulate against the cold. Perhaps that will be a help?"

"The chimneys may have fallen. Your coachman said that hardly a street in Mansfield doesn't have some chimneys thrown down," Nick cautioned.

"But some were all right? In that case, let us pray for the best." She sat with folded hands, still looking a bit shaken. Dust and lime had drifted all over her, in spite of her attempts to brush off. She looked as though she had been inspecting fireplace chimneys.

Come to think on it, Nick might be doing just that before long. Well—he looked down at himself—he needn't bother to change his clothes. What had been his best waistcoat was filthy. His blue coat, always a favorite, had dust and lime ground into it. The knees of his fine pantaloons were covered with dirt from when he had knelt in the graveyard. All in all, he was a disaster. Not even his shoes had escaped—they were covered in thick dust.

Before long they reached the avenue leading to Coxmoor Hall. Nick opened the window, wanting to see immediately what had occurred to the house, if anything.

When it came into view, it appeared as though little had happened to it, the chimneys stood as always. From all he could see, the windows were intact.

"Well? How is it?"

Nick pulled his head back inside to face the elderly lady across from him. "As far as I can see at this distance, you have escaped the worst. The chimneys all stand. No windows on this side are damaged."

She bowed her head, then leaned against Nympha. "I was worried I would leave you a heap of rubble."

"Don't you worry about a thing, dearest." Nympha slipped an arm about her great-aunt, patting her gently on her shoulder. "A good cup of tea and you are bound to feel better. Foley will give us a report once we are inside."

Nick almost smiled. A good cup of tea, the British panacea.

The coach came to a halt before the front of the house. The three left the carriage and stood silently inspecting the edifice for obvious damage.

Foley opened the front door and hurried out to assist his employer inside with the gentlest manner imaginable.

Nympha stood, leaning against Nick as they surveyed the house.

"*It* seems to be all right. How do *you* feel?" She peered up at him, her streaked face all concern.

All at once, Nick felt every ache and pain in his stressed body. He shook his head. "I have had better days."

"You hurt. Come on, Foley will have tea ready, and I will bet he has something stronger for you." She tugged his hand. Nick willingly followed her.

What a disaster this day had been. Not only was the church in shambles, the populace dazed, his plans for Nympha were in abeyance. Until matters were straightened out here, he would have to wait to propose. At least he thought that the best thing to do. He wondered who would tend to Sir Jared's affairs. All that money would do him little good now.

On that thought, he ushered Nympha into the house, meeting Foley at the entrance to the drawing room.

Nick guided Nympha to a chair. He went back to the entry where he found Foley issuing instructions to James and another footman.

When they had departed, Nick gazed about him and didn't see any damage. "How is it here? Mansfield is a shambles. The church isn't usable, and chimneys are thrown down all over town."

"Actually we did not feel it as strongly, from what you describe. There was a strange shaking, a faint rumble. I observed the chandelier swaying gently. Other than that, I could detect little."

Satisfied that the house had likely come off with small damage, if any, Nick returned in time to accept the cup of tea Nympha poured for him. Although he would have appreciated something stronger, oddly enough the tea proved just what he needed.

"Foley says everything is satisfactory," Mrs. Coxmoor said in a subdued voice.

"So he told me. I imagine it is possible that the earthquake is stronger at one place than another."

Nympha swallowed her tea in a gulp. "Do you think it will happen again?"

"I don't know," Nick admitted.

"I shan't sleep a wink tonight." She gave him an anguished grimace.

"I intend to," Mrs. Coxmoor stated. "I noticed there were a number of older people who were badly shocked. I hope none come to a dire end—like Sir Jared."

Talbot, her devoted abigail, came into the room. She walked up to her employer, frowning in concern. "May I suggest you take a nap now, dear ma'am? This has been a dreadful shock for you."

"Perhaps I shall." Without a word of caution to the two others in the room, she departed at once.

"Dear me, she *must* not be feeling herself," Nympha said. "Else we would have had a lecture on proper behavior."

"I appreciate your effort at normalcy, dear girl. You are sure you have no injuries—other than the bruises I spotted when I carried you to the coach?"

"Oh, I daresay I have a few more. That bully who knocked me down was not a lightweight." She held out her arms to show where her gown had been torn.

Nick shook his head in disbelief. "This isn't really the time or the place, my dearest. But today I realized just how precious you are to me. I want nothing more in this life than to make you mine, so I might guard and protect you the rest of your life."

"You wish to marry me?" Her lips parted with a smile, her eyes held stars shining from their blue depths.

He was thunderstruck that she might think anything else. "Of course." He rose to kneel by her chair, hoping she might accept him, not turn away. "Will you?"

"I had hoped, but did not expect to have a proposal when looking like this!"

He glanced down at his clothes and chuckled. "I never in my life imagined I would propose marriage to the light of my life in such a state, either."

She smiled at that. "We are a pair," she pointed out, gesturing to her own dishevelment.

"True, we are in far more ways than our present

clothes. You are my other half, the one for whom I have searched. To think you were under my nose, so to speak, all these years and I didn't know it."

"Well, as to that, I must confess I'd no eyes for you, either." Her admission was wary; her eyes watching him were equally so.

"That is in the past, is it not?" He hoped the sigh she gave was one of relief that he understood.

"Indeed, it is far in the past. I cannot imagine what I saw in your brother, if truth be told. He never paid me the slightest attention, other than to be polite."

Nick smiled. "He always was a well-mannered chap."

"So are you. In fact, I think you quite the hero. You saved me. And you rescued my great-aunt as well. I will never be able to thank you enough."

"I think I can find a means. Although I don't intend marriage as a way of saying thank you, it would give me an opportunity to show you just how I accept your appreciation."

She blushed, a delicate blossom pink that spread from her face down as far as he could see.

"Does this mean you will accept my hand, my offer, and my love?"

"What about your family? I am a nobody." Her eyes gleamed with longing.

"You marry me, not my family."

"Oh, I do love you. I will—"

Talbot rushed into the room, wringing her hands in distress, unaware that she was interrupting a proposal of marriage. "Miss Nympha, your great-aunt has collapsed. I cannot seem to rouse her. Please come at once. I think it is her nerves, miss. She always seems so collected. She hides her nerves."

With a backward look at Nick, Nympha hurried off with the abigail.

Nick decided his first order of business was to change from the ruined garments. He would probably find himself charging off to Nottingham in search of Dr. Graham.

As it happened he was precisely correct.

Nympha stood by her great-aunt's bed, holding a limp hand in hers, and praying the dear lady wouldn't expire of shock. As intrepid as she seemed, she wasn't young anymore, and even Nympha had been badly shaken. "Will Lord Nicholas go to Nottingham to fetch Dr. Graham for us?"

The abigail left the room at once, to come back a few minutes later. "He was on his way to the stables. I believe he anticipated your request."

"How like him," Nympha murmured. If she married him she would have a gentleman who truly cared about people. He had been so concerned for her and her great-aunt at the church.

But could she do that? Marry him? He declared he loved her, but she wondered how she would fit in with his life. Should he stand for the Commons, he would move into London for part of the year. He'd want an accomplished hostess, not a girl from a village with no background in politics or entertaining. As far as she could see she was the worst possible wife for him.

Her aunt moved slightly. Nympha devoted her entire attention to her. There would be time enough later to think about marriage.

Around two hours later, with Nympha hovering over her aunt the entire time, Dr. Graham arrived.

He dismissed Nympha from the room at once.

In the hallway, she found Lord Nicholas waiting.

"I have tea for you in the drawing room. There is nothing you can do for your great-aunt at the moment. Talbot will assist Dr. Graham."

She didn't resist when he guided her down the stairs and into the drawing room. A tray set with china, a plate of biscuits, and a large pot of tea awaited them.

"I do not see why I must be banished. There must be something I could do. Oh, Nick, she looks so white, so helpless. I don't wish to lose her when I have only begun to know her!"

His arms were a haven she could not deny if she tried. She nestled against him a few moments, not thinking of any improprieties.

Her earlier thoughts returned, and she drew away.

"What is it?"

He was far too intuitive where she was concerned. "I was mulling over the possibility of our marriage. I cannot see that it would or could work."

He placed a hand over her mouth. "Do not say it. Never say 'no' to me, dear girl. I'll not give up so easily. What do you imagine the problem to be now?"

"We are from such different backgrounds. You should stand for Parliament; you would be so good there. Yet if you do, I know I am not a proper hostess for the dinners, the affairs you will want to give. I've not the proper training. Managing on a tight budget is what I know best. I've no need for that now. I am all at sea. I scarce know what I shall do."

"Would you allow me to help you? We can both learn at management. We could live here part of the time, at my home down south part of the time. As to my standing for Parliament, I'll not do it if it deprives me of you! You come first before all else."

"Oh, Nick," she whispered. "If only I could accept that."

"Ahem."

Nick and Nympha turned to find Dr. Graham standing just inside the door. His gaze was compassionate.

Nympha hurried to his side. "How is she?"

"Badly shocked. This shake-up at the church was hard for her to take. I have given her something to calm her. Only time will tell if she recovers. There is little else I can do. I'm sorry."

Nympha buried her face in her hands, sobbing quietly into them. She had tried to be brave, as she knew that dear lady would want her to be, but it was very difficult when everything seemed to bleak.

Nick wrapped her in his arms. He spoke to the doctor in quiet tones, trying to learn all he could. It did not look good.

The doctor promised to look in tomorrow, then left.

"Why don't you change your dress, then come back

here? I'll have fresh tea waiting, and you will feel better, I swear."

Since she didn't seem able to reply, Nick picked her up, carrying her to her room. Annie was there, shocked at the state of her mistress when she was set on her feet.

"Help her to change. I'll carry her back down if needs be."

Nympha gave him a watery chuckle. She submitted to Annie's tender care at once.

Nick did as promised. Foley refreshed the tea. The cook added a bit of cake as well as sandwiches, knowing that no one would feel like a Sunday dinner today.

"I guess I am not as strong as I always thought," Nympha confessed when she rejoined him. Annie had put her into the blush sarcenet gown and fixed her tangled curls. With a clean face and hands, her gown presentable, she looked good enough to eat.

"You will do well enough. Think of Letitia Coxmoor's age and all she has seen in her lifetime. She will recover; I feel it. A thing like this won't put her down."

"I hope that is true."

Neither of them went to bed that night. They sat in the drawing room, checking on Nympha's great-aunt from time to time, otherwise simply talking. Nympha dosed for a bit. Nick watched over her with tender regard. His poor little darling had endured an impossible day. Yet she hadn't succumbed to a fit of the vapors as so many women might. She thought she wasn't strong? She was a tower. He just knew her fervent prayers would be granted.

Along about dawn her great-aunt stirred, becoming restless. Talbot fetched Nympha at once.

"Great-Aunt Letitia, I am here. Please say you know me." Nympha was out of breath from her dash up the stairs.

Eyes nearly as blue as her young relative's opened. "Why all this fuss? It must be the middle of the night. Let a body get some sleep." She sounded cross, but to Nympha it was as though she sang praise to the heavens.

"We will. Sleep well." Nympha dropped a kiss on her forehead, then joined Nick in the hall. "I do believe she will be all right. What an amazing woman."

"Come to think of it, you are as well. I am convinced that you could handle anything that comes your way. Consider today. Any other woman would have fainted or had hysterics like Lady Anne. Not you."

"I think I was too frightened to faint."

He touched her chin, raising her face so he could look her in the eyes. "Say yes, Nympha. Say you will marry me."

"That sounds suspiciously like an order," she countered with a bit of her usual spirit back.

"Perhaps it is. I want you for my wife."

"You ought to ask my father."

"I did better than that—I asked Mrs. Coxmoor, and she heartily agreed that we would make a fine couple."

"I do not know." She gazed deeply into his eyes and was apparently pleased with what she saw there. "Yes, I do. I love you dearly, and I will marry you, whenever and wherever you please. Once my great-aunt is restored, that is."

"I can wait. I'd wait however long it takes. But dearest, I do hope it isn't long."

Epilogue

A little over three months later on a lovely June day, Lord Nicholas Stanhope and Miss Nympha Herbert, heiress to the great Coxmoor fortune, were married at the Pailthorpe chapel, since the Mansfield church was not quite restored. She was given in marriage by her father, who then proceeded to perform the ceremony. Her mother, along with two of her sisters and her brother, Adam, sat in the front pews. Mrs. Coxmoor also sat in the front pew, a contented twinkle in her eyes, quite as if she had concocted the entire affair.

Priscilla Herbert attended her sister, and the Earl of Stanhope attended his brother at the altar. The Countess of Stanhope remained at their home with their infant son.

It must be confessed that the couple, now Lord Nicholas and Lady Nicholas Stanhope, had eyes for no one but each other.

Author's Note

Earthquakes are not something we generally associate with England. It is a surprise to most people to learn that London and the country are susceptible to earthquakes. A look at the UK seismicity map reveals an amazing collection of little dots, each representing an earthquake that occurred at a point in recorded history. The worst recorded earthquake in Britain was in 4 April 1884 when twelve hundred buildings were damaged or destroyed over an area of four hundred kilometers in the vicinity of Colchester, between Wivenhoe and Peldon.

The earliest recorded earthquake was a massive one occurring in Kent in 1382 of such intensity that it shook several churches, causing one of them to collapse.

During the reign of Elizabeth I, the earthquake in 1588 was deemed a signal from heaven regarding the legality of her claim to the throne as opposed to the claim of her sister Mary. Both sides insisted it supported their particular view.

In 1759 the earthquake that struck London created great fears among the populace, with the Bishop of London declaring the quake was an expression of the wrath of God at the depravity of the citizens of London.

The weekly *Nottingham Review* reported in 1816 that an earthquake had occurred in the Nottingham area that past week, at the town of Mansfield on Sunday, 17 March:

> At Mansfield the congregation were in the church, when a loud noise was heard, the place shook, and it was supposed, from the dust and lime falling from the ceiling, that a beam had given way; the people instantly sought to make their escape, and from the pressure, several persons were thrown down, and some of them much hurt and trampled upon. There was scarcely a street which had not several chimneys thrown down, the houses cracked, or otherwise injured. The church at Mansfield was much damaged.

Days later the paper reported:

> . . . a "universally respected and regretted" Mrs. Unwin, widow (for 42 years) of the late W. Unwin, esq., died. She had been in Mansfield church during the earthquake, and apparently never recovered from the shock.

All this isn't to say that if one goes to England one is in danger of experiencing an earthquake. That simply isn't the case, and the vast majority of English will go from cradle to grave without so much as feeling a tremor. But as I have related above, earthquakes have indeed happened, and Mansfield truly was rocked by such an event on the vary date that my fictional characters were there.